An Unexp Family for the Rugged Mountain Man

STAND-ALONE NOVEL

A Western Historical Romance Book

by

Sally M. Ross

Disclaimer & Copyright

Table of Contents.

Letter from Sally M. Ross

"There are two kinds of people in the world those with guns and those that dig."

This iconic sentence from the *"Good the Bad and the Ugly"* was meant to change my life once and for all. I chose to be the one to hold the gun and, in my case...the pen!

I started writing as soon as I learned the alphabet. At first, it was some little fairytales, but I knew that this undimmed passion was my life's purpose.

I share the same love with my husband for the classic western movies, and we moved together to Texas to leave the dream on our little farm with Daisy, our lovely lab.

I'm a literary junkie reading everything that comes into my hands, with a bit of weakness on heartwarming romances and poetry.

If you choose to follow me on this journey, I can guarantee you characters that you would love to befriend, romances that will make your heart beat faster, and wholesome, genuine stories that will make you dream again!

Until next time,

Sally M. Ross

Prologue

Oatman, Arizona, 1853

Six-year-old Sophie Thompson tugged at her pink cotton skirt, worried that it had gotten creased while she was climbing under the table looking for Mittens. Her little kitten was forever getting herself trapped in the most inconvenient of places.

She smoothed her skirt again but it was no use—as soon as she removed her hand, the fabric wrinkled again. Sophie looked up at her mother with her pale blue eyes, hoping she would not notice. She had gone to a lot of effort to make sure that Sophie would make a good impression and would not be happy to know that only moments earlier she'd been crawling around the kitchen floor.

"Stop fidgeting," her mother warned.

Sophie straightened her shoulders and folded her small hands behind her back. Her white blouse felt scratchy and beads of perspiration ran down her back as they baked under the hot Arizona sun.

"There they are," her mother said.

She craned her neck, trying to get a look at the buggy now coming in through the ranch gates. Sophie knew how important this meeting was—her mother had spoken of little else for the last few weeks.

As the buggy came closer, the gravel crunched loudly beneath its wooden wheels and Sophie's stomach fluttered wildly. The feeling reminded her of the time she went on a walk with her father. She'd caught a butterfly with checkerboard wings and had cupped it carefully in her hands. As it tried to fly, its fragile wings beat against the skin of her palms. This felt the same, only the fluttering sensation was stronger.

"Remember what I told you," her mother said.

Sophie nodded, but the truth was, her mother had given her so many instructions that morning that she'd forgotten most of them. In one ear and out the other, her father used to joke.

The buggy came to a halt and the door swung open. Sophie's palms were sweaty as she plastered a smile onto her face.

Out of the buggy stepped a large man with copper-colored hair and a beard to match. He had small, dark eyes and a flat nose. He wore a tailored linen suit the exact shade of the bay trees her father had planted near the vegetable garden. Around his neck he wore a silk cravat and his black leather shoes were so well-polished that Sophie was certain she'd be able to see her reflection in them.

"Mrs. Thompson," the man boomed as he stepped down. "What a breath of fresh air it is to see you again."

Sophie looked up at her mother, whose cheeks had turned a pretty shade of pink.

"You do know how to flatter a woman, Mr. Colton," she replied. "And please, I insist that you call me Lauren."

Sophie looked up at her mother again, never having heard her speak in such an affected tone.

Behind Mr. David Colton, another head emerged from the buggy. His son was the spitting image of his father, with the same copper-colored crop of hair and dark eyes. Unlike his father, however, his nose was long and his chin was sharp. Sophie's mother had told her all about Frank Colton. He was thirteen years old and the apple of his father's eye.

Frank climbed down from the buggy and as he did, Sophie saw that he too was dressed well. He wore a crisp white linen shirt and a pair of bay-green trousers that reached just below the knee. It was strange to Sophie to see such well-dressed people. She was so used to more practical, durable clothes like denim pants and canvas vests, the clothes that her father and the ranch hands wore. They seemed entirely out of place to her against the backdrop of the old barn, with its rotting roof and the wonky woodshed. She knew what her father would call them—he'd call them a pair of fancy Dans.

David Colton and his son walked across the narrow stretch of gravel to where Sophie and her mother stood. Sophie did not take her eyes off them, her stomach still fluttering.

"Allow me to introduce my son," Mr. Colton said. "This is Frank."

"It's a pleasure to meet you, Mrs. Thompson," Frank said.

"And you, Frank," she said. "Your pa has told me so much about you."

For a moment, Sophie thought she might be invisible, until her mother placed a hand on her shoulder.

"This is my Sophie," she said. "And Sophie, this is Mr. Colton and his son."

Sophie's mind was racing as she tried to recall the exact words her mother had told her to say. But no matter how hard she tried, they would not come to her, and she felt the hand on her shoulder grow heavier, more disapproving.

"I am sorry," Mrs. Thompson said. "She's just a bit shy."

Sophie looked up at Mr. Colton and she saw his dark eyes harden for a moment, and her throat went dry.

"Why don't we all go inside? I am sure you are all parched from your travels."

Mr. Colton pulled his hard gaze away from Sophie and back to her mother.

"That would be most welcome," he said.

Sophie did not move as her mother led Mr. Colton and his son into the house.

"Sophie?" her mother called back. "Come inside and help me in the kitchen."

Sophie did not want to go into the house; she wanted to turn and run until the house was no bigger than the head of a pin. But she knew how important this was to her mother, and so she took a shaky breath and went back inside.

As Sophie passed the sitting room, she saw Mr. Colton and his son were seated in the two arms chairs by the window. She dropped her eyes as she passed, afraid she might catch Mr. Colton's hard gaze again.

"There you are," her mother said as she stepped into the kitchen. "Really, Sophie. Would it have been so hard for you to say hello to our guests?"

"I am sorry, Ma," Sophie apologized. "I could not remember what you told me to say."

Mrs. Thompson shook her head and sighed. "Well, help me with the lemonade."

A few minutes later, Sophie was seated beside her mother on the threadbare sofa. They'd done their best to get the place into shape for Mr. Colton's arrival, but Sophie knew that her mother was still ashamed by the state of the furniture and the holes in the ceilings and mold on the walls.

"Sophie," her mother said after a few moments. "Why don't you show Frank around the ranch?"

Sophie looked across at Frank, who met her gaze, and she found the same hardness in his dark eyes that she'd seen in his father's eyes.

"That sounds like an excellent idea," Mr. Colton said, putting his glass down on the table. "Frank was just saying how much he is looking forward to living on a ranch."

Sophie looked up at her mother but did not move.

"Go on now, Sophie," she said. "Mr. Colton and I have some things we need to discuss."

"You too, Frank," Mr. Colton said.

Both Sophie and Frank got up from where they were seated and left the room. Neither of them spoke until they were outside.

"What do you want to see first?" Sophie asked.

Frank shrugged. "I don't care."

"I thought you wanted to live on a ranch?"

Frank snorted rudely. "My father just said that to impress your mother."

Sophie frowned. "So he was lying?"

Frank looked down at her and smiled. "I knew you'd be a little goody two-shoes."

Sophie frowned again, not quite knowing what Frank's words meant but clearly understanding the intention behind them was to be cruel.

Frank walked over to the barn and peered inside, and from the way he wrinkled his long nose, she knew he didn't like what he saw.

"Just because our parents are getting married doesn't mean we are family," he said, turning to look at Sophie.

"I know," Sophie said.

They fell into silence again for a few moments. Sophie did not like Frank or the way he was turning up his nose at her home. She loved the ranch and all the memories it held.

"This place is a dump," Frank said, looking around.

"It's not!" Sophie retorted, her face growing warm.

"It is," Frank said. "But I guess that will change after they are married."

Sophie said nothing, but she hated the way Frank knew more things than she did. Like the reason her mother wanted to get married again. After all, her father had only been gone a few months.

"I am bored," Frank whined.

"My pa used to say that only boring people got bored."

"Well, your pa sounds like an idiot," Frank said.

"My pa was the best man in the whole world."

"But not clever enough to stop himself from falling off a horse and breaking his neck."

Sophie's chest rose and fell as she glared at Frank. He knew nothing about her father.

"Stop talking about him," Sophie said, blinking back tears.

"Why?" Frank jeered. "Does talking about your dead daddy make you want to cry? Huh? You big crybaby—"

Without thinking, Sophie kicked out her right foot as hard as she could, and her shoe hit Frank square on the shin. He cried out in pain as he lifted his leg, hopping around for a moment before he turned back to Sophie.

"You're going to be sorry you did that," he said.

Before Sophie had a moment to think, Frank pushed her with all his strength, and she hit the barn wall and fell to the ground with a thud. She lay on the floor, trying to catch her breath, as the blow had pushed all the wind from her stomach.

When she was finally able to breathe again, Sophie pushed herself up onto her knees. Her back ached and her head was pounding. When she was finally able to get to her feet, she used the barn wall to steady herself. She looked around for Frank, but he had disappeared.

As she made her way back around the house, Sophie caught sight of herself in the porch window. Her skirt was covered in dust and her long plait had been shaken loose and strands of hair now hung around her face.

"Goodness gracious, Sophie," her mother said as she stepped into the sitting room.

"What on earth have you been doing?"

Sophie said nothing as she caught Frank's eye.

"I tripped," Sophie lied.

Her mother sighed. "You'd better go upstairs and get changed."

Sophie turned and left the room. She had lied only because she'd been afraid that Frank would tell them that she'd started it by kicking him in the shin. She did not want to get in trouble with her mother.

Sophie did not come back downstairs until Mr. Colton and Frank had gone. As she watched the buggy disappear down through the gate, a wave of relief washed over her.

"Sophie?" her mother said from the other side of the door. "Are you in here?"

"Yes, Ma," Sophie said.

Her mother turned the doorknob and pushed open the door. "What are you doing up here?"

"I was just changing my dress."

Her mother frowned but said nothing for a moment.

"Mr. Colton and his son have gone back to their hotel in town to freshen up," she said. "But they will be back for dinner."

The relief that Sophie had felt only a moment ago evaporated into thin air.

"When you are dressed, come downstairs and help me," her mother said, turning away.

"I don't think you should marry that man, Ma," Sophie blurted, unable to stop herself.

Her mother turned around to look at Sophie again.

"They got hard eyes," Sophie said. "And Pa used to say that the eyes were the windows to the soul."

Her mother sighed softly. "I know this isn't easy and you are too young to understand, but I am doing what is best for us."

Sophie said nothing, but she could not believe that marrying Mr. Colton was the best thing for them.

"Come down when you are dressed," she repeated.

Then without another word, she left. Sophie turned back to the window and sighed. She wished her father were still alive. Things had been so much better then.

Just as her mother had said, Mr. Colton and Frank returned for supper that evening. As Sophie sat at the table in the kitchen, she said nothing. Mr. Colton sat across from her, in the place where her father used to sit. Frank sat beside her.

Despite his fancy clothes and accent, Frank had poor table manners and his arms protruded like the wings of a chicken, leaving Sophie with barely any space to eat her dinner. Yet no one seemed to notice. Her mother barely looked her way as she doted on Mr. Colton, hanging on his every word. Sophie had never seen her mother like this before, so wide-eyed and girlish. She could not really explain it, but it made the hairs on her arms stand up.

"So, son," Mr. Colton said, looking at Frank as he leaned forward in his chair. "What do you think of our new home? Our new family?"

Frank nodded as he looked up from his plate. "I think it's great, Father."

Mr. Colton nodded and smiled. As Sophie watched, he reached across and squeezed her mother's hand. Her mother looked into his eyes and smiled. Sophie looked around and saw that everyone but her was smiling. No one looked at her, no one asked her what she thought, no one cared. She may as well have been invisible.

Chapter One

Oatman, Arizona, 1867

Almost fourteen years had passed since that night. Sophie had eaten thousands of dinners since then and yet nothing had changed. She still felt invisible almost all of the time and when her family did notice her from time to time, she usually just wished to be invisible again.

"Sophie?" her mom called from the sitting room. "Will you come in here, please?"

Sophie sighed softly to herself. She'd hoped they would not notice her but one of the floorboards had betrayed her. She turned around and walked back to the sitting room. She did not go inside but stood, leaning against the doorway.

"Will you stand up straight?" Mr. Colton barked.

Sophie straightened up slightly.

"We want to talk to you," her mother said.

"I was actually just going out for a walk—"

"It's not a question," Mr. Colton said, his dark eyes flashing a warning. "Sit down."

Sophie hesitated. She knew the price of defying him, and it was steep. For fourteen years, she'd felt like a mouse in a house full of cats.

"Sophie, please?" her mother said.

Sophie's shoulders dropped as she stepped into the room. She took a seat on the sofa across from the two armchairs where her mother and stepfather sat. The furniture in the room was new; her mother had it all upholstered again a few months ago, to keep up to date with the latest fashions. That's all she did now, her mother, play house.

"We want to talk to you about your future," her mother said.

Sophie's stomach sank but she said nothing.

"You are twenty this year, Sophie," she continued. "That's old enough to find a husband and to run a household of your own. I was about your age when I got married."

"But I don't want a husband," Sophie said. "Or a household of my own."

Her mother said nothing for a moment as she pursed her lips. Sophie knew this was not her idea, but she'd become so weak over the past fourteen years, so terribly afraid to speak up, that she really no longer had a single thought that was her own. She did whatever *he* wanted.

"There is a man in town," her mother continued. "His name is Mr. Beaumont and he has shown an interest in you."

Sophie's eyes widened in horror. She knew Mr. Beaumont, she'd seen him in church. He was twice her age and his breath smelled of rot and decay from a lifetime of chewing tobacco.

"No, Ma," Sophie said, shaking her head. "Please don't make me marry that man."

Sophie's blue eyes were full of desperation as she pleaded silently with her mother, who still would not meet her eye. Had it truly come to this? Over the years, Sophie had wondered if her mother cared at all for her happiness, and now she knew that she could not. The hurt of knowing this, deep down in the very core of her heart, was almost worse than being forced to marry this old man.

"Mr. Beaumont is a well-respected man in town and is a gentleman," her stepfather said sharply. "He is a good match."

"He is one hundred years old!" Sophie insisted. "You can't make me marry him—"

"I know he is a bit older than you," her mother said. "But he has money and a nice home, he can offer you security and a comfortable life."

Sophie stared at her mother, still refusing to believe they were actually suggesting she marry Mr. Beaumont. That money and security would be worth sharing a bed with that man for the rest of her life.

"What about Frank?" Sophie said. "He's twenty-seven and still not married."

"Are you suggesting that Frank marry Mr. Beaumont?" Mr. Colton asked dryly.

"It's different," her mother said.

Sophie shook her head bitterly. She knew that meant one day Frank would inherit the ranch and everything else, while she would inherit nothing, which was why she needed to get married.

"I won't marry him," Sophie said. "You can't make me marry him—"

"That's enough," her stepfather said. "This subject is not up for debate. You will marry Mr. Beaumont, it's all been arranged."

Sophie did not take her eyes off her mother. "Please, Ma. Don't let him do this."

But as usual, her mother said nothing, and so Sophie got up from the sofa and hurried out of the room.

As she pushed open the back door, Sophie took deep gulps of air, trying to remember to breathe. She pressed her hand to her chest, and her heart was beating a million times a minute.

"So I guess you heard the news then?"

Sophie whirled around to see Frank leaning against the trunk of a large maple tree. He was chewing sunflower seeds, and as she looked at him, he spat a mouthful of shells onto the ground.

"I won't marry him," Sophie said, doing her best to stand up for herself, although she knew it was pointless.

"Of course you will," Frank said. "Even if our father has to drag you down the aisle himself."

"He's not my pa," Sophie said. "And you are not my brother."

Frank smirked as he reached into his pocket and took out another handful of sunflower seeds, which he put in his mouth. Sophie glared at him as he chewed loudly with his mouth open.

Neither of them spoke for a moment, but Frank did not take his eyes off her. She was used to this—Frank had found pleasure in her pain for years. Their relationship had been decided on that very first day they met and the passing of time had only made it worse. Frank had never grown out of being a bully.

"Father's been planning this for a while," Frank said. "To marry you off. But he was just waiting for the best offer."

Sophie frowned. "What do you mean?"

Frank smirked again. "Are you really that naive?" he jeered. "You're a broodmare, who Father sold off to the highest bidder."

Sophie's stomach turned. Was Frank telling her the truth? Had her stepfather really sold her off, as if she were just another ranch animal? Yet it made sense. Mr. Beaumont had no children of his own. After he died, the ranch would become Sophie's. Her stepfather wanted Mr. Beaumont's land, and the price was her freedom.

"You can't be surprised," Frank said, shaking his head in disbelief. "After all these years, you still haven't learned, have you? Nothing you say or want matters in this family. Even your own mother doesn't care about you."

Frank was not wrong and Sophie knew it. She'd lost her father when she was six years old and she'd lost her mother the day she remarried. She'd been alone for fourteen years, but Sophie knew that she'd lived under her stepfather's thumb for too long. She needed to escape this future that she did not want. All she needed to figure out was how to get away.

"I know what you are thinking," Frank said.

Sophie met his eyes and she saw a glimmer of amusement in them.

"That maybe you could run away," Frank continued, his tone mocking. "But you know he'd find you."

Sophie said nothing but she knew Frank was right. If she ran, he'd find her and bring her back. So she needed another plan, a way that her stepfather could not get to her.

"Well, as much as I'd like to stand around all day chewing the fat. I've got work to do," Frank said as he turned away. He paused, turning back to her. "Oh, before I forget to tell you—I hear Mr. Beaumont is looking forward to having lots of children."

Frank waggled his eyebrows at her suggestively before he turned to go and Sophie felt bile rise in her throat.

Sophie turned and ran, as if trying to outrun her fate. She passed the barn and the stables and the cattle grazing in the eastern pasture. She ran until she found herself at her father's grave and she fell to her knees, out of breath.

"I wish you were still here," she said.

The headstones of Thompson family graves stood out against the blue sky that seemed to stretch out toward forever, like some waveless sea. The oldest of those tombstones belonged to Sophie's great-grandfather and great-grandmother. The limestone had weathered over the years in the sun, wind, rain, and snow. Lichen in various textures and colors grew around the tops and sides, like some feathery blanket keeping the dead warm. Weeds grew from the base of the stones, a testament to the neglect over the years. Sophie could not recall the last time her mother had come to pay her respects, certainly not since marrying Mr. Colton.

Ever since her father's passing, Sophie had come here nearly every day to talk with him. She had no idea if he could hear her, but it brought her comfort just being near to him. She'd barely got the chance to know him in the short years before he was taken from her, and yet Sophie felt closer to him than anyone else in the whole world.

Sophie did not know how long she sat there, staring at the tombstone. She only turned when she heard footsteps. The ranch foreman, Charlie Briggs, had been there for as long as Sophie could remember. He was an old man now, with a white beard, and yet he was still cowboying as if he were a young man. Over the years, Charlie had become a friend to her. Sometimes he was the only person in the whole world that she could talk to, besides her cat, Mittens. Charlie had no family of his own, and sometimes Sophie felt as if she were almost like a daughter to him.

"You all right?" Charlie asked. "You've been sittin' here a long while."

Sophie said nothing for a moment as Charlie sat down on the ground beside her, the bones in his knees creaking as he did.

"You wanna talk about it?" he asked.

"They are going to make me marry Mr. Beaumont," Sophie said.

Sophie looked sideways to see Charlie frowning in disapproval. "But he's an old man."

Sophie shrugged. "My stepfather has it all arranged."

"What does your ma have to say about all this?" Charlie asked.

Sophie shook her head. "Nothing. She never has anything of her own to say."

Charlie put a hand on her shoulder. "So what are you gonna do?"

"I don't know," Sophie said. "But I can't marry that man."

Charlie looked thoughtful all of a sudden. "I might have an idea. Come with me."

A flicker of hope sparked in her chest as she and Charlie got up off the ground. She followed him to the ranch hand quarters located behind the barn. She hesitated a moment, turning to look at the house, to see if someone was spying on her from the window. She was not allowed near the ranch hand quarters, not under any given circumstances.

"Wait here," he said as he disappeared into his small room.

Sophie waited outside the door but her stomach was in knots, in case Frank suddenly turned up and found her there. A few moments later, however, Charlie emerged from the room and handed her a newspaper.

"What is this?" she asked.

"Read it," Charlie instructed, pointing to a black and white advertisement printed on the page.

A Bachelor of ability, good moral character, 29 years of age, born and reared under Southern skies, is anxious to correspond with a good woman between the ages of 18-25 with a view to matrimony.

Address with the Editor

Sophie frowned as she looked up from the advertisement.

"You should apply," Charlie said.

"What?"

"If you have a husband, then your stepdaddy won't own you no more," Charlie explained.

Sophie said nothing for a moment. What Charlie said was true, a husband would protect her. But could she really marry a total stranger? At least this man in the advertisement was younger, but she had no idea what he would be like.

"This could be your chance to escape," Charlie said. "Your only chance."

Sophie looked down at the advertisement again. She'd been racking her brain all afternoon for a way to get out of marrying Mr. Beaumont and now she had a way. Sophie sighed softly as she gazed out into the distance. She'd lived nowhere else but here; this was where her father was buried and where she'd known happiness.

Yet it was also a place of great pain and hurt for her. This place had taken her father, and with it, her family. She knew deep down that there was nothing for her here anymore, not if she wanted some kind of life of her own. If she stayed, she would always be at the mercy of her stepfather.

"You're right," Sophie said, nodding. "If I write a letter, will you take it into town for me?"

Charlie nodded. "Let me fetch you some paper and a pen."

So, with Charlie's help, Sophie wrote a letter to the mysterious bachelor and gave it to him to post. As she made her way back to the house, all she could hope was that he would write back to her soon, before she was pushed down the aisle and into the arms of Mr. Beaumont.

***

"Are you ready, Mittens?" Sophie asked.

The gray-blue cat was curled up in a ball at the base of her bed, but opened one round yellow eye at the mention of her name.

Mittens was fourteen years old, and was Sophie's best friend in the whole world. Over the years, it was Mittens who listened when Sophie needed someone to talk to and who slept beside her every night. In her heyday, Mittens was an excellent ratter, but she was old now and spent most days sunning herself in the window.

Sophie sighed softly as she walked across the room. One week had passed since she'd been informed of her impending marriage to Mr. Beaumont and the idea had not softened even slightly on Sophie's heart.

On the vanity table was a wooden crate she had taken from the barn. It was usually used to transport chickens but it would do for Mittens. Sophie had taken great care making it as comfortable as possible for the old cat using an old wool scarf to fashion a makeshift bed.

"I know you'd rather stay cuddled up on the bed," Sophie said softly. "But I can't leave you behind, Mittens."

She carefully picked up the cat and carried her over to the crate. She lowered her inside and then closed the top. Mittens looked up at her, her thin tail swishing from side to side with annoyance at being disturbed from her restful slumber.

"Don't look at me like that," Sophie said. "I'm doing this for us."

Sophie hoped it was true. She had thought about leaving Mittens behind, but she was her only friend, and the one good thing she had in her life. The journey would not be too comfortable but it wouldn't be long, half a day south at most.

Sophie exhaled slowly as she looked around the lamp-lit room. It was a full moon outside, and pale moonlight came through the narrow gap in the curtains. Her small carpetbag sat on the bed; she'd packed carefully, taking only what she needed and leaving everything else behind. The only thing she'd taken of value was a pearl brooch that had once belonged to her grandmother.

The letter from Mr. Simon Jones was tucked carefully into the pocket of her skirt. It had come that morning and Charlie had collected it from town. Sophie had opened it with trembling hands and her heart had lifted in relief as she read the words. He'd asked her to come at her earliest convenience and the tone of the letter sounded pleasant. His handwriting was as neat as a pin, slightly feminine even, but what did that matter? He wanted her.

After reading the letter, Sophie knew she had to go right away. They were having luncheon with Mr. Beaumont the next day and she had to leave before then. So, with Charlie's help, she made plans to leave in the early hours of the morning. There was a local rancher, a friend of Charlie's, who delivered eggs to the neighboring town. He left two hours before dawn to make it there in time. He would give Sophie a lift and from there she would catch a train to Shadow's Ridge.

"All right," she said. "I guess it's time to go."

Sophie lifted the wooden crate with Mittens into her arms. She then reached for the carpetbag, careful to balance the crate on her forearm as she did. Sophie walked over to the door and opened it slowly, trying not to make too much noise. Before stepping out into the hallway, she took one last look around her room. *This is goodbye*, she thought.

Sophie heard a floorboard creak in the bedroom across from hers and her heart stopped. She held her breath, waiting for Frank to open his bedroom door and ruin everything. But the house fell silent again and Sophie quickly hurried down the hallway and into the kitchen. She pushed open the door and stepped out into the cool night air. She made her way across the moonlit garden toward the barn. As the building came into view, she could see the tall, thin silhouette of Charlie.

"Did anyone see you?" Charlie asked as she approached.

"I wouldn't be here if someone had," Sophie replied.

"Right," Charlie agreed. "Come on, we'd better get going."

Charlie took the crate carrying Mittens from her, and together they hurried down the road toward the entrance to the ranch. Just as they reached the road, Sophie heard the crunching of gravel and turned to see the silhouette of a horse come to view at the top of the road.

A few moments later, a rancher dressed in a felt Stetson and a burgundy bandana around his neck came to a stop on the side of the road. The wagon he drove was full of crates of eggs and Sophie was certain it was not an easy feat getting all those eggs safely to their destination.

"Charlie," the man said gruffly as he tipped his hat to them.

"Appreciate you doing this, Clyde," Charlie said as he walked around the side of the wagon and put the crate carrying Mittens down beside the eggs.

"Climb up, Sophie," Charlie said.

But Sophie hesitated a moment and turned to him.

"I could never have done this without your help," she said.

Charlie nodded. "Well, your pa was a good man, and he'd want you to have the chance at being happy. I just wish I could have done more to help you these past years..."

His voice trailed off and Charlie bent his head.

"You've been a real friend to me," Sophie said. "And I will never forget your kindness."

Before Charlie had a chance to respond, Sophie threw her arms around him and hugged him tightly. He smelled like pipe tobacco and fresh hay.

"Come on now," Charlie said kindly, patting her on the back. "It's time you were on your way."

Sophie nodded as she dropped her arms and blinked back tears. Charlie gave her a hand up and she climbed into the seat beside the rancher.

"Travel safe," Charlie said.

Sophie tried to smile as the rancher tipped his hat in Charlie's direction. He then clicked softly under his breath and the wagon began to roll forward. As they made their way down the road, Sophie turned in her seat and saw that Charlie was gone and the road behind them was empty. Sophie turned back and looked out as the road stretched before them. As she did, she was overwhelmed by the fact that she was leaving her whole world behind, with no idea what the future held.

Chapter Two

Shadow's Ridge, Southern Arizona, 1867

Simon Jones woke up to the wails of the baby. He was screaming with such raw intensity that it seemed to reverberate off the walls, the same way thunder did during a storm. Simon rolled over in bed, pulling his pillow over his head, but it did nothing to block out the noise. Just like thunder, it was a force of nature.

Grumbling under his breath, Simon pushed the blanket off and swung his legs over the side bed. He winced slightly as his feet touched the cool wood. He walked over to the window and in the distance, he could see the first subtle glow of dawn coming over the mountains.

Simon went to the small dresser and filled the large porcelain bowl with water. He leaned over and splashed his face, once and then again, the cool water waking him up. When he was finished, he reached for the small towel and patted his dark beard dry.

He then opened the long, narrow top drawer and removed the small tortoise-shell comb and pulled it through his unruly curls. He was in desperate need of a haircut and a shave, but had not found the time for either. There were no mirrors in the house, but from the reflection he'd caught in the window the day before, he looked more like a mountain man than ever.

Simon reached for his blue denim pants and rust-colored shirt hanging over the back of the chair. He dressed quickly, the cool dawn air licking against his bare skin. When he'd laced up his boots, he headed downstairs.

As he stepped into the kitchen, he found his cousin, Jenna, sitting at the table. Her long, auburn hair was disheveled and she had large, purple rings under her eyes. The baby, who was quiet now, suckled hungrily at the bottle she held in her thin hand.

"He's about as loud as a hurricane, I reckon," Simon muttered as he walked over to the kettle. "Is there coffee?"

"In the pot," Jenna said, her voice thin and tired.

Simon walked over to the china hutch and peered inside, but there were no clean cups. He turned to the sink to see a stack of dirty dishes.

"I am sorry," Jenna apologized. "I meant to wash those last night."

"It's fine," Simon said, trying to hide his irritation. He walked over to the sink and found a mug that he rinsed out with cold water.

"Was he up all night?" he asked.

"And then some," Jenna sighed. "Every time I tried to put him down, he screamed. I must have walked a thousand miles last night carrying him up and down. I am at my wits' end with this colic."

"Didn't the midwife say you could give him some whiskey?" Simon asked. "To calm him down?"

Jenna nodded but furrowed her brow in disapproval. "I just don't feel right giving a baby whiskey."

"Well, we can't keep going on this way," Simon insisted. "You can barely stand up, you're so tired, and you've got no time to do anything else. I'm barely keeping up with the ranch work, and yesterday I fell asleep in the middle of milking the cow."

Simon was reaching his own wits' end. He'd been wearing the same shirt for three days because neither he nor Jenna had found the time to do any laundry. He'd also eaten nothing but beans on bread since the baby was born.

Between all the ranch chores and keeping a roof above their heads, dishes and laundry just didn't get done. Simon knew Jenna felt badly about not keeping on top of the housework, but he couldn't spare any time away from the ranch.

"What about getting someone to help?" Jenna asked.

Simon frowned. Jenna had suggested this a few weeks ago, but he'd brushed it off. His quiet, undisturbed life had already been completely uprooted by her and the baby. The last thing he wanted was to add someone else into the mix. Besides, they couldn't afford a housekeeper, they were barely scraping by as it was.

"We can't afford it," Simon said.

"We don't have to hire someone," Jenna said.

"So what?" Simon said dryly. "We find someone who wants to work for free?"

"We could place an advertisement in the newspaper," Jenna said.

Simon turned to her, frowning. "I've told you that I don't want a wife."

"I know," Jenna said. "But you wouldn't have to be involved—"

Simon raised his eyebrows.

"Well, you don't have to be *that* involved," Jenna said. "I'll show her around and teach her about the ranch and how you like things done—"

"Jenna, this place is crowded enough," he said, gritting his teeth.

"I know you like to be on your own," Jenna said. "And if you'd have your way, you'd live alone in these mountains for the rest of your life. But you've made space for me and the baby, can't you make space for one more person?"

Simon said nothing for a few moments as he busied himself pouring coffee into his mug. He loved his cousin—she was the only family he had, and that was the reason he'd agreed to help her.

He and Jenna had been estranged for years, but when she'd arrived on his doorstep two months ago with a newborn baby in her arms, he had promised to help. He'd opened his home to them without explanation, and he had been trying to adjust but was struggling. Simon had gotten so used to being on his own, and he liked it that way. Still, he'd done it all because Jenna was family, and you never turned away family.

"I don't want to get married, Jen," Simon said as he carried the coffee over to the table. "I am sorry, but that's how I feel. We'll get by just us, I am sure that things will get easier—"

"Simon..."

Simon looked over at her and he saw tears in the corner of her eyes.

"What is it?" he asked. "What's wrong?"

"I am scared you are going to be angry with me," she whispered.

"What did you do?" he asked, unable to hide the mixture of fear and annoyance he was feeling in that moment.

"She's already on her way," Jenna said, sounding both apologetic and apprehensive.

Simon said nothing for the moment as he lowered his chin toward his neck and frowned. The baby gurgled in Jenna's arms.

"Who?" he asked, although deep down, he already knew the answer.

"Her name is Sophie Thompson," Jenna said.

Simon's eyes widened as he stared at his cousin. She'd gone and done it without his permission. She'd applied for a mail-order bride who was on her way right now.

"Jenna, what have you done?" Simon said, his tone full of brisk energy.

"I am sorry," Jenna pleaded. "I am just so tired and everything is just so hard and I just thought that maybe if we had some help..."

Jenna's voice trailed off as Simon stared at her. "Your ma was my ma's favorite sister, Jenna, and we grew up together. So when you arrived at my door with a baby and no husband, I didn't ask any questions. Even now, I haven't asked you who the father is or why you won't give the child a name. I have kept my nose out of your business, so tell me, why do I not deserve the same courtesy?" he demanded.

The frustrations of the past few weeks were bubbling to the surface and Simon could not stop them. He was angry with her, with what she had done. Jenna had marched into his life and turned everything upside down, and now she had the gall to insist that he must get married?

"For Pete's sake, Jenna!" Simon cried, forgetting all about the baby as he banged his hand on the table, causing the coffee to spill. "What were you thinking?"

The baby, who was asleep, began to wail again, and Jenna's face crumpled.

"I thought I was doing a good thing," she cried.

"You were thinking about yourself, as usual," Simon retorted.

Jenna opened her mouth and closed it again but remained silent.

Without another word, Simon turned away from his cousin and marched out the back door and toward the stables.

***

Perspiration trickled down Simon's back as he shoveled fresh hay into the horses' stalls. It was midmorning and he had not been back into the house to speak with Jenna. He was still too mad. So instead he focused on his work, trying to distract himself.

However, as he finished shoveling straw into the last stall, a shadow crossed the open doorway and he turned to see Jenna.

"What do you want?" he asked, not trying to hide his annoyance.

"I know you are mad at me," Jenna said. "But I thought I was doing the right thing."

Simon snorted but said nothing.

"Well, you may not believe me," Jenna said. "But that does not change the fact that Miss Thompson is coming here."

Simon stopped shoveling and turned to her. "Well, that sounds more like your problem."

Jenna said nothing, but Simon could see the hurt in her eyes, and his heart twinged with guilt. He was not a cruel man, not by any standards, but he knew the life he wanted for himself and it did not include marriage. He liked the life he had, alone on his mountain with no one to talk to but his horse. It was the kind of life he had chosen for himself and he wasn't ready to give it up. Jenna still remembered how he was before his parents died, but he'd changed.

"Jenna," Simon sighed. "You are my family and I love you. I told you the day you arrived with the baby that you could stay for as long as you needed to, and I mean that. But I won't marry this Miss Thompson and that is the end of it."

"Will you not just think about it?"

"I have, Jenna," Simon said.

"I know that Rachel hurt you—"

Simon's jaw tensed at the mention of her name. "I don't want to talk about Rachel."

From inside the house, the baby started to cry, and Jenna gave Simon one pleading last look before she turned and hurried inside.

Simon rested the fork against the wall and ran his hand through his dark curls. It wasn't fair of Jenna to bring up Rachel, or to put this all on him. He'd been alone for years and he liked it that way.

Simon left the stables and headed north, toward the boundary of the ranch. As he approached the tall blackjack pine, he stopped. This was his favorite spot on the ranch, where the mountains stretched out before him as far as the eye could see. He always came here when he needed to clear his head.

The Jones ranch had been in their family for three generations, nestled in the mountains, a steep walk from the town of Shadow's Ridge. The town, established over one hundred and fifty years ago, got its name from the long shadows the mountains cast every afternoon. Their family, who had come from England, had bought the ranch for almost nothing. They saw the potential in it when others had only laughed. His great-great-grandfather had bought a herd of sheep, and the rest, as they said, was history.

Their ranch wasn't the biggest or the grandest in the area, but to Simon, it was his little piece of heaven on earth. He tended to his herd of sheep and supplied the town with wool. His great-grandfather had been a green-fingered man and had established an orchard of fruit trees.

Every year, Simon would harvest apricots, apples, peaches, figs, and plums, and turn them into jams and preserves, which he also sold to the town. It was a simple life, but it was his, and after everything that he'd been through, it was the life he needed.

A cool breeze blew in from the west, causing the firs on the blackjack pine to sway and dance above his head. He sighed deeply, knowing he could not stay there forever but wishing he could.

Simon gave himself one more minute before he turned and headed back to the ranch. It was past lunchtime but he was not hungry. Instead, he loaded up some fresh hay in his wheelbarrow for the sheep. When this was done, he checked on the water troughs and the fences. By the time he was done, it was late afternoon.

As Simon walked back toward the stables, the wind picked up and the barn was whistling as the wind passed through the openings in the wood. Simon turned to the east, wondering if the wind was blowing a storm in, but the sky was clear.

Simon frowned as something in his gut told him that the wind was blowing something in—something that threatened to change his life, not temporarily like Jenna and the baby, but forever.

Chapter Three

A chilly wind blew through the train station, causing Sophie's skirts to sway back and forth like a boat on the ocean. She craned her neck, looking right and then left, but she saw no one. The train station was empty, except for her, and Mittens, of course.

Sophie had been sitting on that bench for over two hours, waiting for Mr. Simon Jones to fetch her. Her buttocks were numb from sitting for so long and her neck was stiff from looking around for him all afternoon. Mittens, who was still in her crate, sat on the bench beside Sophie, waving her tail irritably.

"I know," Sophie said. "I am irritated too."

It had been a long day and Sophie was tired. She felt grimy from all the traveling and her stomach grumbled hungrily.

"Miss?"

Sophie looked up to see a young porter looking down at her.

"Are you all right?"

She nodded, doing her best to look confident.

"Well, the last train has come in for the day," the porter said. "So the station will be closing soon."

"Oh, right, of course," Sophie said. "Well, I am sure he will be here any moment."

The porter nodded but there was a crease of uncertainty between his brows. Without another word, he turned and walked away, but out of the corner of her eye, Sophie could see him talking with the train station master and panic rose in her chest. She knew she was being paranoid but she did not want them asking questions about where she'd come from and whether she was alone.

So, without another thought, Sophie got up from the bench, picked up the crate and her bag, and hurried out of the station onto the street.

She stood on the street for a moment, looking around her, but it was as empty as the station. It was getting late and soon it would be dark. Sophie knew she needed to get to the ranch before the sun set.

As she walked down the street toward a row of buildings, Sophie hoped to find someone who could give her directions. This was all so new and unfamiliar; it unsettled her. She'd not seen much of the world under her stepfather's careful curation, but she'd known her ranch and her little town. But this town was different; it earned its name, Shadow's Ridge. Everything felt devoid of light here, where strangers kept to the shadows. She wished that Charlie were there.

As Sophie passed by the saloon, she heard raucous laughter, and suddenly the door of the building opened. A man stumbled out, almost falling as he tried to regain his balance.

Sophie did not move for a moment and the door to the saloon opened again, and this time another man stepped outside. He was tall and well-dressed in a fitted blue suit. His dark hair was pushed back from his face, and he had startling blue eyes.

He walked over to the drunk man and put his hand on his shoulder. "Maybe it's time to get home to your wife?"

Sophie could not help but notice he had an English accent. The drunk man nodded before he turned and stumbled down the road. The man in the blue suit did not move for a moment, but then turned to look at Sophie.

"You don't look familiar," he said, not taking his steely eyes off her. "Are you from around here?"

"No," Sophie said. "But I am looking for directions to the Jones ranch."

The man in the blue suit raised an eyebrow but said nothing.

"Do you know where it is?" she asked.

"It's a long walk," he said. "At least two miles from here."

"I don't mind," Sophie said.

"How about I walk with you?" he offered.

There was something in his voice, in his eyes, that told Sophie it was not a question, and her heart began to race.

"No, thank you," Sophie said. "I am sure I can find it myself."

She turned to go, but as she did, the man suddenly reached out and grabbed her wrist. Sophie looked up at him, her eyes widening in shock, and for a moment she could not speak or move.

"Let go of me," she said, coming to her senses.

But the man did not let go. Sophie had grown up with Frank, and so she knew a bully when she saw one.

"Let go," she repeated. "Or I'll scream."

The man in the blue suit smirked, but before either of them could say more, the door of the saloon opened a third time, and this time, a man with a round face and a bowler hat stepped out.

"Come on," he said. "Harry's finished dealin' and he reckons he can win back what he lost off you last time."

The blue-suited man turned back to Sophie. Her breath caught in her chest as he gazed at her with those cool eyes and she was sure she could see a hint of regret in them. Then, without another word, he dropped her wrist and turned to go.

As soon as he was gone, Sophie turned and hurried down the road, wanting to get as far away from that saloon and that man as possible. Her heart was beating so fast she was sure it would leap out of her chest at any moment. However, she had only gone a short way when she walked right into an older woman.

"Watch where you are going," the older woman grumbled. "You nearly knocked me right off my feet."

"I am sorry," Sophie said, out of breath.

The older woman frowned at her. She was short and her dark hair was pulled back into a tight bun, revealing her gray roots.

"Who are you?" she asked, somewhat suspiciously. "You're not from around here."

"No," Sophie said. "I am looking for the Jones ranch."

Just as the blue-suited man had done, the older woman raised her eyebrows in surprise.

"Just keep following this road," she said. "It's quite a walk and steep as a wall."

"How will I know if it's the right place?"

SALLY M. ROSS

"Just keep going until you can't go no more," the woman said. "It's about two miles up the road and there is a sign on the front gate, so you can't miss it."

"Thank you," Sophie said gratefully.

Without another word, the older woman bustled away and Sophie continued down the road and out of town.

Just as the older lady had said, the road to the ranch was steep, and as Sophie climbed higher and higher, her legs began to ache, as did her arms and shoulders from carrying the wooden crate. She grumbled under her breath as beads of perspiration ran down her back. The tendrils of ash-blonde hair that had come loose during the climb now clung to the sides of her face and neck. Mittens peered through the gaps in the crate, her yellow eyes wide with curiosity.

Eventually Sophie spotted a gate ahead and she exhaled in relief. As she approached the gate, she saw a sign that said "Jones" and she knew she had finally arrived.

The sun had long since sunk below the hills and so she could not see much as she walked up the road. However, in the twilight, she could make out the silhouette of a large building, which must've been the barn. Across from the barn was another building, larger still, which she figured must be the farmhouse.

Sophie approached the house, but as she reached the two narrow steps that led up to the porch, she hesitated a moment. This was it.

Sophie exhaled shakily as she climbed the steps and walked across the porch. Some of the wooden planks creaked and groaned under her weight. When she reached the front door, she lifted her right hand and rapped on the door. Then she waited, but she heard no sounds from inside the house, and so she rapped again. Still nothing.

She turned and went back across the porch and down the two stairs. She walked around the side of the house, peering into windows as she did. But most of the rooms were dark and the windows were so full of grime, it was difficult to make out if anyone was inside. As she came around the back of the house, she suddenly heard voices from inside. She walked to the back door and knocked again. This time, she heard a chair scrape back and heavy footsteps.

A moment later, the door opened, and a tall man with a thick beard and wild curls stood in front of her. He was taller than any man she'd ever seen, so tall his head almost touched the top of the door frame. Sophie was certain she'd never encountered such an intimidating presence in her life. As Sophie's eyes traveled the length of his body, from his feet to his head, she finally met his eyes. She was surprised to see that, despite his size and ruggedness, he had soft brown eyes, kind eyes.

Before Sophie could say anything, a baby began to cry, and she looked around the man to see a woman seated at the kitchen table with a squirming bundle in her arms. Sophie's brows furrowed as she took in the scene. This had to be the wrong house, surely?

"I'm sorry," Sophie said, shaking her head. "I must be in the wrong place..."

She stood a step back, confused. The sign at the gate had said "Jones" but this man could not be Simon—he had a wife and a baby.

"Are you Miss Thompson?" the woman asked as she got up from the table and walked over to the door.

Sophie frowned again as she slowly nodded. The woman was pretty, with auburn-colored hair and green eyes. However, she was pale, and the skin across her cheekbones was taut. The large purple rings under her eyes indicated to Sophie that she was in desperate need of a good night's sleep.

"You're not in the wrong place," the woman said. "I am Jenna and this is Simon."

Sophie said nothing for a moment, trying to figure out exactly what was happening.

"I'm Sophie," she said.

"You should come inside, Sophie," Jenna said.

Simon stepped aside but Sophie did not move. Her mind was racing at a million miles a minute. She had no idea what situation she'd gotten herself into and yet she had no choice. She'd run away from home and had nowhere else to go. It was dark and she knew no one in this town. So, despite the sinking sensation in the pit of her stomach, Sophie stepped inside the kitchen.

"Come and sit," Jenna offered as the baby wiggled in her arms.

"I think I'll stand," Sophie said, still holding the wooden crate in her arms.

No one said anything for a few moments, but Sophie saw Jenna give Simon an apprehensive look as she bit her bottom lip. Simon, on the other hand, was silent, his arms now folded across his chest.

Something about their silence irritated Sophie. After all, she'd come all this way, and now she was standing in this strange kitchen with no explanation.

"Will someone tell me what is going on?" Sophie asked.

"Are you sure you don't want to sit down?" Jenna offered again, the baby still fussing.

Sophie did not move.

"Okay," Jenna sighed. "I know this is going to be a bit of a shock—"

The bundle in her arms went rigid all of a sudden, and the baby's cry was a primal sound, quite unlike anything Sophie had ever heard before.

Jenna rocked the baby back and forth but the crying did not stop; in fact, it only grew louder. Mittens was moving around now, unsettled by the noise and looking for a place to escape it, but there was nowhere to go.

"I am sorry," Jenna said, blinking back tears.

Before Sophie could say anything, Jenna hurried from the room, and the baby's cries grew distant. Sophie turned to Simon, who was watching her.

"So?" she said, locking her gaze on him. "Are you going to tell me what is going on?"

Chapter Four

Sophie's question hung in the air between them for a long moment. He could hear Jenna in the bedroom upstairs, the baby still wailing as she tried to soothe him.

Simon had been surprised when he'd opened the door to find this messy, attractive young woman standing there with a cat in a chicken crate. He could see it in her eyes, a spark he'd never seen in anyone else before. She was different, and he had not expected to be interested in her, but part of him was, and he knew once he told her the truth, he'd be closing that door.

"Well?" Sophie said, her blue eyes glinting with confusion and frustration. "What is going on here? Are you already married? Is that your baby?"

She fired questions at him without taking a breath, and despite everything, Simon found himself slightly amused by her prickliness.

"No," Simon said, shaking his head. "Jenna is my cousin and the baby is hers, not mine."

Sophie's shoulder relaxed a little but she continued to frown.

"Don't you want to sit?" Simon offered. "Maybe put the cat down?"

Sophie glanced down at the crate but did not move. "If you are not married, then I don't understand why you don't seem pleased that I am here."

Simon exhaled deeply. "I am not pleased that you are here, because I am not the one who wrote to you."

"What?" Sophie said, her mouth popping open in shock to reveal a set of perfectly straight teeth.

"My cousin, Jenna, was the one who put the advertisement in the paper, she is the one who invited you to come."

Sophie stared at him, clearly quite unable to believe the words coming from his lips. He had not been the one who advertised for her?

"But why?" Sophie asked, shaking her head in disbelief. "Why would she do that?"

Simon shrugged. "Because she thinks she knows what's best."

They fell silent for a moment, but Simon could almost hear Sophie's brain working as she processed the information.

"So let me get this straight," Sophie said. "You don't want to marry me?"

"No," Simon said. "I don't want to marry anyone."

"Why not?" Sophie asked.

"Excuse me?" Simon said, taken aback by her frankness.

"Why don't you want to marry me?" Sophie asked. "Is there something wrong with me?"

"What?" Simon said, bewildered by the sudden confrontation of her tone.

"Why don't you want to marry me?" Sophie insisted, her blue eyes bright with determination.

"I don't know you," Simon argued.

"Well, I don't know you either," Sophie challenged. "But I came all this way to marry you."

Simon was certain he'd never met someone so argumentative in all his life. Yet he could not help but find her spirit alluring.

"And I am sorry that happened," Simon said. "But it was not my doing. I never put the advertisement into the paper and I never promised that I would marry you—"

"So what now?" Sophie asked. "What are we going to do? Because I can't go back. I need to find a husband."

Simon said nothing for a moment before he ran his hand through his hair and sighed. Sophie looked less fierce now and more afraid. He did not understand her fear but he wasn't willing to try to understand it—he couldn't, he wouldn't, get involved in her.

"You are welcome to stay the night," he said. "And in the morning, I'll drive you back to the train station—"

"You don't understand. I can't go back," she repeated, shaking her head.

Simon opened his mouth, but before he could respond, Jenna reappeared in the doorway. She did not have the baby with her, so she must have finally managed to get him to sleep.

"Did you tell her?" Jenna asked, looking at Simon.

He nodded.

"Sophie," Jenna said, her eyebrows pulled together in sympathy. "You must be starving. Can I make you something to eat?"

Sophie shook her head. "I am not hungry, but if you have a bowl of milk for Mittens—"

"Mittens?" Jenna asked, frowning.

"My cat," Sophie replied, indicating with her eyes to the wooden crate in her arms.

"Of course," Jenna said as she hurried to the pantry.

Sophie put the crate on the ground and undid the latch on top. She then reached in and lifted out a gray-blue cat with bright yellow eyes. Jenna returned with a saucer of milk and handed it to Sophie, who put it on the ground at her feet, and the cat began to drink. Simon was not a cat person, he'd never been one. They made him sneeze and his eyes got all watery.

No one spoke for a moment and the only sound to be heard was Mittens licking up the milk. The tension in the air was palpable.

"I'd better go and check on the horses," Simon said, needing some air.

Without a word, he turned and left the kitchen. It was dark now, but he knew the place like the back of his hand. As he entered the stables, he lit the small paraffin lamp and walked over to the first stall. His horse came up to him, putting his large head over the side of the stall, and Simon scratched his nose. Horses were so much simpler than people, and Simon often spent time with them, enjoying the quiet, uncomplicated companionship.

Simon felt badly about Miss Thompson and the whole situation; he could sense a desperation in her, although he did not quite understand it. Still, it was not his doing and he did not want to marry her.

It was late by the time Simon returned to the house. He'd hoped to discover that everyone had gone to bed, but when he stepped into the kitchen, Jenna was seated at the kitchen table.

"I need to talk to you," she said.

"Aren't you supposed to sleep when the baby sleeps?" he asked.

"Simon, please."

He sighed as he walked across and sat down at the table across from her.

"Where is she?" he asked.

"In the spare room," Jenna said. "She was tired."

Simon nodded but said nothing.

"Simon, won't you let her stay, please?"

Simon shook his head as he leaned back in his chair. "I've already told you, I don't want to get married."

"But can't you change your mind?" Jenna asked. "She's pretty and she seems to have a good head on her shoulders."

"I don't want to get married, Jenna," Simon argued.

"Well, she made it all the way to the ranch by herself," Jenna reasoned. "And she grew up on a ranch, so she'd be helpful."

Simon could hear how much Jenna wanted her to stay, but it was *his* life that would alter if he married her. He was the one who had to make all the sacrifices, not her. "I am sorry, Jen. But the answer is still no."

Without another word, Jenna was on her knees at his feet.

"Jenna, come on, get up," Simon insisted, but she did not move.

"The baby is not getting better, Simon," Jenna said, taking his hands as she looked up at him. "And I am hanging on by a thread. We need her help, please don't send her away."

Simon got up from the chair and helped Jenna to her feet. "You need to rest. You're just tired—"

"Please think about it, Simon, please."

Simon sighed. "All right," he agreed. "I'll think about it."

Jenna reached over and put a hand on his cheek. "Thank you," she said, her tone brimming with relief and gratitude.

Simon sat at the table for a long while after Jenna had gone to bed. He knew things weren't great, but he hadn't realized just how desperate his cousin was for someone to help out. In truth, Simon had lived alone for so long that he'd forgotten how to read people, how to read their emotions. He'd barely asked his cousin anything about her situation or how she was feeling, and he hadn't realized it until now. Her decision to put that advertisement in the paper had been an act of desperation, an act she may Not have taken had Simon been more present, more willing to listen.

Simon knew that he would do anything for family, and maybe Miss Thompson's arrival was as much his fault as his cousin's, but could he really marry a stranger? If he married Sophie, it would be the end of his solitude. Could he do it for Jenna, for the baby? He did not know, but he would have to make a decision soon, and he just hoped it would be the right one.

***

Simon did not sleep well that night. He woke up whenever the baby did and then lay awake, thinking about Sophie and Jenna and what he was going to do. Around midnight, he fell into a deep sleep, and woke up just as the birds were starting to chirp outside his bedroom window. The whole house was quiet and he'd forgotten what that was like. For a long moment, Simon did not move, enjoying the sounds he'd missed, the rustling of the leaves in the morning breeze and the distant crow of the roosters.

Simon got out of bed and quickly dressed before heading to the kitchen. As he approached, he heard Jenna talking to Sophie, and he hesitated a moment to listen.

"You're so good with him," Jenna said.

"According to my ma, I was a colicky baby," Sophie said. "And a tight swaddle was the only thing that kept her sane."

"Well, I can't thank you enough for sitting up with him," Jenna said. "I don't remember the last time I slept for more than an hour."

"I don't mind," Sophie said. "He's a sweet thing."

The two women fell silent for a few moments. Simon could not help but be impressed by the way Sophie had managed to calm the baby, how perfectly comfortable she sounded.

"May I ask you something?" Sophie said.

"Of course," Jenna said.

"Why haven't you given him a name yet?"

Jenna did not answer right away, but Simon listened closely. It was something he'd wanted to ask her for weeks. It was odd to him that the baby had no name.

"I guess I just thought that if I gave him a name, then it would make this all real," Jenna confessed. "And not some bad dream."

Simon's heart caught in his throat.

"I get it," Sophie said. "Sometimes it's easier to pretend than to face reality, but in the end, it catches up with you eventually."

"I just didn't see my life turning out like this," Jenna said.

"I know what you mean," Sophie said wistfully.

Simon frowned at the regretful longing in her voice and he thought back to the night before and how she'd insisted that she could not return home. Despite not wanting to know her reasoning, he could not help but feel curious. Why would such an attractive young woman, one coming from obvious means, by her mannerisms and way of dress, want to come to a remote mountain ranch and marry a stranger?

"I am sorry," Jenna apologized. "For pretending to be Simon and putting that advertisement in the paper. I really thought that he'd change his mind."

The two women fell silent and Simon stepped into the kitchen.

"Mornin'," he said.

"Morning," Jenna said, but Sophie remained silent.

Simon shifted on his boots for a moment, feeling like an intruder. He looked at Sophie for a moment, unable to ignore how attractive she looked in the soft morning light, her ash-blonde hair like a halo around her face. However, the instant she met his gaze, he dropped his eyes.

"I'd better get out and start on those chores."

Without another word, Simon walked across the kitchen and out of the back door. The sun was rising over the top of the mountain, casting a warm glow across the ranch. Simon usually loved this time of day, the peaceful quiet of the world waking up, but that morning, his mind was somewhere else.

Simon and Jenna had always been more like siblings than cousins. Jenna's mother was the favorite sister of Simon's mother, and both women had only had one child. Jenna was a few years younger than Simon but it had never mattered to them. Growing up, Jenna and her parents lived in town; her father was a cobbler and her mother a homemaker.

For as long as he could remember, Jenna had always been a free spirit. A spirit as wild as her mop of curly auburn hair, his mother used to say. Then, when Jenna was thirteen, her parents were caught in a blizzard and never made it home. After that, Jenna moved from town to the ranch, and she and Simon spent every day together.

Simon's parents hoped that the ranch, the simple life, would settle Jenna down some, but it never did. When she turned nineteen, Jenna left the ranch in search of a different life. She wanted more, something bigger. That same year she got a job singing for patrons at the saloon in town.

Simon and Jenna grew apart after she left the ranch. Unlike his parents, Simon didn't care about the fact that she was a dance hall girl, but she felt further away from him, as if they were existing in two entirely different worlds. A year slipped by and then another. Then, when Simon was twenty-two, his parents were killed in an avalanche on the ranch. After his parents died, Jenna came for the funeral, but she was a stranger to him now. He was day and she was night. There was never any real animosity between them; it was just the course that their lives had taken.

Simon had not even known his cousin was pregnant until one night, almost two months ago, she arrived on his doorstep with a newborn baby. Jenna had hidden her pregnancy from him, from everyone, in fact. It was not hard to understand why she'd kept it secret. Having a baby out of wedlock came with consequences. So Jenna had run away from town, and all the people who would shun her and the baby, and she'd come to Simon. He had not thought twice about letting her stay; she was his family.

Yet in the weeks that followed, Simon could see that Jenna was different. That light, that Simon loved so much about her, was gone. Perhaps it had gone out a long time ago or perhaps it was the trauma of being a new mother, but she'd become a watered-down version of who she once was.

It was no secret that over the past few years, life had bent them out of shape, and Simon had changed too. After his parents passed, he grew used to his own company. He had turned inward and become his whole world. He liked it that way. It was easier that way.

In truth, he'd never been very good at making friends. When he was a boy, he attended the school in town, but never saw the point in books and longed to be working the land with the sun beating down on his back. His parents had allowed him to drop out of school when he was eleven to work on the ranch. Simon did not miss having friends, as he'd always been better with animals than with people, unlike Jenna, who everyone loved.

From the stables, Simon heard the baby wailing again, and he sighed. He and Jenna had spent the past eight weeks surviving, but not really living. If he had his way, he'd tell them all to leave, but he knew he couldn't. As soon as he'd opened his home to Jenna and the baby, everything had changed.

Now he was the closest thing to a father that baby had, and Simon knew that if his own father were still alive, he'd tell him to marry Sophie and try to give the child some sort of family, a support system. Life was not going to be kind to him and it would not be his fault; all he did was be born.

While it was Jenna who'd opened the door to Sophie and invited her into their lives, it was up to Simon to decide what to do next. As much as he did not want to get married, he felt backed into a corner. If he sent her away, their lives would remain as they'd been the last eight weeks; they'd be surviving. He knew by getting married he'd be sacrificing the life he wanted, but with Jenna and the baby, that life was lost to him already.

The horse whinnied softly and Simon turned to look into his brown eyes.

"Looks like our bachelor days are over," he said.

The horse blinked at him and Simon sighed. He'd marry Sophie, and with any luck, he'd get some clean shirts and a hot meal, because that was what he was marrying her for—so that they could stop surviving and start living again.

Chapter Five

Mittens sat on Sophie's lap, purring loudly as she scratched her lightly behind the ear.

"At least one of us is happy," she said quietly.

Sophie was sitting on the porch step in the warm morning sunshine. Simon had not come in for breakfast, so she and Jenna had eaten alone. Sophie had offered to do the dishes so Jenna could put the baby down for a nap.

Mittens yawned and tucked her head under her paw and Sophie sighed to herself. She'd hardly slept a wink last night with everything that had happened. She felt as if she were in limbo now, waiting for her fate to be decided. She hoped that by some miracle, Simon might change his mind, but it was as likely that he'd come around the side of the house any moment and tell her to hit the dusty trail.

Sophie had only left home a day ago but it felt like a lifetime. She knew that if Simon told her to go, she'd be in trouble. She had no money for a train ticket, and even if she had money, she had nowhere to go. All of her father's relatives were dead, and she could not trust her mother's relatives not to tell on her. No, she was at the mercy of Simon Jones, and she was annoyed that she'd escaped one man only to be at the mercy of another.

"Maybe we should just go," Sophie said to Mittens. "At least then it would be our choice."

The cat opened one yellow eye and Sophie sighed again.

"You're right," she said. "We don't have anywhere to go."

Sophie looked up at the large mountains that surrounded the ranch, their peaks touching the sky. There was a stillness

57

here, a peacefulness that she hadn't experienced in a long time. But with that sense of peace was a sadness too, because as much as she wanted to belong to this place, she didn't.

"It's something special, isn't it?"

Sophie nodded as Jenna walked across the porch and sat down next to her on the step. She'd changed out of her night clothes and was now dressed in a dark green cotton skirt and white blouse. It suited her well, setting off her dark auburn curls.

"I moved here for a while after my parents died," Jenna said. "Simon and I spent a lot of time wandering these mountains, pretending that we were explorers on some kind of epic journey."

There was a wistfulness in Jenna's voice that Sophie knew well. She'd spent a great deal of her life longing for her lost childhood.

"Why did you leave?" Sophie asked.

Jenna did not answer right away and as Sophie turned her head, she could see something in Jenna's green eyes. Regret, perhaps?

"I was young," Jenna said. "I thought I knew what I wanted..."

Jenna's voice trailed off at the sound of gravel crunching under heavy boots, and a moment later, Simon came around the corner. Mittens, who'd been fast asleep, was startled by his sudden arrival and jumped off Sophie's lap and ran under the porch.

"Can I have a word?" he asked, looking at Sophie.

Sophie nodded as Jenna got up from the step.

"I should go and check on the baby," she said.

Sophie's stomach was a ball of knots, she could not read Simon's intentions in his face or his body. If he decided to take her back to the train station, where would she go? Her fate hung in the balance, the awful silence between them.

Simon did not speak until Jenna had disappeared into the house. Sophie looked up at him expectantly, her shoulders tense.

"I don't want a wife," he said plainly.

Sophie's heart sank.

"But I can see that we need some help around here," he said. "Especially with the baby and everything—"

Sophie held her breath, hoping her face did not betray the desperation in her heart.

"So I will honor Jenna's promise to you and marry you," Simon said, rather stiffly. "But it will be a business arrangement. A marriage of convenience and nothing more than that. You will help around the house with the cleaning, cooking, and such, and in return, you will get the roof over your head and meals. Is that clear?"

Sophie did her best to ignore his tone of voice, which suggested he was speaking to a child or someone hard of hearing. This was what she wanted—she could stay, and that was the most important thing.

"I never expected anything more than that," Sophie said. "Thank you."

Simon nodded once before he turned to go, but as he did, he hesitated. "I'll go into town this morning and make the arrangements."

Then, without another word, he was gone, leaving Sophie alone. Her shoulders dropped in relief as Mittens peered out from under the porch to make sure Simon had gone.

"Did you hear that, girl?" Sophie said. "We get to stay, after all."

***

Sophie sat beside Simon as the small buggy bumped down the road. It was late afternoon and the sun was already sinking below the tree line, and long shadows stretched across the road, broken up by intermittent stretches of sunlight, like the keys of a giant's piano. In the back, Jenna sat with the baby in her arms. The motion of the buggy had rocked him to sleep only moments after they'd left the ranch.

Sophie looked down at her hands clasped tightly in her lap. Despite wanting this marriage, she was nervous. This was all so new, so strange, and the man sitting next to her was as stiff as a board. It was obvious that he could not hide his discomfort, which didn't help her nerves.

As he had said, Simon had done into town earlier that day to speak to the minister at the local church, and had returned shortly after to say that he was available to marry them that very afternoon. When Sophie told the news to Jenna that she was staying, she was happy enough that she almost hugged her. Sophie was relieved at least someone was pleased she was staying.

The small town of Shadow's Ridge came into view and as they turned into the main street, people were milling about in front of the various shops. Out of the corner of her eye, Sophie saw Jenna shrink back, as if she were trying to make herself very small.

As they passed by the general store, Sophie was surprised that no one tipped a hat or waved a hand to them; instead

An Unexpected Family for the Rugged Mountain Man

they just stopped and stared, their expressions dark. It really was a shadow town.

"People in this town aren't very friendly," Sophie noted.

Neither Simon nor Jenna responded, but Sophie did not notice. They were passing by the saloon and her heart started to race. She'd not forgotten the man in the blue suit, nor those steely blue eyes. The thought of them still sent a shiver down her back.

The baby began to niggle and Sophie turned to see Jenna, whose face was now as white as a sheet, and her hands were trembling.

"Jenna?" Sophie said, twisting around in her seat. "Are you quite well?"

"Just a little nauseous," Jenna said. "Must be the windy road."

Sophie nodded. "Take deep breaths," she advised.

Sophie turned back to see the small chapel in front of them. It was made of stone and had a thatched roof. Around the chapel was a low wall made from the same stone. The tops of several gravestones were visible, all covered in soft green lichen. A large oak tree grew beside the church, offering shade to those who rested there.

Simon brought the buggy to a stop on the road opposite the church and they all climbed down. Jenna had the baby in her arms as they crossed the road and Simon pushed open the small wrought iron gate that squealed on its hinges.

As Sophie stepped inside the churchyard, she thought back to that day her mother had married her stepfather. She could remember every detail of that day. How her mother had stood across from that man and promised to love and obey him. Sophie could remember the burning in her chest. It was a feeling she'd never forgotten, and she knew hating someone was wrong, but she'd hated her mother for betraying her father and marrying a monster.

"You okay?" Jenna asked, touching her arm.

Sophie nodded.

"Welcome," a warm voice greeted them.

Sophie looked up to see a tall, gray-haired man standing at the church doors. He was dressed in a dark wool coat and a clerical collar. He smiled kindly at them as they approached and his warmness helped to loosen the knots in Sophie's stomach.

"Will anyone else be joining us today?" he asked.

Simon shook his head. "No," he said. "It's just us."

The minister's eyebrows lifted in surprise, but only momentarily before he recovered himself and smiled again. "Let's get started then, shall we?"

They all followed the minister into the small church. Rows of benches were on either side of the room with a narrow aisle down the middle. At the front of the church was a large, paneled window and the afternoon sun shone through it, casting the room in a warm glow. When they got to the front of the church, Jenna took a seat on one of the benches while Sophie and Simon joined the minister in front of the window.

"Are you both ready?" the minister asked.

Sophie caught Simon's eye, and she saw the same apprehension in them that she felt in her chest. The truth was that this was not the future she'd wanted for herself. Sophie had always wanted to marry for love and to find her equal in another. Yet love, a family, they were both lost to her now.

"I'm ready," Sophie said.

***

They arrived back at the ranch just as the first stars began to appear in the sky. No one had spoken much of the ride back. The baby was restless and cried most of the journey, despite Sophie and Jenna's best efforts to calm him. It was quite a relief to everyone when they could finally get out of the buggy. Simon went straight to the barn to do the chores that he'd missed that afternoon while Sophie and Jenna went inside. Mittens was there, waiting at the back door for them.

"Shall I get something on for dinner?" Sophie offered.

"Please," Jenna said gratefully. "I am going to see if I can get him down for a nap."

Jenna disappeared, leaving Sophie alone in the kitchen. To tell the truth, she wasn't a very experienced cook. Her stepfather had hired a cook at the ranch and so she'd never had much opportunity to practice. Still, this was her job now and she needed to make the best of it.

By the time Jenna got back to the kitchen, Sophie had managed to get a pot of water on to boil and had found four rather sad-looking potatoes in the pantry. She'd also found a piece of salted pork and some beans. It was by no means a feast but it would have to do.

"I haven't had much time to get into town," Jenna said. "With the baby being so fussy and everything."

"What about Simon?" Sophie said.

"Simon doesn't go into town," Jenna said. "He prefers to be here."

"Why?" Sophie asked.

Jenna shrugged. "It's just how he is."

Sophie did not ask any more questions, turning her attention to the potatoes, which had so many eyes it was as if they were all watching her.

Sophie was setting the table when Simon came into the kitchen.

"Where's Jenna?" he asked as he walked over to the sink to wash up.

"The baby woke up," Sophie explained.

Simon nodded but said nothing.

Sophie walked back over to the coal stove and carried across the dishes but as she did, Mittens suddenly raced through her legs after a rat, and Sophie got such a fright at the enormous size of the rodent that she dropped the bowl of beans and it went crashing to the floor.

"Oh no," Sophie groaned as she kneeled to scoop up the beans.

Simon walked over to her and handed her a cloth. "Maybe we should put that cat of yours in the barn," he said. "Keep her from getting under everyone's feet."

Sophie looked up at him and frowned. She had not spent one night away from Mittens in fourteen years and she was not about to start now.

"She can't sleep in the barn," Sophie said, her tone full of indignation. "And besides, she's being useful, she's catching rats—"

"She's leaving fur all over the house," Simon argued. "Animals belong outside, in the barn."

"Well, if you are going to make her sleep in the barn, you'll have to make me sleep out there too," Sophie argued.

Simon said nothing for a moment but he tilted his head slightly, to indicate that he was considering it. Sophie got up from the floor, forgetting all about the beans and putting her hands on her hips.

"Mittens is my family," Sophie said. "And we are married, so now she is yours too, and if you don't like it, you can go out and sleep in the barn."

"This is my house," Simon said, gritting his teeth.

"Well, it's my house now too," Sophie said, her blue eyes flashing.

Sophie saw the muscle in Simon's jaw tense, but she would not stand down. She'd been bullied all her life and she was tired of it. Between her stepfather, Frank, and even her own mother, Sophie had lived a half-life, and she was having no more of it. This was a fresh start for her and she intended things to be very different.

"I think I've lost my appetite," Simon said.

Without another word, he turned and walked out of the kitchen.

"Good!" Sophie cried after him. "There wasn't enough food for you anyway."

Sophie exhaled deeply as she looked at the mess on the floor at her feet. Her cheeks were hot as she kneeled back down and continued to scoop up the beans. They had been married for less than four hours and they were already fighting. Still, she would not apologize for standing up for herself. She was his wife, but she would not obey him. She was done obeying men, and if Simon couldn't deal with that, he could very well go and sleep in the barn.

Chapter Six

Simon waited for everyone to be in bed before he went to the kitchen to get something to eat. The house was quiet for a change, and it reminded him of how it used to be, before Jenna and the baby arrived. It was hard to believe only eight weeks ago he'd been enjoying his life of solitude, without anyone to worry about, save for himself.

Simon lit the small paraffin lamp and searched the pantry for some food, but all he found was a piece of hard bread and some jerky. He took the jerky and sat down at the kitchen table, enjoying the peace and quiet. Somewhere outside, an owl called.

The jerky was as tough as old boots, but it was better than nothing. As he ate, the cat suddenly appeared in the doorway, its bright yellow eyes unblinking as she stared at him.

"What do you want?" Simon asked rudely. "Don't you think you've caused enough trouble for one night?"

The cat continued to stare at him for a moment longer before she turned and ran back down the hallway, her long tail pointed straight up at the ceiling. Simon heard her scratching at Sophie's bedroom door; there was a click of the latch as the door opened and then closed again.

"Stupid cat," Simon muttered to himself.

He knew deep down that he probably should have been a bit more tactical with Sophie about her cat, but he really wasn't a cat person. Still, he'd made the decision to marry her and so he knew he should make more of an effort. After all, Simon knew how much an animal could become the most important thing in your life. Maybe that could even be something they had in common, a small thread to connect them together in this new life.

Simon finished the piece of jerky and then got up from the table and made his way back to his bedroom. He needed to get some sleep before the baby woke up again.

But as Simon lay in bed the night, sleep evaded him. It was frustrating, because he was tired, but his brain was too awake. He lay staring at the ceiling for a long time, and eventually drifted to sleep. However, he woke with a start when he heard his horse, Buckaroo, neighing loudly from the barn. It was a deep, throaty sound, and Simon knew that it meant trouble.

He got out of bed and grabbed his rifle from the top of the wardrobe. He then threw the bedroom door open and raced outside to the stables, grabbing a lamp on his way out of the kitchen.

He got there in time to find the coyote with his strong jaws buried in the Buckaroo's flank. The horse was bucking wildly, its eyes rolling back in his head, but the coyote would not let go. Simon pointed his rifle in the air and fired; the shot was enough to scare the coyote into letting go, but before Simon had the chance to take another shot, the coyote ran off into the night.

Simon put down the rifle and hurried over to the horse, who'd stopped bucking, but he was furiously pacing the length of the small stall.

"Whoa, boy," Simon said gently. "I just want to take a look, okay?"

He reached out and placed his hands on the horse's neck to calm him down, and when he'd stopped pacing, Simon lifted the lamp to get a better look. There were several bite marks on the flank and leg, and they were deep. The biggest risk now would be infection, which was why Simon needed to get it cleaned.

Carrying his lamp, Simon hurried from the stables to the barn and fetched clean water and a bottle of turpentine. He then went into the kitchen and found some clean cloths before he returned to the horse, who was groaning softly. Simon climbed into the stall and hung the lamp from a nail in the wall.

"It's all right, boy," he said. "We will get you patched up and as good as new in no time."

Using the clean water, he rinsed the bite marks first. He then poured turpentine onto the clean cloth and dapped it into the wounds. Buckaroo flinched in pain and Simon placed his left hand on his neck to soothe him.

"Almost done," he said.

Once he'd finished cleaning the wounds with turpentine, he used another cloth to cover the wounds. He was concerned that the horse wasn't putting any weight on his leg, but it might just be because he was in pain. It was difficult to tell in the lamp light, and Simon knew he'd have a better idea in the morning if he'd need to fetch the farrier.

"You did great," Simon said, rubbing the horse's neck. "I'll come back and check on you in the morning. Try to get some sleep."

Simon turned to go, unhooking the lap off the nail as he did. He'd been so busy making sure the horse was all right that he had not stopped to consider how the coyote got into the stables. He was always so careful to latch the doors, as they often had coyotes around the stables and barn at night.

Simon's mind was working so furiously that he did not notice Sophie at first. She was standing in her nightdress in the middle of the back garden. Her long ash-blonde hair hung down her back and shoulders like a silvery curtain. She was barefoot and her arms were wrapped around her chest. Simon realized that he also was undressed, wearing nothing but his flannel night pants, and he suddenly felt slightly self-conscious.

"What happened?" she asked. "I heard the gunshot."

"Coyote got into the stables," Simon explained.

Even from where he stood, Simon saw Sophie's face pale.

"Are the horses okay?" Sophie asked.

"We just got the one horse," Simon said. "And he's bit quite bad, but I'll be able to get a better look in the morning."

Sophie nodded but as she did, she bit her bottom lip.

"What is it?" Simon asked.

"I think it's my fault," Sophie said.

Simon frowned. "What do you mean?"

"Earlier tonight, before bed, I couldn't find Mittens. The last time I saw her was when she was chasing that rat, and I thought maybe she'd chased it into the stables. So I went to look and I must have not latched the door properly on my way out—"

Simon knew it was a mistake, but the anger was already rising in his chest.

"How could you be so careless?" he snapped. "I thought you grew up on a ranch!"

"I am sorry," Sophie apologized.

"Being sorry doesn't change the fact that my horse got seriously injured this evening because you were looking for your stupid cat," Simon exploded.

Sophie flinched but said nothing as Jenna emerged from the house, pulling her dressing gown around her body.

"What in the heavens is going on?" she asked, looking from Simon to Sophie.

"Ask her," Simon said, glaring at Sophie.

Sophie said nothing, but Simon could see she was trembling.

"Simon?" Jenna pressed.

"She left the latch off the stable door," Simon said, gritting his teeth. "A coyote got in and attacked Buck."

"Is he all right?" Jenna asked.

Simon shrugged. "I cleaned him up but will only be able to take a proper look in the morning. I'm worried he's injured his leg, he won't put any weight on it."

Jenna nodded. "Okay, well, there is nothing else to be done until the morning then, so we should all probably get to bed."

No one moved for a moment.

"I am sorry," Sophie apologized again.

Simon said nothing as he turned toward the house but he hesitated a moment and turned his head. "A good cowboy learns from his mistakes. So I sure hope you learn from this one."

Then, without another word, he headed inside the house.

***

Simon was up with the sun the next morning. He went straight to check on Buckaroo and was surprised to find Sophie there. She had the horse's head cradled in her arms and she was talking to him softly. The way she spoke to him it was plain how bad she felt; even from where he stood, her whispered words were full of regret. He knew it had been an accident, but the idea that he could have lost his horse still outweighed his sense of goodwill toward her.

Simon cleared his throat and Sophie turned around.

"I was just checking on him," Sophie explained.

Simon said nothing as he walked over. As he removed the cloth and examined the bite marks, he could sense Sophie watching him. Simon then ran his hand down the horse's leg. As far as he could tell, the leg wasn't broken, it was most likely just a sprain. But even a sprain would put him out of business for a few weeks, which meant that Simon was without a horse.

"How is he?" Sophie asked.

"He'll heal, as long as the bites don't get infected."

Sophie nodded and they fell silent for a few moments.

"Simon—"

"I've got other chores to do," Simon said, cutting her off.

He then turned and exited the stables, leaving Sophie alone with Buckaroo.

***

Simon returned to the house after finishing all his chores. He yawned widely as he approached the house, feeling exhausted, and the day had only just begun.

"He's never going to forgive me," Sophie said from inside.

"He will," Jenna said. "He knows you didn't do it on purpose."

"And he hates Mittens."

"Just give him some time," Jenna said. "He's used to being on his own."

The kitchen fell silent and Simon stepped inside.

"I've made eggs," Jenna said. "Why don't you sit down?"

Simon took a seat across from Sophie as Jenna placed a plate of eggs in front of him. Sophie had the baby swaddled up in her arms.

"I have some news," Jenna said as she took her seat and Sophie handed her the baby.

Simon turned to look at her.

"I've given the baby a name," Jenna announced. "His name is Oliver, after my pa."

"How nice," Sophie said.

Simon nodded. "It's a good, solid name."

Jenna looked pleased and Simon was relieved. It was strange to him that his cousin had taken so long to name the baby. But finally she had, and he couldn't help but feel that Sophie had done one good thing at least.

After the events of the night before, Simon had been angry at Sophie, probably more than she deserved, and he felt his heart soften toward her in that moment. Still, he had married her for Jenna, not for himself and he needed to focus on what was important—making sure his horse got better and keeping the ranch running.

Chapter Seven

After breakfast that morning, Simon went back out to work. He'd hardly said two words to Sophie over breakfast and had kept his eyes averted. She still felt so stupid that she'd not latched the door properly after searching for Mittens.

Sophie had just finished the breakfast dishes when Jenna came back in the kitchen.

"He's asleep?" Sophie asked.

Jenna nodded.

Sophie was glad that the swaddling was helping. It had only been a couple of days but the dark circles under Jenna's eyes were already fading a bit and she looked better rested.

"How about I show you around the ranch?" Jenna asked. "You've been here two days but no one's given you the proper tour."

"Sure," Sophie agreed. "I'd like that."

"Come on then," Jenna said.

Sophie followed Jenna out of the back door and into the warm sunshine. Mittens followed them too, stopping every now and again to sniff at a blade of grass or peer up at a bird in a tree.

"How big is the ranch?" Sophie asked.

"About five hundred acres," Jenna said.

Sophie nodded. Her family's ranch was four times bigger than this one and employed eight ranch hands to help.

"Does Simon have anyone to help him around the ranch?" Sophie asked, looking around.

"He used to," Jenna said. "I don't know the whole story, but after his parents were killed, there was a lot of debt left behind. Simon sold what he could and got rid of all the hands, and he's been doing it alone ever since."

"It sounds like a lot of work for one person," Sophie said.

"It is," Jenna agreed. "But I think he likes it that way."

They fell silent again as Jenna led her to the orchard around the back of the barn.

"What trees are these?" Sophie asked, looking around with interest.

"Apples here," Jenna said. "Apricots over there and plums and figs at the back there."

"What do you do with all the fruit?" Sophie inquired.

"Simon turns it into jam and sells it in town," Jenna said.

"Simon makes jam?" Sophie asked, unable to hide the disbelief in her voice.

Jenna laughed and shook her head. "I know, he doesn't seem like the home industries type, but my cousin can make a mean jar of jam."

The picture of the very masculine Simon wearing an apron and holding a wooden spoon was too much for Sophie and she could not help but smile. It was also very apparent that she did not know Simon very well and she could not help but feel intrigued.

"Come on," Jenna said.

She led Sophie through the fruit trees to the edge of the property, which dropped off in a steep ledge. In the distance, the sheep were baaing loudly, and Sophie could see an eagle circling up in the sky above their heads. It felt to Sophie as if she were standing on the precipice of the world.

"It's so beautiful here," Sophie said. "So peaceful."

Jenna sighed softly. "When I was younger, all I wanted was to be in town, where the excitement was, not stuck out here with the sheep and the birds."

"Do you still feel that way?" Sophie asked.

"No," Jenna sighed sadly. "Not anymore."

They fell silent for a few moments, staring out into the horizon.

"Can I ask you something?" Jenna said.

"Of course," Sophie replied, turning to look at her.

"Why don't you judge me?" Jenna asked, her dark brows furrowed

Sophie frowned, not really understanding what she meant.

"Everyone judges me," Jenna continued. "Well, maybe not Simon, but he's my family, but everyone else does. You saw the way they treated us yesterday when we drove through town, as if we were a family of pariahs."

Sophie thought back to yesterday and the people on the street, with their stony faces and creases of disapproval. The way the shadows passed over their faces and how Jenna recoiled from their view as if she were terrified to be seen. To be truthful, Sophie had not understood it.

"It's not my place to judge you," Sophie said. "I don't know your story."

"No one knows my story," Jenna said bitterly. "But that does not stop them from treating me like a Hester Prynne."

Sophie said nothing. She did not know who Hester Prynne was, but she knew how it felt to be an outcast. She'd been an outcast for most of her life, not even feeling as if she had a place in her own home.

From the house, Oliver woke up from her nap, and Jenna sighed.

"Why don't you take a walk?" she said. "Get to know the place."

Sophie nodded as Jenna turned back toward the house. Once Jenna was gone, Sophie walked back through the orchard and then past the barn and stables. Mittens stopped following her, choosing instead to lie down on a patch of dirt in the warm sunshine.

Sophie walked for a long time, not in any particular direction. There was just so much to see, from the bright red cardinals chattering away in the treetops to the aromatic junipers that brushed against her skirt.

Sophie had grown up on a ranch but it had always felt like a prison. After her mother remarried, her stepfather had insisted she stay close to home and convinced her mother that a girl's place was indoors and not on the back of a horse.

No matter how often she snuck out to ride, Frank would always find her and bring her back, and she'd be punished. Sometimes her stepfather would lock her in her room for days on end. They'd tried to break her spirit, but Sophie had refused to give them the satisfaction.

A movement out of the corner of her eye caused Sophie to turn her head and see Simon. He was topless, and dripping with water. The drops caught the sunlight, making him shine. In the daylight, Sophie could really see him now, from the arch of his shoulders to the V on his lower abdomen near his hips.

His shoulders were as broad as two men put together, and his upper arms were as thick as the trunks of whitebark pines. She knew she should look away, but it was as if her eyes refused to listen to her brain.

Suddenly Simon looked up and caught her eye, and Sophie's cheeks burned as quickly as she looked away.

"What are you doing all the way out here?" Simon asked, pulling his shirt over his wet shoulders.

"I was just taking a walk," Sophie said. "Getting to know the place better."

Simon was struggling to get his shirt on and Sophie was doing her best to keep her eyes averted, her cheeks still pink.

"You shouldn't be wandering around the place," Simon said. "You could fall and hurt yourself."

Sophie's embarrassment turned to irritation.

"So I should just stay inside?" she asked. "Is that where women belong?"

Simon frowned. "I just don't want you to go missing because I haven't got the time or the horse to come looking for you."

"Well, you don't have to worry about me," Sophie said. "I can take care of myself."

Just as the words left her lips, the longest snake she'd ever seen, with red, black, and white bands, slithered past her, and Sophie got such a fright that she almost jumped into Simon's arms.

"It's harmless," Simon said, his lips twitching in amusement.

"I knew that," Sophie said, smoothing her skirts. "What are you doing out here, anyway?"

"Bathing," Simon said. "There is a spring just on the other side of those pines."

Simon's muscular arms popped into her mind again and her cheeks flushed.

"Well, I'd better be getting back to the house," Sophie said.

"I'll walk with you," Simon said.

"I don't need an escort," Sophie insisted. "I can make it back on my own."

Simon rolled his eyes. "The farrier is coming to look at Buckaroo. So I am going in that direction, but if you prefer, I can walk three paces behind you so you don't feel so indignant?"

Sophie had the strongest desire to stick her tongue out at him. "Fine. Let's just go."

Together they walked back toward the house but neither of them spoke. Sophie kept casting sideways glances at Simon, hoping he might talk to her, open up a bit, but he kept his eyes forward. He was the most perplexing man she'd ever met. He had such kind eyes but he was so rough around the edges. She could not help but wonder if he'd always been this way or if, like her, he'd been shaped by the casualties of his life.

"Are you worried about Buckaroo?" Sophie asked. "Is that why you've asked the farrier to come?"

"I'd like a second opinion," Simon said. "He's the only horse we have now and if he can't work, well, what good is a horse that can't work?"

Sophie said nothing as she glanced at Simon again. His voice was hard but his eyes betrayed him. She knew he was softer than he liked to let on. Buckaroo was more than just a working horse, he meant something to Simon.

"I am sorry," Sophie apologized. "About leaving the door unlatched."

"Least said, soonest mended," Simon said.

Sophie nodded as she glanced at Simon again. She'd not really had any time to talk with him these last couple of days. He was always out on the ranch and when they did talk, it usually turned into an argument. Maybe this might be the time to try and get him to come out of his shell and talk to her.

"Jenna showed me the orchard," Sophie said, doing her best to keep the conversation flowing. "I don't think I've ever seen such healthy trees. Jenna said you make jam in the fall."

"I do," Simon confirmed.

Sophie waited, hoping he'd give her a bit more but he didn't.

"Who taught you to make jam?" she asked. "Was it your ma?"

Simon nodded and without intending to, Sophie sighed in exasperation, and he turned to her with his eyebrows raised.

"What?" he asked her.

"Why won't you talk to me?" Sophie asked.

"Why do you ask so many questions?" Simon retorted.

"Because I am trying to get to know you," Sophie said. "After all, I am your wife."

Simon stopped and turned to her.

"Sophie," he said. "I was clear with you about all this, you are my wife only in name. We don't need to get to know one another. You just need to fulfill your end of the bargain."

Sophie frowned. "So because this is a marriage of convenience, we can't be friends?"

"I don't need any friends," Simon said. "If you need someone to talk to, go and talk to Jenna—"

"Fine," Sophie said, her eyes glowering. "I will."

Simon flung out an arm as if to say 'be my guest' and Sophie stormed off toward the house. By the time she reached the back door, tears were streaming down her face in a mixture of frustration and disappointment. Since she was six years old, Sophie had felt invisible in her own home. She'd hoped that when she left and came here that things would be different, but Simon was no different from her stepfather. All he wanted was for her to be quiet and finish the mending.

Chapter Eight

The farrier confirmed what Simon thought—Buckaroo had sprained his leg. It was a relief to Simon that it wasn't a fracture or a break, but it would still take a few weeks to heal. He'd struggle without a horse but there was no help for it. The ranch did not have the money to get a second horse. He would be doing a lot more walking in the weeks to come.

Once the farrier had left, Simon headed over to the barn. It was almost the end of May and Simon was behind on shearing. Jenna and Oliver's arrival had thrown a spanner in the works and now he needed to play catch up. In the past, Simon had his ranch hands to help him, but this time he'd have to hire a team.

He'd need help with the shearing and the skirting and sorting. It was a big job, admittedly too big for him to handle on his own, so he'd have to go into town and advertise for a team to help. During the war, when Simon was serving, his father had also been forced to hire men, as most of the ranch hands were fighting.

The wool they sheared every year was their biggest moneymaker, and Simon had to get it done right. A few weeks ago, the only person he was responsible for was himself, but now he had three other mouths to feed.

It was a lot for him to wrap his head around, a wife and a baby. It was a future he'd not wanted but now had. Still, he was determined to make the shearing a success and keep a roof over their heads. It was what his father would expect of him.

By the time Simon finished sharpening the shearing tools, it was midafternoon. He'd been so focused on his work that he'd forgotten about lunch, but his stomach was now grumbling and so he headed inside to find something to eat.

Inside the kitchen, he found Jenna at the table with baby Oliver asleep in his Moses basket beside her. Jenna's auburn hair was tied back from her face and she did not notice Simon at first. She was reading a letter, and as her mouth traced the words, Simon saw the creases in her brow deepening.

"Who's that from?" Simon asked as he stepped inside.

Jenna jumped in surprise and almost dropped the paper she was holding.

"You wouldn't believe it," Jenna said. "It's from my Uncle Earnest."

Simon frowned. "Your father's youngest brother?"

Jenna nodded. "He's driving cattle and they are coming through Shadow's Ridge. He was writing to ask if I'd meet him for dinner tonight."

Jenna's uncles had never really taken much of an interest in her. After both her parents were killed, they came to the funeral but did not want to take any responsibility for her. As far as Simon knew, they never wrote or tried to contact her, until now.

"I wonder what he wants," Simon said thoughtfully.

"Well, that's why I thought I would have dinner with him," Jenna said. "And find out. He and the driving team are camped just outside of town."

Simon said nothing as his stomach grumbled loudly again.

"Is there anything for lunch?" Simon asked.

"Sophie went into town earlier and bought some things," Jenna said. "There is fresh bread and cheese in the pantry."

Simon nodded and then fetched the cheese and the bread. He'd tried not to think too much about Sophie and their conversation that morning. He felt bad being so short with her, but that was what they'd agreed upon.

"Will you watch Oliver while I am town?" Sophie asked.

Simon frowned. "Can't you take him with you?"

"You know that I can't," Jenna said.

Simon knew she was right, of course. "Well, can't you ask Sophie?"

"She said she wasn't feeling well," Jenna said. "She's in her bedroom, lying down."

"Jenna—"

"Please, Simon," Jenna said. "I won't be long and he'll probably sleep most of the time anyway. I'll feed him before I go."

Simon wanted to refuse, but there was a quiet yearning in her eyes.

"Okay," he sighed. "I'll watch him."

"Thank you," Jenna said. "And Sophie's here if you need any female advice."

Simon took a bite of his sandwich, not feeling very hungry anymore. He had no idea how to care for a baby; what if he started crying or got hungry? He was a rancher, not a governess. He just hoped that Jenna would hurry back soon.

***

Simon stared at baby Oliver and frowned. He was lying in his Moses basket, his tiny hands grasping the blanket as he cooed softly. But there was a smell radiating from the little boy that was definitely amiss. How could Simon not have considered this might happen?

"It's okay," Simon said to himself. "You are a grown man. You can do this."

He gingerly picked up Oliver in his arms. With his right hand, he took the blanket out of the basket and spread it out of the kitchen table. Then he laid the baby down on the table and lifted his shift and then the linen chemise. As he did, the smell grew more pungent and his eyes started to water.

Simon took a deep breath and unfastened the two pins, and the soiled diaper fell. Holding his breath, Simon removed the diaper from under Oliver and placed it on the chair. However, he had not thought further than removing the diaper. He looked around for a cloth to wipe him but there was nothing in his grasp.

"What are you doing?" Sophie said from the doorway, her lips twitching.

"What does it look like?" Simon grumbled.

"Why are you doing it on the kitchen table?" Sophie asked.

"I don't know," Simon said, his tone slightly exasperated. "I've never done this before."

Sophie did not move but her blue eyes were lit up in amusement

"Are you just going to stand there and watch or are you going to help me?" Simon said

"I think I'll just watch," Sophie said.

Simon turned to her, his eyes pleading.

"Fine," Sophie sighed as she walked over to the kitchen table. "Move over."

Simon did not need to be asked twice. He stepped away from the baby.

"I need some damp cloth and a fresh diaper," she said. "Jenna keeps both in the top drawer of her dresser."

"Okay," Simon said.

He hurried down the hall to Jenna's bedroom and returned moments later with the cloth and nappy.

"Wet the cloth, please," Sophie asked.

Simon carried it over to the sink and wet it before he gave it back to Sophie. She quickly cleaned Oliver up as if it were the easiest thing in the world.

"Diaper, please," Sophie said.

Simon handed her the diaper. As he did, his fingers brushed hers and he dropped the diaper, his heart racing.

"Sorry," Simon said, reaching down and retrieving it.

Sophie took it from him but Simon was distracted by the way his heart had started to race at her touch. It did not make any sense.

By the time his heart rate had returned to normal, Sophie had used the pins to fasten the clean diaper and pulled down Oliver's chemise and shift.

"There we go," she said, picking up Oliver and smiling. "All clean."

Sophie put Oliver in his Moses basket and he continued to coo happily.

"Where is Jenna?" Sophie asked, looking up at him.

"Her uncle was passing through town," Simon said. "And invited her to come for dinner."

Sophie nodded.

"How are you feeling?" Simon asked. "Jenna said that you weren't well?"

Sophie raised an eyebrow. "Are you supposed to care?"

Simon sighed. "Just because I said I didn't want to be friends doesn't mean I'm a total hardcase."

"That's good to know," Sophie said.

Simon said nothing as Sophie walked over to the coal stove and put the kettle on to boil. He could not blame her for being cool with him—he'd made the boundaries very clear—but he had also not expected the warmth of her skin to make his heart race the way it did. It was confusing but undeniable.

"Any idea what time Jenna will be back?" Sophie asked.

Simon shook his head.

"What do you feel like for dinner?" Sophie asked.

"Anything," Simon said. "I am not too fussed."

Sophie nodded and then disappeared into the kitchen, emerging with chicken pieces. As he watched her prepare the chicken, Simon could not help but notice how pretty Sophie was, with her ash-colored hair and pale blue eyes. As she worked, she pursed her lips in concentration, and there was a tiny crease between her dark brows.

"I've never made fried chicken before," Sophie said. "So no complaint if it isn't how you like it."

"You didn't do much cooking back home?" Simon asked.

"Not much, no," Sophie said. "We had a cook."

Simon raised his eyebrows. The truth was that he did not know much about Sophie's past, hardly anything, really. All he knew was what Jenna had told him. Sophie was from a ranch in the northern part of Arizona. She'd left home to start a new life and that was all they knew.

"So your family is wealthy?" Simon asked.

"It's rude to talk about money," Sophie said.

Simon scoffed. "That's what rich people say."

Sophie looked at him and sighed. "My stepfather was wealthy."

"Stepfather?" Simon said. "What happened to your pa?"

"He died when I saw six," Sophie said. "He fell off his horse and broke his neck."

"I am sorry," Simon said.

"Me too," Sophie said. "You know what made it worse was that my stepfather used my pa's accident? He convinced my ma it wasn't safe for a girl to be on a horse, that there were much gentler pursuits. They sold my horse without even telling me..."

Sophie's voice trailed off as she shook her head. Simon watched her dip another piece of chicken in the beaten egg and then into the flour. From the tightness in her jaw, it was plain to him that her stepfather was the one she'd run from, and although he did not know all of it, he knew she was carrying the weight of her own past.

"I am sorry that happened to you," Simon said.

Sophie shrugged. "It was a long time ago."

"Still, it couldn't have been easy—"

"It's okay," Sophie said. "You don't need to feel sorry for me. We aren't friends, remember?"

Simon said nothing and the room fell silent. Oliver's dark eyelashes were fluttering as he began to fall asleep.

"I'm going to put him down for the night," Simon said.

Sophie nodded and Simon picked up the Moses basket by its two handles and carried it carefully out of the kitchen, down the hall and into Jenna's bedroom. He carefully lifted Oliver out of the basket and into the wooden crib beside the bed.

The baby's face crumpled for a moment as Simon put him down but then smoothed again. Simon waited a while to make sure he was asleep. When he was certain, he turned away, but as he did, something under the bed caught his eye— the corner of a piece of paper. He leaned over to retrieve it and without thinking, he unfolded it.

Jenna, the letter began.

You can't keep me from my son. I want to see him.

If you keep ignoring me, I'll be forced to take other measures.

J.

Simon suddenly heard Jenna's voice in the hallway and he slipped the letter into his pocket just as she came into the room

"What are you doing in here?" she asked, accusingly.

"I was just putting Oliver down."

Simon frowned as he took in his cousin's pale face.

"What happened?" he asked.

"Nothing," Jenna said. "I just got a bit lightheaded on the way home. I wanted to lie down."

"Jenna—"

"Please, Simon," she said. "I just need to lie down."

Simon hesitated a moment and then left the room, the letter still tucked safely in his pocket. Jenna closed the door behind him and Simon hesitated outside of her bedroom for a moment.

"Supper's almost ready," Sophie said as Simon stepped back into the kitchen. "Did I hear Jenna just then?"

"She's gone to bed," Simon said.

Sophie frowned slightly as she turned the chicken over in the bubbling lard.

"I am just going to go and check on Buckaroo," Simon said. "I won't be long."

Simon headed out the back door and to the stables. As he stepped inside, he walked over to Buckaroo and scratched his nose.

"How you feeling, boy?" Simon asked.

The horse whinnied softly as Simon stroked his neck. He then filled his food and water trough. Before leaving the stables, Simon reached into his pocket and pulled out the note. He read it again and when he was finished, he stared at the signature, wondering who it was. Obviously whoever this J character was, he was Oliver's father. But why had Jenna never mentioned him?

To be fair, Simon had never asked her, but he'd assumed that Jenna had not told the father, or perhaps he'd not been around to tell. Yet it was obvious this was not the case. What worried Simon was the tone of this man—it felt threatening.

Did he feel threatened because Jenna would not let him see his son, and why was this the case? Surely if he wanted to know Oliver, then he'd be willing to marry Jenna and they could be a family?

Simon frowned, all these unanswered questions buzzing loudly in his head. He knew that he'd have to talk to Jenna about this, and as much as he did not want to get involved, if there was the slightest chance she could marry and Oliver could become legitimate, then he had to try.

Chapter Nine

Sophie had not intended to open up to Simon about her father's passing or how her stepfather had sold her horse without telling her. He'd made it pretty clear he was not interested in being her friend, so she did not wish to be his either. But talking about her past had made her feel closer to him, despite her feelings. She'd never really been able to talk about how she felt, mainly because no one cared to listen. Yet, last night, Simon had been sincere in his responses to her, something Sophie was not used to.

The next morning, Jenna was unusually quiet. She had large purple rings under her eyes again. Sophie had not heard Oliver wake more than once or twice in the night, so she could not help but wonder if something else was keeping Jenna from her sleep.

"How was the dinner with your uncle?" Sophie asked as she beat the eggs.

"It was fine," Jenna said shortly, not looking up from the stove.

Sophie nodded. It was evident from her response and the way her shoulders stiffened that she did not wish to talk about it.

Sophie handed Jenna the bowl of beaten eggs, and she poured them into the pan.

A short while later, Simon entered the kitchen, finishing the morning chores. He looked over at Jenna and then at Sophie and frowned. Usually they were talking and laughing, but that morning, the room was as tense as Jenna's shoulders.

"Everything okay?" he asked.

"Fine," Jenna said. "Why wouldn't it be?"

Simon said nothing as he walked over to the sink and washed his hands. Then he took his seat at the kitchen table.

Jenna served the eggs, bacon, and beans without a word. Oliver was niggling in his Moses basket, but Jenna did not seem to notice, so Sophie went and picked the baby up, and rocked him.

"So, how was dinner with your uncle?" Simon asked.

Jenna, who was still holding the empty egg pan, suddenly dumped it into the sink with a loud crash.

"Why is everyone so interested in how the dinner went?" she cried, whirling around to face them, her pale cheeks now flushed.

Both Sophie and Simon stared at her with wide eyes but said nothing. Sophie did not understand why Jenna was so upset; had something happened at the dinner? Perhaps her uncle had given her bad news.

"I am going for a walk," Jenna said tensely.

Then without another word, she left the kitchen.

"What was that all about?" Sophie asked as she looked at Simon.

Simon sighed and shook his head, but there was something in his eyes that told Sophie he knew more than he was letting on about what just happened.

"Do you know something?" Sophie asked.

Simon shook his head. "No. Well, not really."

Sophie said nothing as she waited for him to elaborate.

"I found a letter in Jenna's room last night."

Sophie frowned in disapproval.

"I didn't intend to find it," Simon said defensively. "I mean, I wasn't looking for it."

"Did you read it?" Sophie asked.

He nodded, looking slightly abashed. "It was from Oliver's pa. Asking to see the baby."

"What?" Sophie said, her mouth popping open in surprise.

"It wasn't a nice letter," Simon continued, his jaw tense. "He was threatening her."

Sophie frowned. Of course, she did not know anything about Oliver's father, but she had assumed he was unaware of the baby's existence.

"I think Jenna went to meet Oliver's pa last night," Simon said.

"Why do you think that?" Sophie asked.

"Well, she hasn't spoken with her uncles in years," Simon reasoned. "And when she returned last night, she was out of sorts, pale and shaky. And just now, with the frying pan—"

Sophie said nothing for a moment. Simon was not wrong. Jenna's behavior this morning was out of character.

"I was going to talk to her," Simon said. "About the letter, but maybe it's better if you do it."

Sophie chewed the inside of her cheek thoughtfully.

"I mean, Jenna is my cousin, but this might be a better conversation for two women."

Sophie knew what Simon was getting at. Jenna might feel more comfortable talking to Sophie about how little Oliver had come to be, and yet the two had only just met.

"She might not like me prying," Sophie said. "After all, we don't know each other very well—"

"Would you try?" Simon asked, his face softening

Sophie looked into his brown eyes, and they were brimming with concern for his cousin and the baby. She knew that this was important to him, and so she would try to talk to Jenna.

"All right," Sophie sighed. "I'll talk to her after I've put Oliver down for his morning nap."

***

Sophie stepped out of the house into the morning sunlight, which bathed the porch in its warm glow. She gazed out in search of Jenna and saw her sitting on a fallen tree not far from the barn. She took a deep breath and walked down the porch steps and across the garden. As she approached, Jenna did not turn to her, but continued staring into the endless horizon.

"May I sit?" Sophie asked.

Jenna nodded but still said nothing as Sophie sat beside her. The two women sat in silence for a time. Sophie cast a sideways glance at Jenna, who was lost in her thoughts, and Sophie thought she looked sad.

"Are you all right, Jenna?" Sophie asked, turning her head to look at her.

Jenna exhaled deeply, her pale face drawn. "Not really," she admitted.

"Do you want to talk about it?" Sophie asked.

Jenna did not answer immediately; her green eyes were thoughtful, and a lone strand of auburn hair had escaped her plait and now danced in the morning breeze across her narrow shoulder.

"I want to tell you," Jenna said, still not looking at Sophie. "But before I do, I need you to promise this stays between us. You can't tell anybody, especially not Simon."

A small crease formed between Sophie's brows as she carefully considered Jenna's request. Sophie was sure that Simon would ask her what she and Jenna talked about, and yet she also knew that this secret, whatever it was, was not hers to share.

"You have my word," Sophie promised.

Jenna exhaled again before she turned her head and looked at Sophie.

"I did not go and meet my uncle last night," Jenna said. "That was a lie."

So Simon had been right about that part, at least.

"So, where did you go?" Sophie asked.

Jenna put her bottom lip as if she were wrestling internally with her decision to entrust Sophie with this secret. "I went to see Oliver's pa."

The words hung between them for a moment, and Jenna watched Sophie carefully, scared of how she might react.

"He lives in town?" Sophie asked.

Jenna nodded, her face growing paler until she was almost translucent.

Sophie wondered if she should mention the letter, but she did not want to get Simon in trouble, so she decided against it. Jenna's hands were trembling, and so Sophie reached over and clutched them tightly in her own hands.

"It's okay," Sophie said, not breaking eye contact. "You can talk to me."

Jenna exhaled again as she blinked back tears. "I haven't told anyone. Not a single soul. I was just so ashamed."

Sophie waited as a tear rolled down Jenna's cheek and onto her cotton skirt.

"I was so stupid," Jenna said. "I should never have…"

Her voice trailed off, and she shook her head as another tear fell, and then another. Sophie let go of Jenna's hands to retrieve a small white handkerchief from her pocket, which she handed to her.

"Here," she said.

Jenna took the handkerchief and dabbed her eyes.

"Jenna," Sophie said. "Tell me what happened."

Jenna shook her head again as she clutched the handkerchief tightly in her fist, so tightly that her knuckles turned white.

"I don't know if Simon told you," Jenna said. "But I used to be a dance hall girl."

Sophie tried to hide the surprise on her face, but she failed, and Jenna nodded.

"I guess he didn't tell you," she said.

Sophie said nothing for a moment. Growing up, she had heard about dance hall girls from the maids that worked in the ranch house. According to them, these young women worked in saloons entertaining the male patrons by singing and dancing. They were dressed in brightly-colored skirts with ruffles decorated with fringe, lace, and sequins. Sophie could not imagine such a lifestyle; it seemed exciting and risqué.

"You're judging me," Jenna sighed.

"No," Sophie said quickly. "I am not. I'm just surprised, that's all."

Jenna shook her head, smiling sadly. "When I left the ranch, it was because I wanted more," she said. "So I moved into town, but every job I could do seemed so small. I didn't wish to be a seamstress or work in the post office. I wanted something more exciting than that."

"So what happened?" Sophie asked.

"One day, the saloon owner stopped me in the street and told me I was pretty. He asked if I could sing or dance, and I told him I could sing. He offered me a job right there on the spot. I didn't agree immediately. I knew what people would think, what my aunt and uncle would think. But it felt like exactly what I'd been searching for. So one night, I turned up at the back door of the saloon, and that was it—I became the saloon's most popular girl."

Looking at her now, it was hard for Sophie to imagine Jenna with rouge on her cheeks, her green eyes bright with laughter and excitement. She tried to picture her in colorful red ruffled petticoats and green sequins, but it was almost impossible to pair this pale-faced, deflated woman with the picture she'd conjured up in her head.

"I liked working in the saloon," Jenna said. "For the most part. I missed Simon and my aunt and uncle, but I didn't write or visit. I wanted to, but I was worried that they'd turn me away, afraid of the shadow my job would cast on their good name."

Sophie, of course, had also heard about the reputations of dance hall girls from the maids. They were notorious among the wives whose husbands frequented the saloons. Sophie had not understood much of what the maids meant then. However, she'd come to understand much more as she grew older.

"We weren't like they said," Jenna insisted, her eyes hardening as she misread Sophie's expression. "We earned money doing what we were good at—singing, dancing, and flirting. I made sure the other girls kept on the straight and narrow. Despite what everyone thought, we never did anything untoward—"

"I believe you," Sophie said in earnest.

Jenna's expression softened slightly. She'd stopped crying but was still twisting the handkerchief between her fingers.

"I'd been working at the saloon for nearly a year the first time he came in," Jenna said, an edge to her voice. "Of course, I'd heard about him; he was all the girls could talk about. He came from England and made his fortune on the railroad. He wasn't only the talk of the saloon. He was the talk of the town. A young, good-looking, wealthy bachelor had all the mothers falling over their feet to get to the seamstress so that their daughters would all be dressed in the latest fashion, should one of them be fortunate enough to catch his eye."

Sophie said nothing as she listened closely to Jenna's story.

"He tried to catch my eye all night," Jenna continued. "But I ignored him. I had my regulars and didn't think it was fair to them to suddenly turn all my attention to him. Besides, he had quite enough attention as it was. The next night, when he came in again, he tried to catch my attention again, and this time, he tried harder. He came right up to me and asked my name."

Jenna paused and looked far away in that moment, as if she were back in the saloon all those months ago.

"He was handsome," Jenna said. "That was true, but there was something in his eyes, a coldness that didn't sit quite right with me. Still, I treated him like everyone else; he was a paying customer, and he was generous. Our boss, Jamie, had made it pretty clear that we were to treat him better, to give him whatever he wanted..."

Jenna's voice trailed off, and a shadow crossed her face.

"He'd been in town for about a month, and he'd come into the saloon almost every night. Some nights we talked and other nights we didn't, but not one night did I not feel those eyes on me, watching me. Then, one night, Jamie had gone to bed; he'd had too many drinks with the patrons and was snoring up a storm upstairs. The other girls had gone home, and it was just me. I was just about to lock up when I heard someone coming in the door. It was him. He sat down at the bar and asked for a drink, and I served him one, although now I wish I had told him to go."

The regret in Jenna's voice was palpable and she shook her head, the corners of her mouth were turned downward.

"He talked as he drank," Jenna continued. "About how he was engaged to a girl in town, about his family back in England. Yet he never took his eyes off me for one moment—"

SALLY M. ROSS

Jenna shivered, and Sophie reached out to her, but Jenna shook her head, and Sophie dropped her hand again.

"I don't know if he planned it," Jenna said, the raw emotion plain in her face and voice. "Or if he just saw his opportunity and took it. I've thought about that night so often, the way the lamps cast long shadows across the ceiling. How he'd done what he did, without a hint of remorse, as if he were just taking what was rightfully his."

Sophie had not realized that she'd been holding her breath until her chest started to burn. She wanted so much to comfort Jenna, but no words would do justice to what had happened to her.

"I went to work the next day," Jenna said. "And he came in early in the evening. He pretended as if nothing had happened, and I did the same. It wasn't until weeks later that I discovered I was pregnant."

"Why didn't you go to the sheriff?" Sophie asked.

Jenna scoffed and shook her head. "I knew what he would say. He'd say that it was my word against his. There were no witnesses."

Sophie frowned, but she knew Jenna was right. She'd grown up knowing that in this life, women were at the mercy of men. She'd been at the mercy of her stepfather and Frank all her life, and her mother had just watched it happen. There was no justice.

"Did you tell him?" Sophie asked. "About the baby."

Jenna shook her head. "No, I didn't tell anyone. I left my job and locked myself away for months. Of course, people found out soon enough, and I could barely go out to buy milk and eggs without people judging me and spurning me. I knew that after the baby came, I had to escape the town, so I came here."

"And you've never told Simon what happened?" Sophie asked.

"I can never tell him the truth," Jenna said, shaking her head. "There is no telling what he would do if he knew what had happened."

Sophie nodded. She could understand Jenna's reluctance. It was clear to anyone that Simon loved his cousin and would do whatever he needed to do for his family, even if it meant ruining his own life.

"So why did you go and see him last night?" Sophie said, frowning.

Jenna sighed. "He's written several times. Asking to see Oliver."

Sophie's brows furrowed deeper. "But why?"

"I don't know," Jenna confessed. "I went to see him last night to tell him to leave us alone, but as I approached the house, I saw him through the front room window. He was with her—his fiancée. So I turned around and came right back home."

"How did he find out about Oliver?" Sophie asked. "Did you tell him?"

"Of course not," Jenna said. "I haven't spoken to him since that night. But maybe he pieced it together somehow. I mean, it's no secret in town."

Sophie frowned, her mind full of the terrible things that had happened to Jenna and how hard it must have been for her all these long months. She now understood why Jenna had found it hard to name the baby and why she'd felt so desperate for help.

"I am so sorry that happened to you," Sophie said, touching her shoulder.

Jenna did not recoil from her touch this time, and the two women sat silently for a long while.

"So what happens now?" Sophie asked.

"I don't know," Jenna sighed. "But I won't let him be part of Oliver's life, or mine."

Sophie nodded, a small crease in her brow. It did not make sense to her that this man should want to know Oliver. After everything Jenna had told her, he was to be married and was a respected gentleman in the town. Why would he risk that all now? It did not make any sense.

"I'd better go and check on Oliver," Jenna said, getting up.

Sophie nodded as Jenna turned and walked back to the house. Sophie continued to stare out across the horizon but her heart was heavy. It wasn't right that something like this had happened to Jenna, but what could be done? This man, whoever he was, obviously had wealth and status, and that made him believe he was untouchable. She was all too familiar with men like that, and while Sophie had managed to escape, she worried for Jenna.

After a little while, Sophie got up, and as she walked back to the house, she caught sight of Simon by the barn. What was she going to tell him when he asked what Jenna had said? She couldn't tell him the truth; it was not her truth to tell. But she knew this secret might only wedge them further apart.

Chapter Ten

Simon watched Jenna and Sophie from the porch. While he couldn't hear what was being said, he saw the tears on Jenna's cheeks and the way Sophie placed a comforting hand on her shoulder. He knew that something was very wrong.

After they'd finished talking, Simon headed around the house to check on Buckaroo but he could not stop thinking about Jenna, and so after he'd checked on the horse, he sought Sophie out and found her alone in the kitchen. She was making biscuits, pouring buttermilk into the center of a thick batter of flour, butter, salt, and baking powder. Mittens was asleep on the kitchen chair in the sun, but as Simon entered the room, she opened one yellow eye.

"Where's Jenna?" he asked.

"She took Oliver for a walk in his carriage," Sophie said.

Simon nodded and looked at Sophie expectantly, but she said no more as she continued to stir the buttermilk into the batter.

"So what did Jenna say?" he asked.

Sophie stopped stirring and looked up at him, regret in her eyes. "I can't tell you."

Simon frowned in confusion. "What do you mean?"

"I can't tell you," Sophie repeated.

Simon stared at her, his confusion turning to frustration. "You have to tell me. She's my cousin."

"It's not my secret to share," Sophie said apologetically.

Simon gritted his teeth. "Sophie—"

"There is nothing that you can say that will change my mind," Sophie said as she looked away from him, picked up the wooden spoon, and continued to stir the batter.

Simon stared at her for a moment or two as he bristled with annoyance before he turned and left the kitchen. Part of him admired Sophie's loyalty, but it had been him who had asked her to talk to Jenna in the first place.

***

Simon did his best to busy his mind during the morning, and there was a lot of work to be done. But he still could not stop thinking about Jenna's secret. The last couple of months, he'd been able to bury his head in the sand and pretend nothing was amiss, but that note, this J character, had changed everything. He now wanted to know the truth— what had happened to his cousin?

Simon walked back to the house at midday for lunch. He'd found the kitchen empty but could hear Sophie and Jenna in her bedroom. He walked through the kitchen and down the hallway. Jenna's bedroom door was open and he found the two women leaning over Oliver's crib, their brows furrowed in concern.

"What is going on?" he asked as he took a step into the room.

"Oliver has a fever," Sophie said.

Simon looked over at the crib to see Oliver, his cheeks red and flushed. Jenna stood beside her, frowning as she placed her palm over the baby's forehead.

"Is it serious?" Simon asked.

"We don't know," Sophie said.

Simon frowned as he looked at Jenna again. She was tense with worry. He could tell by the stiffness in her shoulders. He did not blame her for being concerned; both of their mothers had lost children. He'd had two siblings, one who'd died when he was three, and another before her first birthday.

"It's Friday," Simon said. "Which means the doctor will be in town; we could take him."

Jenna nodded.

"Buckaroo's not up to pulling the buggy," Simon said. "So we will have to walk."

"I'm coming too," Sophie said.

A short while later, they were heading down the road and out through the entrance to the ranch. Oliver was swaddled in a blanket, his cheeks still flushed. Now and then, he coughed, and it sounded as if something were rattling around in his lungs. Jenna's face was pale as she held the baby tightly in her arms.

No one spoke as they descended the rocky road toward town. Usually, Simon enjoyed the walk, but today he hardly noticed the mountains or the trees whispering to one another. He was setting the pace, but his legs were much longer than Sophie and Jenna's, who were struggling to keep up.

As they reached the town, Jenna grew paler still.

"Do you want me to take him?" Sophie offered.

"No," Jenna said shortly. "But thanks."

Shadow's Ridge did not have a resident doctor, but shared a doctor with two neighboring towns. The doctor only came to town once a week on a Friday, where he operated out of the boarding house.

As they approached the two-story wooden building, Simon saw a line of people snaking around the side of the square boarding house. He glanced over at Jenna, whose head and eyes were tilted down.

They joined the end of the queue, and as they did, Simon was not immune to the whispers and stares from the residents of Shadow's Ridge. Still, he did his best to ignore them. He'd never been popular in town; people thought he was strange to want to live all alone on the mountainside, and after Jenna arrived with Oliver, people had finally found a valid reason not to like him.

The line moved slowly, and it was torture to have to listen to Oliver cough and cry in discomfort.

"Are there usually so many people?" Sophie asked as she glanced down at Oliver in concern.

"Not usually," said an older man standing behind them. "But the grippe has been making its way around town."

The older man coughed suddenly, not bothering to duck his head into his elbow, as drops of spittle landed on Simon's face.

This was one reason he hated towns. There were too many people breathing all over one another all day and not enough fresh air to keep diseases at bay.

Eventually, they made it to the front of the line, and as they stepped into the boarding house, they were directed to the common room where the doctor had set up his makeshift clinic. Various patients sat in chairs around the fireplace while a friendly-looking nurse felt their foreheads, checked their blood pressure, and offered words of comfort. The four windows in the room were wide open, but there was no breeze, and the whole place still smelled of sickness.

"We'll wait here," Simon said.

Jenna nodded as she carried Oliver over to where the doctor was waiting.

Simon and Sophie stood waiting for Jenna. As they did, Simon overheard two women whispering behind them.

"I hate to say it, but it might be best if the grippe takes that poor baby."

Simon stiffened as he balled his hands into fists at his sides.

"What kind of future has he got?" the woman continued. "With no father to speak of and a soiled dove for a mother."

The other woman clicked her tongue in disapproval, and Simon, now shaking with anger, was ready to give those women a piece of his mind for talking about his family in such a manner. Before he had the chance, however, Sophie marched right up to them.

"How dare you?" Sophie said loudly.

"Excuse me?" the woman said, feigning innocence.

Everyone in the room had now turned to see what all the commotion was about.

"*'Judge not, that you be not judged,'*" Sophie said, quoting from the Bible. "You should both be ashamed of yourselves. He is just an innocent child."

Both women were now red in the face as Sophie's blue eyes flashed with anger. Simon could hardly take his eyes off her.

"Well, we were having a private conversation—" the one woman said.

"Well, perhaps next time you should have your private conversation in private and not in a boarding house full of people," Sophie spat.

One woman puffed with indignation, while the other looked more abashed at being called out in front of everyone.

"Perhaps you should be saving your hard words for your sister-in-law," the woman challenged. "After all, she is the one who obviously needs them."

From where he was standing, Simon saw Sophie's hand quiver and he admired her restraint.

"Just don't talk about my family again," Sophie said. "Ever."

Then, without another word, she turned and walked back to where Simon stood. Sophie's cheeks were flushed and her blue eyes were shining, and Simon could not help but think that even in a temper, she was beautiful. She took her place beside him again and Simon felt a rush of admiration and gratitude toward her. She'd stood up for Jenna, for their family, and that meant more to Simon than he could put into words.

Everyone's eyes were still on the two women trying to recover their composure after Sophie's dressing-down.

"What's going on?" Jenna asked as she walked over to them with Oliver in her arms.

"Nothing," Sophie said. "What did the doctor say?"

"He has the grippe," Jenna said. "But his fever is broken, and the doctor said we should watch him closely."

Oliver looked a bit better now—his face was not as flushed, and his eyes were more alert.

"Come on," Simon said. "Let's get out of this wretched place."

Simon did not need to ask twice, and he, Jenna, and Sophie left the boarding house. As soon as they stepped out into the sunshine and fresh air, Simon felt better. Sophie's cheeks were still slightly pink and Simon would not soon forget the dressing-down she'd given those two busybodies. He'd discovered a newfound respect for Sophie and her protectiveness of their family.

***

Oliver fell asleep on the walk back up to the ranch, so they did not talk much as they did not wish to wake him. Sleep was the best medicine, after all.

When they arrived back at the ranch, Jenna went to her room to settle Oliver into his crib, and Sophie and Simon went to the kitchen. No one had eaten lunch, and it was now nearly suppertime.

"I'll just make some gravy for the biscuits," Sophie said.

Simon nodded as he took a seat at the kitchen table. "Thank you for what you said today. At the boarding house."

"I still can't believe they'd think something like that, let alone speak it out loud," Sophie said, shaking her head. "How can people be so uncharitable?"

"They are small people," Simon said. "With small lives, and bringing down others makes them feel bigger, more important."

"It's sickening," Sophie said, her tone a mixture of disgust and disappointment.

"It's life," Simon said, shrugging.

Sophie said nothing for a moment as she stirred the brown gravy now simmering in the frying pan. She was frowning, her dark brows meeting almost in the middle.

"What is it?" Simon asked.

"Do you really believe that?" she asked.

"You saw it today with those women," Simon reasoned. "That's why I prefer to be on my own, here in the mountains and far away from those poisonous people in town."

"But you can't really believe that everyone is bad?"

Simon shrugged. "You told me about what your stepfather did, how he treated you. Surely you know better than anyone that the world is made up of bad people."

Sophie looked thoughtful again.

"It's true," she said. "My stepfather and stepbrother did not treat me well, nor did my ma. But then I met you and Jenna, and I was just a stranger who showed up at your door with a cat in a crate, and you made me a part of this family. Isn't that evidence that not all people are bad?"

Simon said nothing for a moment as he thought about Sophie's words. She'd revealed so much of herself to him that day. She'd proved that she was not only loyal and brave, but that she was strong, strong enough to find a splinter of hope in a world of despair.

"The gravy is ready," Sophie said.

She plated some biscuits and poured a generous amount of gravy over them before she walked across to Simon and placed them down on the table in front of him.

"This was my pa's favorite," Sophie said, smiling to herself.

"Biscuits and gravy?"

Sophie nodded, still smiling. "I don't remember much about him, but I remember how much he loved biscuits and gravy, and he always got drops of gravy in his beard. After my ma married Mr. Colton, we didn't have it anymore because he called it 'peasant food.'"

Simon frowned. The more Sophie revealed about her stepfather, the more he disliked the man.

"You never said what made you leave?" Simon asked. "I mean, aside from the obvious."

Sophie did not answer right away.

"They wanted me to marry," Sophie finally revealed. "Mr. Colton, my stepfather, made a business deal with this old rancher, and I was the price he paid."

"He sold you off?" Simon said, his eyes wide with disbelief.

Sophie nodded. "I know I shouldn't have been surprised. He never treated me as if I were his own daughter. But I knew I could never marry that man, so I ran."

Simon had never known anything but love from his parents, so it was hard for him to imagine what it must have taken for Sophie to leave her home and all she knew behind.

"After I wrote and applied to the advertisement that Jenna posted, I often wondered if I was doing the right thing," Sophie continued. "I was running from one marriage right into another one, this time to a total stranger."

"How did you know you were doing the right thing?" Simon asked with interest.

"I didn't," Sophie said, shaking her head. "But I knew that for the first time in my whole life, *I* was making a decision. No one told me what to do; it was my choice to come here."

Simon could hear the hint of pride in Sophie's voice, and he felt she deserved it. It was no small feat what she'd done; she'd run toward the life she wanted, and Simon, better than most, knew what it meant to fight for the kind of life that made you happy.

"I know that this wasn't the life you wanted," Sophie said, her eyes sympathetic. "Being married, a house full of people—"

"Maybe not," Simon agreed. "But I had a choice too. I chose to marry you."

As the words left his mouth, Simon realized how much had changed in such a short time. He'd married Sophie for Jenna's sake, and yet only now was it starting to feel like the right choice.

"But you didn't do it for yourself."

"No," Simon agreed. "But I did it for my family."

Sophie sighed softly. "I envy you," she said. "To have known what a real family is and to care enough about someone that you'd put their happiness before yours. It's powerful, that kind of love—transformative."

Simon looked into Sophie's eyes. He'd been so focused on Jenna and what this marriage would mean to her that he had not realized what it meant to Sophie. She was so desperate for a real family that she could not see how dysfunctional they actually were, an island of misfit toys.

"Do you want some more biscuits and gravy?" Sophie offered.

"Please," Simon said, offering up his plate.

Sophie got up and filled his plate, and Simon watched her as she did. He was grateful in many ways that she was there, but he did not know if he could give her what she so desperately wanted—a real family.

Chapter Eleven

Sophie woke up with a start. She'd kicked off her blankets in her sleep, and the back of her neck was damp with perspiration. It took her a moment to orient herself and remember where she was.

She'd been dreaming of her family's ranch, and it had felt so real, as if she were back home. In the dream, she was a girl, no older than five or six. She and her father were riding a horse, and Sophie could feel the warmth of the sun on her skin and the smell of desert lavender drifting through the air. She'd been so happy she thought her chest would burst, but in an instant, the sky clouded over.

Sophie looked down to see the hands on the reins were no longer her father's and her heart caught in her throat. When she turned, her father was gone, and in his place was Mr. Colton. Then Sophie was no longer a little girl; she was her, and her stepfather's hands were around her neck, pressing tighter and tighter as she kicked against the sides of the horse, desperate for air. But he would not let go, and suddenly she was falling from the horse, and then she'd woken up in her bed.

Sophie reached up and touched her neck with her fingertips. Even now, she could still feel him, but how was that possible? He was miles away with no idea where she was. Yet Sophie could not shake the hollow feeling in her stomach.

After that nightmare, Sophie struggled to fall back to sleep. Every time she closed her eyes, she saw Mr. Colton's face, the vein in his temple throbbing madly as he squeezed the life from her.

When morning finally came, Sophie was relieved to get up and dressed. As she pulled on her stockings in the nippy morning air, Sophie's mind was still on her nightmare, and she wished she could shake the images from her head and smash them on the bedroom floor.

A short while later, she was dressed, and as she turned around to make the bed, she frowned. Where was Mittens? The blue-gray cat was always curled up at the bottom of her bed, but she was not there. Sophie hadn't seen her since the afternoon before when they'd gone to town to see the doctor.

"Has anyone seen Mittens?" Sophie asked as she stepped into the small kitchen.

Jenna was at the stove cooking eggs while Simon was seated at the table with Oliver in the Moses basket.

"No," Jenna said, shaking her head. "I haven't seen her this morning."

"Or last night," Simon added.

Sophie frowned. Ever since arriving at the ranch, Mittens had stayed close to home.

"I saw her yesterday afternoon," Sophie said. "She was sitting on the porch when we walked to town. I hope she didn't try to follow us and get lost."

As Sophie spoke the words, her heart sank. What if Mittens had tried to follow them? Cats usually had good instincts when it came to finding their way home, but this was an entirely new terrain, and she could easily have lost her way.

"Let's eat breakfast," Jenna suggested. "And then we can go out and look for her."

Sophie nodded, but she had no appetite. Her stomach was in knots over the fact that she hadn't noticed Mittens was missing until that morning.

"Hey," Simon said supportively. "I am sure she's around."

Sophie gave him a tight-lipped smile but said nothing.

As soon as breakfast was over, Sophie left the house and walked all the way to the entrance of the ranch. She cupped her hands over her mouth.

"Mittens?" Sophie called. "Kitty-kitty-kitty."

Sophie continued down the road calling her cat over and over again, hoping she would emerge from a bush and rub herself against Sophie's skirts as she so loved to do. However, after half an hour of calling, there was still no sign of Mittens.

Sophie turned and headed back toward the house. Perhaps Mittens was trapped in one of the bedrooms, and they hadn't heard her calling. There were so many places that she could be hiding.

As Sophie reached the house, she heard Simon calling for Mittens. She was grateful to him for helping; she knew how busy he was, and that he did not particularly like cats, so it meant a lot to her.

Sophie disappeared into the house. She searched every bedroom, peering under beds and into wardrobes, but there was no sign of the old gray cat.

"I searched all around the barn and stables," Jenna said as she stepped into the kitchen. "Simon's gone further out to look."

Sophie nodded but her stomach sank. Where was she? Mittens had been her faithful companion for fourteen years and had journeyed here with her to start a new life. She could not bear to think of losing Mittens.

She was the last link Sophie had to her old life, and she was so much more than just a cat. For so long, she'd been the only one who'd listened to her. On the days when Frank pinched her under the dinner table or her mother took her stepfather's side over hers, Mittens was always there.

When Mr. Colton nailed her bedroom window shut for leaving the house, Mittens had curled against her back as she cried bitterly into her pillow. The cat had been there for her countless times simply by being there, and without her, Sophie felt lost.

"Sophie?" Jenna said, her tone urgent.

Sophie turned toward the kitchen window to see Simon carrying Mittens carefully in his arms. Even from a distance, she could tell something was wrong. Without a word, Sophie rushed out of the back door.

"What happened?" she cried.

"Found her caught in a snare on the boundary," Simon said. "Heard her crying for help."

"Is she hurt?" Sophie asked as she took Mittens from him and cradled her in her arms.

"The snare was around her neck, but the wound should heal," Simon said. "I think she's probably pretty hungry and thirsty too."

Sophie turned and hurried back inside, entirely forgetting to thank Simon for his heroics. Simon followed her into the kitchen.

"What happened?" Jenna asked.

"She was in a snare," Sophie said. "Can you fetch me a saucer of milk?"

Jenna nodded and hurried to the pantry, emerging with a pail of fresh milk. She removed the cloth from the top of the pail, dipped the ladle into the milk, and emptied the contents carefully into a saucer, which she then placed on the kitchen table.

Sophie sat down, and Mittens leaned forward and began to drink. As she did, Sophie saw the damage the snare had done. The fur around her neck was gone, and in its place was an angry red cut that went all the way around. Flakes of dried blood were visible in the fur on her head and back. Sophie hated to think of Mittens struggling, hurting herself in her desperation to escape from the snare.

"It's good she's drinking," Simon said. "Once she's finished, I'll take a look at that wound and get it cleaned up."

Sophie looked up at him. "Thank you. I don't know what I would have done if you hadn't found her."

"Well, as you said, she's your family," Simon said.

Sophie smiled at him before she turned her attention back to Mittens, who was on her second helping of milk.

"Don't give her too much at once," Simon warned. "It might make her sick."

After the second saucer, Sophie followed Simon out to the stables with Mittens. He cleaned her wound carefully as Sophie held the cat. As he worked, Simon kept sneezing, and Sophie saw his eyes turning bloodshot.

"You really are allergic to cats?" Sophie asked.

"Did you think I was making it up?"

"Kind of," Sophie confessed.

Simon smiled wryly as he shook his head. "I'm done. You can take her to rest."

Sophie carried Mittens back into the house and to her room, where she put her on the bed.

"I think your adventuring days are over," she said. "It's a quiet life for you from now on."

The cat blinked her large yellow eyes sleepily and curled up on the bottom of the bed. Sophie watched her for a moment, her shoulders relaxing in relief. Mittens was safe. She now needed to think of a way to thank Simon for finding her, and she wanted to make it a special thank you to really show him her gratitude.

***

Sophie kept a close eye on her cat all the rest of the day, but it was clear that Mittens had no intentions of moving. She'd also been thinking of how to thank Simon and had come up with what she hoped was a good idea.

After checking on Mittens again, Sophie made her way to the kitchen. As she passed Jenna's bedroom, Sophie found her asleep beside Oliver. She smiled to herself at how peaceful they looked, and she crept past so as not to disturb them.

She then collected the wet sheets and carried them outside to hang up in the afternoon sunshine. They really should have been hung up much earlier, but she'd forgotten all about them in their search for Mittens. In fact, between poor Oliver being ill and Mittens getting caught in a snare, Sophie was looking forward to a more peaceful afternoon.

As she hung the sheets up, pegging each corner securely to the line, she thought about Jenna and baby Oliver. With everything that had been going on, Sophie had not had time to really think about what Jenna had told her the morning before. But now she could not help but worry. Why did Oliver's father want to be part of her life? She did not understand it, and it was this uncertainty that gnawed at her insides.

Then, of course, there was Simon. While he had not broached the subject with her again, which was a relief, Sophie could not help but feel that it was not the end of the matter. She would not break her promise to Jenna, but how could she evade Simon forever? S

ophie understood why Jenna did not wish her cousin to know the truth, but he could protect them if he did. Whoever Oliver's father was, he was an evil man, and Sophie knew she needed to talk to Jenna again and convince her to tell Simon the truth.

Chapter Twelve

"Can I ask you a favor?" Simon asked as he looked across at Sophie.

She nodded, her empty spoon hovering in midair above her bowl of warm oats. They were all seated around the breakfast table. Mittens was curled up in the Moses basket with Oliver and both of them were fast asleep.

"When you go into town this morning, will you stop at the farm store and ask the owner to place an advertisement in the window?"

"Sure," Sophie said. "What's it for?"

"A shearing team," Simon said. "Sheep need to be sheared by this time next week."

"Why don't you ask Mr. Fields?" Jenna suggested.

Simon shook his head. "Those Fields boys wouldn't know a shearing blade from a butter knife. I need a good team, quick and experienced."

Jenna nodded but said no more. Simon had been waiting for an opportunity to talk with her about that letter, and with Sophie going to town that morning, he might finally get a chance.

"Thanks for breakfast," Simon said, getting up. "I'll see you later."

"Is there anything special you'd like from town?" Sophie asked.

Simon frowned. There was nothing special to be found in that place.

"No, thanks," he said.

Simon fetched his hat off the hook on the door and headed out to the barn. He busied himself until he saw Sophie heading down the road toward the gate and then headed back inside to talk with Jenna.

"Everything all right?" Jenna asked as she looked across at him from where she was wiping down the table.

Simon wasn't usually back in the house until lunchtime, so he could understand his cousin's concern.

"You got a minute to talk?" he asked, shifting in his boots.

Again, Jenna frowned. He wasn't usually the one who liked to talk, but Sophie had refused to tell him anything, so he didn't have much of a choice.

"Sure," Jenna said. "Let me just finish up here."

Simon waited outside the back door as Jenna finished the breakfast dishes. She came out, wiping her damp hands on her apron as she squinted in the bright morning sunshine.

"What is it that you wanted to talk about?" she asked, raising a hand to shield her eyes.

Simon cleared his throat as he reached into his pocket and pulled out the crumpled note he'd found in Jenna's bedroom. As he did, he saw Jenna's face pale.

"Have you been going through my things?" she asked, her tone full of accusation.

"No," Simon said defensively. "I was putting Oliver down for his sleep and I found it."

"And you read it?" Jenna asked, her brows furrowed.

"I didn't intend to read it," Simon said.

Jenna exhaled sharply. "It's none of your business, Simon—"

"Where did you go the other night?" he asked, cutting her off. "Did you go and see Oliver's pa?"

Jenna paled again, her green eyes betraying her.

"How come you never told me he lives in town?" Simon asked. "That he wants to get to know Oliver—"

"Because it doesn't matter!" Jenna said, her voice rising. "He's never going to meet Oliver."

Simon frowned. "He's his pa."

Jenna said nothing as she shook her head.

"Jenna," Simon said, trying to reason with her. "I don't know this man, but don't you think that if you just gave it a chance, maybe you could even get married and give Oliver a real family?"

As the words left his mouth, Simon knew that they were the wrong ones, and Jenna's face hardened like stone.

"You have no idea what you are talking about," she said, her voice dangerously low.

"Then tell me," Simon insisted.

"I can't," Jenna said, her voice cracking now. "I can't tell you, and please, don't ask me again."

Without another word, Jenna turned and went back into the kitchen, closing the door behind her. From inside, Simon heard a sob escape her chest and the creak of the wood as she pressed up against it. He waited for a moment in case she might come back out, but she did not, so he slipped the crumpled paper back into his pocket.

For the rest of the morning, Simon thought of little else than his conversation with Jenna. He could understand why she might have hard feelings against this man; he should have offered to marry her right from the start. But if she had the choice to give Oliver a father and a proper home, why would she not even try?

Simon wondered if he might be able to track down this J character and talk to him, and find out more about the situation. He knew Jenna would never approve, so he'd have to keep it from her.

***

Jenna kept her distance for the rest of the morning, probably worried that Simon would broach the topic of Oliver's father again. However, it was clear to him from their earlier conversation that she wouldn't tell him what was going on or what had gone on, so he was determined to find out on his own.

Sophie was not back for lunch and when Simon entered the kitchen, he found it empty. The whole house was quiet and Simon frowned to himself as he walked into the pantry to find something to eat. He found some of the leftover biscuits they'd had for dinner, some cheese, and a piece of salted pork. It wasn't much of a lunch for someone who'd been working the land all morning. Still, it was better than nothing.

Simon ate alone at the kitchen table as he had done many times before. He enjoyed his solitude, but he could not help looking toward the door now and then, hoping that Sophie or Jenna might come in. He never thought he'd admit it, but he'd gotten used to them being around and the house was almost too quiet without them.

When he was done, Simon carried his plate to the sink, and as he rinsed it in the cold water, he heard the front door open and then close. There was a rustling in the hallway and a few moments later, Sophie stepped into the kitchen, her face pink with exertion. She was carrying her basket over one arm and a large brown bag.

"Hello," she said brightly as she carried everything to the table and dumped it on top, sighing as she turned to Simon. "How are things?"

"Fine." Simon shrugged.

"Did you eat?" Sophie asked as she looked around the kitchen, frowning.

"I did," Simon said. "I don't know where Jenna and the baby have got to, sleeping, I suppose."

Sophie nodded as she began to unpack her basket, but suddenly she stopped and turned to Simon again, her face falling.

"What is it?" he asked, frowning slightly.

"I forgot to stop in at the farm store and post your advertisement," Sophie admitted, her blue eyes apologetic.

Usually, something like this would have annoyed Simon to no end, but today it gave him the opportunity he needed.

"I'll go back this afternoon," Sophie volunteered.

"Don't bother," Simon said. "I forgot there were a few things I needed from the farm store, so I'll go myself."

"Are you sure?" Sophie asked.

Simon nodded. "I am sure you've got chores to be doing."

Sophie nodded as she reached into her pocket and retrieved the advertisement, which she handed to him. Simon hesitated.

"Before I go, can I ask you something?" Simon asked, meeting Sophie's eyes.

She nodded, her lips parting slightly.

"Are you going to tell me what you and Jenna spoke about the other day? What you learned about Oliver's pa?"

Sophie shook her head. "I am sorry," she said. "But I can't."

Simon looked at her for a moment, sensing some regret in her answer but seeing the loyalty in her eyes. She would not tell him and so now he must do what he needed to do.

"All right," he said. "Well, then, I'll see you this evening."

Simon turned and retrieved his hat from the hook. Then without another word, he left the kitchen and headed for town. He never willingly went into Shadow's Ridge, but he needed the answers that he wasn't getting at home.

As Simon entered the main street, he made a beeline for the farm store. Simon hoped that he would find the place empty; he wasn't in the mood for small talk.

The Shadow's Ridge farm store was a single-story wooden building. It had a broad porch in the front and large windows that let in the natural light. The inside of the store was spacious and airy, with a center aisle running from the door right to the back of the store. The walls were lined with shelving and in front of these shelves was a long, U-shaped counter made of solid wood.

As Simon made his way across the store, he passed by the bins of animal feed and the various troughs and pails on display. Across from the livestock supplies, he noted the small selection of boots and hats hanging from hooks by the window. Near the back of the store, they kept a small selection of farming equipment—scythes, plows, harnesses, and the like.

As he approached the wooden counter, he spotted the store owner, Mr. Burns, with a feather duster, dusting off the bottles of liniments.

When Simon cleared his throat, the man turned to him.

"Mr. Jones," he said, not bothering to hide his surprise.

It was true that Simon usually had his supplies delivered to him at the ranch rather than come all the way into town.

"I need to place an advertisement in the window," Simon said.

Mr. Burns raised an eyebrow but said nothing as Simon removed the advertisement from his pocket and slid it across the counter. Mr. Burns picked it up and read it, squinting slightly as he tried to decipher Simon's rather scribbly handwriting.

"That'll be a penny," he said.

Simon reached into the pocket of his denim jeans and extracted a penny, which he handed to Mr. Burns.

"Anything else?" Mr. Burns asked.

Simon shook his head before he tipped his hat to the man and then turned to leave the store.

As he stepped back onto the dusty main street, Simon turned left instead of right, which would have taken him back home. He passed by the seamstress and the general store before he took a second left and found himself in front of the saloon.

Simon had never stepped inside a saloon; he'd never had reason to, yet here he was. Unlike most of the buildings in Shadow's Ridge, the saloon was built of stone, just like the church. All those years ago, the town's founder had built the chapel and saloon first. The chapel was for the good Christian men and women, and the saloon was for the drunkards and gamblers. He'd been an inclusive man, the founder of Shadow's Ridge, there was no arguing that point.

Simon approached the two swinging doors leading into the saloon. He hesitated a moment, wondering if he should just go home and forget the whole thing. But he'd come all this way, so he took a deep breath, pushed the doors open, and stepped into the dimly lit room. His eyes took a moment to adapt to the sudden change in lighting. A few paraffin lamps burned in the corners, but they were nothing compared to the bright sunshine outside.

As his eyes adjusted, Simon saw the long wooden bar against the back wall, bottles of whiskey and gin lining the shelves. Also on display behind the bar were a collection of glasses in all shapes and sizes, as varied as the patrons themselves. Along the front of the bar were stools, mostly empty but for the two occupied by hunchbacked men with graying temples and sagging jowls.

There was another room off to the right of the bar, which Simon guessed was for the gamblers.

Off to the left of the bar was a small, raised stage, and as Simon's eyes brushed over everything, he thought of Jenna working in this dingy, dim place, its walls adorned with old wanted posters, horseshoes, and elk antlers. He had never allowed himself to think much about Jenna as a dance hall girl. He did not judge her for it, but he did not understand why someone would want to be trapped in a place like this when they could be up in the mountains, breathing the air and falling asleep under the stars.

The barkeep was behind the wooden bar, polishing glasses with a grubby rag. He was tall, not as tall as Simon, and well-built. His dirty-blonde hair was pushed back from his broad face. The bridge of his nose deviated from its natural alignment, a token of the job, Simon guessed.

"Sit down," the barkeep said. "I'll be right with you."

Simon sat down and waited, watching the man polish the glass before returning it to the wooden cabinet behind him.

"What can I get you?" he asked.

"I didn't come for a drink," Simon said.

"Well, then you're in the wrong place," the barkeep said dryly.

"I am looking for some information," Simon said. "About a girl who used to work here."

The barkeep said nothing.

"She worked here about a year ago."

The barkeep shook his head and shrugged. "Sorry, I only started working here a few months ago, so I can't help you."

He picked up another glass and began polishing it, and Simon had the sneaking suspicion the barkeep wouldn't have helped him even if he could. Simon got up from the stool and turned to go.

"You can try the old house at the end of the road," one of the saggy men at the bar said.

Simon turned around to look at him.

"Some of the girls rent rooms there," the man explained. "Maybe one of them knows something."

Simon nodded. "Thanks."

"If you are really grateful, you can buy me a drink," the man said, slurring slightly.

"I think you've had enough."

Without another word, Simon turned and left the saloon. As he stepped outside, he squinted in the bright sunshine. He walked down the road toward the old house that had once belonged to the undertaker. However, he'd died ten years ago, and his son had chosen instead to rent out the house instead of take over the family business. Shadow's Ridge hadn't had an undertaker since.

The garden in front of the old wooden double-story house was overgrown and full of weeds, and the gate hung crooked on its hinges. The house itself had been handsome in its prime, but now the paint was peeling, and the roof was missing slates.

Simon walked up to the house, hoping that he was not on some wild goose chase, trusting the words of a drunkard.

A one-eyed ginger cat watched him from across the porch as he approached the front door. He rapped loudly on the wood and waited, but there was no reply. He knocked again, louder this time.

"Hold your horses!" a woman yelled from inside. "I'm coming."

Simon took a step back and a moment later, the door opened, and a woman stood in front of him, wearing a dressing gown. Her feet were bare, and her dark hair was wrapped up in papers.

"Who are you and what business do you have waking a woman from her beauty sleep?"

Simon was so taken aback by her appearance that he was momentarily lost for words, but the woman was watching him with her eyebrows raised.

"I was hoping I could talk to someone," he said. "About a girl who used to work in the saloon—"

"I am going to stop you right there," the woman said, crossing her arms. "We have a code, so no one is going to be telling you anything."

"A code?" Simon said, his eyebrows furrowing.

The woman shook her head in disgust.

"You cowboys think you're the only ones with a code. But just because we don't spend all our time strapped to a saddle doesn't mean we haven't got integrity."

"I wasn't suggesting that," Simon said. "I just need some information—"

"We've got a code," the woman repeated. "And I need to be up for work in two hours, so if there is nothing else?"

"Please," Simon implored. "Her name is Jenna Wilder, she left the saloon about a year ago."

Simon saw a look of recognition on the dark-haired woman's face, and for a moment, he thought she might tell him something. But then she shut the door and was gone, leaving Simon with none of the answers he was looking for.

SALLY M. ROSS

Chapter Thirteen

Sophie saw Simon returning from town through the front room window. She was surprised to see that he was empty-handed; perhaps the farm store did not have what he needed and he'd ordered it.

The house was quiet. Jenna had been holed up in her bedroom most of the day. Sophie noticed that she was sleeping more these days, and she wondered if it had something to do with her secret. She could not imagine the weight of something like that, what it took out of you, and to make matters worse, Oliver's father was now trying to get back into her life.

Sophie turned away from the window and looked around the wide room. She had not spent much time in the front room, but it was pleasant. Its large windows allowed in the afternoon sunlight and although the furnishings were simple, it was bright and airy. It reminded her of how her house used to be before her mother remarried.

After Sophie's mother married Mr. Colton, he insisted that they replace all the furniture in their home. He'd called their home quaint, but he'd said it in a way that made quaint sound like something pathetic. Most of the furnishings in their home had been from her father's family, passed down from generation to generation, yet they were discarded as if they'd meant nothing.

Sophie could still remember the day she came downstairs to a house she no longer recognized. Her father's favorite rocking chair lay at the bottom of a huge pile of chairs and tables on the grass outside, twisted and broken under the weight.

She could remember her mother coming upstairs to talk to her, how she'd insisted that they were just things and did not mean anything, but she was wrong. Those things were all Sophie had left of her father; they told a story.

In the distance, she heard a woodpecker tapping furiously at the trunk of a tree, and she sighed softly. It did no good wallowing in the past; she knew that, but sometimes the memories snuck up on her, triggered by nothing more than the way the light was falling or a scent on a breeze.

Sophie shook her head, refocusing her mind on the here and now. She'd finished her chores for the day, so she decided to check on Jenna and the baby.

She walked across the front room, out the door and down the hallway to Jenna's bedroom. She knocked gently, but there was no answer. The door was slightly ajar and so Sophie peered around into the room. The drapes were drawn, but a narrow beam of light shone between them. Compared to the front room, the air in the bedroom was stagnant and heavy. Sophie saw Jenna asleep on the bed, curled up in a ball, and in the wooden crib beside her, Oliver was awake, his blue eyes lighting up as he saw Sophie.

"Hi, sweet boy," Sophie cooed. "Do you want to come and walk with me for a bit?"

Sophie reached into the cot and lifted Oliver into her arms. As she did, the little boy smiled, revealing two bright pink gums. He was a handsome little boy, with his mother's auburn curls and blue eyes. His face was as round as the moon and he had a tiny button nose.

Sophie carried Oliver out of the house and into the fresh air. Mittens was sitting on the porch railing, her bright yellow eyes half-closed as she bathed in the warm afternoon sunlight.

"You stay here, Mittens," Sophie warned.

The cat opened its eyes but did not show any signs of moving.

"Shall we go and see Buck?" Sophie asked Oliver.

She carried Oliver to the stables, and as soon as Buckaroo saw her stepping through the door, he whinnied in greeting, sticking his large head over the side of the stall.

"Hi Buck," Sophie said, rubbing his nose.

Oliver cooed in delight as the horse pressed his wet nose against him and Sophie smiled at the innocence of it all.

"One day, you can learn to ride him," Sophie said. "I am sure your Uncle Simon will teach you—"

Sophie heard heavy footsteps and turned to see Simon step inside the stables. His dark hair was pushed back from his face, revealing his high brows, and his dark shirt was damp with perspiration.

"What are you doing here?" he asked shortly.

Sophie frowned. "We were just visiting with Buck."

Simon said nothing as he walked over to the wall where the horse tack was hung, and he removed a lead and a halter.

"What are you doing?" Sophie asked.

"Going to take Buck out and stretch that leg," Simon said. "See how it's moving."

Sophie nodded. "Can we come along?"

Simon shrugged. "It's a free country."

It wasn't the most enthusiastic response, but Sophie was more used to Simon's ways now. Something had turned him grumpy, but she would not let that spoil her afternoon.

Simon slipped the halter over the horse's head and then led Buck out of the stables. Sophie followed with Oliver in her arms. She was relieved to see that Buck was hardly limping anymore. With any luck, he'd be back at work before too long.

A short distance from the stables was a large paddock that housed about fifty sheep. They were all huddled together on the opposite end, like some giant ball of wool.

Simon led Buck in through the gate, closing it behind him again. Sophie and Oliver stood, watching through the railings as Simon led Buck in a circle, starting him in a walk, then a trot, and then a canter. Sophie enjoyed watching Simon.

He was so much more comfortable around animals than he was around people. His whole body took on a new form; he flowed effortlessly, every muscle in his body working harmoniously as he led Buck in a wide circle around him. Simon was usually wound so tight, he was always ready to snap, but here he took on his true form; she could see that as easily as she saw the puffy clouds in the sky above them.

"How's he doing?" Sophie asked.

"Good," Simon said, not taking his eyes off the horse. "He's almost got full movement back in his leg."

Sophie was pleased. She still hadn't forgiven herself for leaving the stable door unlatched, and the sooner Buckaroo was back to his old self, the sooner she'd feel less guilty about the whole awful ordeal.

Sophie watched Simon for a while longer. Oliver was now asleep in her arms. She knew she should head back to the house and get supper going, but just as she'd made up her mind, she spotted Jenna racing across the grass toward them. She was wearing her nightdress, her long auburn hair flowing down her back and her green eyes wide with panic.

"You can't just take him!" she shrieked. "I woke up and he was just gone!"

Sophie was so surprised by her outburst that she did not know what to say.

"Give him to me," Jenna said, almost wrestling Oliver out of Sophie's arms.

Oliver's eyes popped open and he began to cry, having been so abruptly awakened from his sleep.

Then without another word, she turned and walked back to the house, leaving both Sophie and Simon's brows furrowed in concern and confusion.

"What was that all about?" Simon asked.

Sophie shook her head. "I have no idea."

However, that wasn't entirely true. Sophie had some ideas. She knew that Jenna was scared of Oliver's father and what he might do. But had she thought he'd come into the house and taken the baby? It seemed incomprehensible, but seeing the panic in her eyes, Sophie wondered if this was not what had happened.

"I'll go and see if she's all right," Sophie said.

Without waiting for Simon to respond, Sophie turned and returned to the house. She stepped in through the back door, but the kitchen was empty. She could hear Jenna muttering to herself from her room.

"Jenna?" Sophie said, stepping cautiously into the room.

Oliver was in his crib, still fast asleep, and Jenna stood beside him.

"I am sorry I scared you," Sophie apologized.

Jenna turned to look at her and Sophie saw a million emotions—fear, anger, embarrassment.

"Do you want to come to the kitchen?" Sophie said. "I can make us some tea."

Jenna hesitated a moment and then nodded.

Sophie led the way into the kitchen and walked over to the stove to put on the water while Jenna sat at the table. She was still very pale and she was trembling slightly.

"I am sorry," Jenna said, her voice thin. "I overreacted."

Sophie turned to her and met her eyes.

"I didn't want to wake you," Sophie explained.

"I know," Jenna said, nodding. "I just woke up and I can't really explain it, but I had this feeling in the pit of my stomach like something bad had happened, and the crib was empty and my mind went in a million different directions."

Sophie nodded sympathetically. "You don't think he really would try to take him?"

Jenna shook her head as she exhaled shakily. "I don't know," she admitted. "I don't know what he wants."

Sophie could understand Jenna's fears. The worst was not knowing.

"Maybe you should try and talk to him," Sophie suggested. "Like you planned the other night."

"I am not sure that I can," Jenna confessed. "The other night, when I saw him through the front room window, smiling and laughing with his fiancée, it brought everything back—that night, how he looked at me. I am not sure I can face him."

Sophie nodded. After leaving her home, she was still scared that her stepfather might find her. She never wanted to look him in the face again.

The water in the kettle started to boil and Sophie carefully filled the teapot. She then carried it over to the table and placed it down. She fetched two cups from the china hutch and the sugar bowl.

"Thanks," Jenna said gratefully as she reached for the teapot and poured the tea.

The two women drank their tea in silence for a little while. The day was turning over outside, the light growing fainter by the minute.

Sophie could see the lines of worry on Jenna's face. She looked old, much too old for a woman of her age. She reached across the table for Jenna's hand.

"Whatever happens, we will keep Oliver safe," Sophie promised.

"But how?" Jenna asked, shaking her head. "He's rich and powerful and takes what he wants. I know that better than anyone."

Sophie said nothing for a moment as she held Jenna's gaze. "You have to tell Simon the truth. He can protect you both."

Jenna said nothing, but Sophie could see it in her eyes that she knew she was right.

"What if Simon does something reckless?" Jenna said anxiously.

"We won't let him," Sophie assured her.

Jenna nodded and Sophie squeezed her hand supportively. She knew they needed to tell Simon the truth, but despite her assurances to Jenna, Sophie had no idea how she'd stop Simon from flying off the handle when he finally learned the truth.

Chapter Fourteen

Simon latched the stable door and then headed for the house. It had been a long, frustrating day, but seeing Buckaroo on the mend had turned the day around some. He was confident after a few more days of rest, Buck would be back in the saddle again.

Sophie was standing over the stove when Simon came into the kitchen. She was so lost in her thoughts that she did not hear him enter.

"Everything all right?" he asked, recalling Jenna's strange behavior at the paddock that afternoon.

Sophie jumped, startled by his sudden arrival.

"Sorry," Simon apologized, walking over to the sink to wash up.

Sophie shook her head, her cheeks slightly flushed. "I was a million miles away."

Mittens was hanging around Sophie's skirts, waiting for her to drop a piece of fat on the floor for her to eat.

"Where's Jenna?" he asked.

"She's gone to bed," Sophie explained, not meeting his eye.

Simon frowned. "Without supper?"

"She wasn't hungry," Sophie said as she stirred beans.

Simon said nothing for a moment, but he could tell that Sophie was holding back, and after the day he'd had, he was sick of no one talking.

"What happened with Jenna this afternoon?" he asked, his tone hard.

Sophie hesitated. "She wants to tell you herself."

Simon sighed in frustration. "Then where is she?"

"Simon," Sophie said levelly, "I promise, she's going to tell you everything. You just need to give her some time."

There was something in Sophie's eyes, a compassion that soothed Simon's irritability and frustration. He sighed again as he shook his head.

"This is why I prefer the company of animals," he grumbled under his breath.

Simon caught Sophie's lips twitching.

"Why don't you sit?" she said. "Supper will be ready in a minute."

Simon turned and walked over to the table. He sat down as Sophie began to plate his dinner.

"How was your trip to town?" she asked, placing a large pork chop on his plate. "Did you manage to put in your advertisement?"

"I did," Simon said, frowning slightly.

"What is it?" Sophie asked as she put the plate down in front of him.

"I just need to find the right shearing team," he said. "Things were so much easier when we had ranch hands who knew the place and the sheep."

Sophie carried her plate and sat down opposite him.

"You can't hire anyone?" she asked.

"No," Simon said, taking a mouthful of beans. "The flock got a disease the same year my parents died and we are still recovering from the losses. I had to let go of all three men that year."

Sophie frowned, her brow creasing.

"Had to sell off most of the horses too just to keep the place afloat," Simon continued. "All but Buckaroo."

"I am sorry that happened," Sophie said.

Simon shrugged. "Can't change it."

They fell into silence for a while and the only sounds were their cutlery scraping against crockery and the distant call of an owl waking up from its daytime slumber.

"Well, at least you've got us now," Sophie said.

"That's true," Simon agreed.

Sophie's questions got him thinking. In many ways, his solitude had been forced on him these past few years, and now he could not help but wonder if he really did enjoy being on his own, or if he'd just gotten so used to it?

"I have something for you," Sophie said suddenly.

Simon frowned but said nothing.

"Wait here," Sophie said.

She hurried out of the kitchen, returning a few moments later with a white handkerchief. She handed it to Simon, who took it, still frowning.

"A handkerchief?" he asked in confusion.

"Open it," Sophie said.

Simon lifted the fabric to reveal a pearl brooch nestled in the material. The broach was shaped like a crescent moon, with large pearls on the outside and smaller ones on the inside. They were ornately set in gold and Simon was sure it was worth a pretty penny, although he did not know why Sophie was giving it to him.

"Thank you," Simon said. "But I don't think I'd find an occasion to wear it."

Sophie rolled her eyes. "It's not for you to wear. It's for you to sell."

"Sell?" Simon said, shaking his head. "I can't sell it. It's yours."

"I want you to have it," Sophie insisted. "As a thank you for finding Mittens."

"It's too big of a thank you," Simon argued, looking down at the brooch again.

"Please," Sophie said. "It's not helping anyone sitting in a drawer in the bedroom. But if you sell it, you can buy something for the ranch."

Simon looked up from the brooch to Sophie. No one had given him something so valuable before. But to him, it was more than the brooch; it was the thought behind it. She knew how much he cared for the ranch and she wanted to help save it. Simon exhaled as he folded the handkerchief back over the brooch and clutched it tightly.

"Thank you, Sophie," he said, with all sincerity.

"You saved the most important thing in my life," Sophie said, smiling slightly. "So I thought that I could return the favor."

Simon rarely had a reason to smile anymore, but he smiled then.

"Are you relieved to know the muscles in your face still work then?" Sophie teased.

"Ha ha," Simon said dryly.

Despite everything that had gone wrong that day, Simon *was* smiling, and it was thanks to Sophie. He had been adamant that they would not be friends, but perhaps he'd been too hasty in that regard.

***

Jenna was not up the following day when Simon ate his breakfast, although he kept expecting her to appear. He could not shake the sensation that she was avoiding him.

Simon spent the morning moving all the various flocks of sheep into the pasture closest to the house. He was unsure how soon he'd find a shearing team but wanted to be ready when the time came. It was hard work; sheep were not the most intelligent animals, and Simon had never gotten another sheepdog after his father's dog passed away some years ago. A dog would have made shorter work of it.

It was past lunch by the time Simon returned to the house. He was tired and hungry, and as he stepped into the kitchen, he stopped dead in his tracks. Seated across the table from Jenna was the woman he'd spoken to at the undertaker's house the afternoon before. She looked a little different now that she wasn't wearing night clothes and didn't have papers in her hair, but Simon recognized her immediately.

"Well, I'd best take my leave," the dark-haired woman said, eyeing Simon with dislike before she turned back to Jenna. "And don't be a stranger. The other girls and I miss you."

"I won't, Rose," Jenna said. "I promise."

She got up to show out the dark-haired woman, Rose, and Simon watched them go, his heart racing. There was no chance that this was a coincidence. She'd come to tell Jenna that he'd been asking questions.

Simon considered leaving before Jenna returned, but he knew that was cowardly and so he stayed glued to the spot. When Jenna returned to the kitchen, her face was stony as she glared across at Simon.

"You wouldn't talk to me—" Simon said defensively.

"And so what?" Jenna said, throwing her arms in the air. "You thought you'd just go and ask questions about me all over town? Is it not bad enough that I can barely show my face in public without making things worse?"

"I wasn't trying to make things worse," Simon said. "I was just trying to figure out what is going on."

"Nothing is going on," Jenna said, her pale face flushed.

"What about the letter?" Simon pressed. "What about Oliver's pa?"

"Jarrett is not his pa..."

Jenna's voice trailed off as her green eyes widened. She hadn't intended to say his name, but she had, and now he knew who Oliver's father was.

"Jarrett?" Simon asked, unable to hide the astonishment in his voice. "As in Jarrett Davidson?"

Jenna said nothing, but the truth was written across her whole face.

"Jarrett Davidson is Oliver's pa?" Simon confirmed, still unable to wrap his head around it.

"He's not his pa!" she exclaimed loudly. "He will have nothing to do with Oliver's life or mine, and I need you to stop asking questions and stay out of my business."

"But Jenna—"

"No, Simon," Jenna insisted. "Stay out of it."

Without another word, she turned and left the kitchen. Simon heard the bedroom door slam shut a moment later. He did not move; he still couldn't believe it. Oliver's father was Jarrett Davidson. He did not know the man personally, but knew he'd come from England and made his fortune on the railroad.

He'd moved to Shadow's Ridge after he became engaged to a business partner's daughter. It was no wonder Jenna did not want the news getting around. It was bad enough to mess around with a single man, but an engaged one?

Still, if it was Jarrett who sent the letter, then what was he trying to do? Why did he wish to be part of Jenna and Oliver's life if he was already engaged? Simon had wanted answers, but this revelation had only left him with more questions.

Simon pondered Jarrett's motivations for the whole afternoon but could not figure it out. Jarrett was a wealthy man, but he also had a lot to lose should news of his child get out in society. It could mean the end of his engagement and important business partnerships. Yet he was writing threatening notes to Jenna, insisting she let him see the baby.

By the end of the day, Simon was no more than wiser as to Jarrett's intentions, but now that he knew who Oliver's father was, he felt a pressing need to get things straightened out.

The best way he could think of doing that was to speak with Jarrett himself.

***

The next morning Simon headed into town, telling neither Sophie nor Jenna about his plan, as he knew neither of them would approve. Jenna had not eaten dinner with them the night before, and to be frank, Simon was worried about his cousin.

Jarrett Davidson lived in a large house at the end of Oak Street. Simon had passed by it on only one occasion, but it was the type of house someone did not easily forget. It was a two-story brick house with white shutters and a bright red door. The porch wrapped around the entire building and the front gardens were immaculate. Not a single blade of grass was out of place.

As Simon approached the gate leading up to the house, he stopped for a moment. He'd thought about what he would say all the way from the ranch, yet he still was not entirely sure. Still, he'd come all this way.

Simon reached over to unlatch the small gate leading up to the house, but as he did, the front door opened and a woman stepped out. She wore a pinafore over her blue ankle-length dress and a small white cap. Her brown hair was tied in a neat bun at the back of her head. Simon guessed she was the Davidsons' housekeeper.

"Can I help you?" the housekeeper said. "If you are wanting something to eat, you should come around the back."

Simon grimaced, wondering if he really did look so rough that she thought he was a beggar.

"I am looking for Mr. Davidson," Simon said. "My name is Simon Jones."

"Is Mr. Davidson expecting you?" she asked.

"No," Simon said. "But I just need a moment."

The housekeeper frowned and for a second, Simon thought she might turn him away.

"Wait there," she said. "I'll see if he's available."

The housekeeper turned and disappeared back into the house. A few moments later, a dark-haired man in a fitted blue suit appeared. Simon had never met Jarrett Davidson before, but he knew immediately this was him.

"I'd like a word, Mr. Davidson," Simon said. "If you have a moment."

Simon felt his steely blue eyes traveling from his old leather boots up to his threadbare Stetson as he measured his worth.

"What is this about?" he asked.

"My cousin," Simon said. "Jenna Wilder."

Jarrett said nothing for a moment, but Simon saw his shoulders tense under the immaculately tailored material of his suit.

"Why don't you come in?" he invited.

Simon unlatched the gate and walked up the path. As he stepped onto the porch, Jarrett turned and went inside and Simon followed.

The inside of the house was equally as impressive as the outside. Along the walls of the wide hallway were framed newspaper articles, all about Jarrett's business successes. There were also several portraits of still individuals in lace collars, unsmiling and frozen in time.

Simon was led down the hallway. As he did, he caught sight of himself in a large, gilded mirror, and in contrast to Jarrett, he did look wild, with his shoulder-length hair and unkempt beard.

Jarrett pushed open a door that led to a brightly lit study. A large desk was near the window and a grandfather clock, as tall as Simon, rested against the one wall. As in the hallway, the walls were decorated with tales of his railroad triumphs.

"Why don't you take a seat?" Jarrett offered, indicating with his eyes to a high-backed chair.

"If it's all the same to you, I think I'll stand," Simon said stiffly.

Jarrett shrugged. "Suit yourself."

Jarrett walked over to a small silver drinks cart and pulled the stopper from a crystal decanter filled with whiskey. He filled a glass before he turned to Simon.

"Drink?" he offered.

"No," Simon said. "Thank you."

Jarrett picked up his glass and took a swig, oblivious to the fact that it was barely past breakfast.

"So Jenna is your cousin?" he asked as he locked his gaze on Simon.

"That's right," Simon said, shifting his feet.

He could not quite put his finger on it, but there was something about this man's eyes that unsettled him. Perhaps it was because they were devoid of any emotion, so cold and unfeeling.

"And she asked you to come here?" Jarrett enquired before taking another sip.

"No, she doesn't know that I am here."

Jarrett raised his eyebrows as if he did not quite believe him

"But I found this," Simon said, reaching into his pocket and removing the note.

He handed it to Jarrett, but he did not take it.

"I don't know what your cousin has told you—"

"She hasn't told me anything," Simon interjected. "Which is why I am here."

Jarrett took another sip from his glass before he walked across the room and took a seat behind the desk. He sat back casually in his chair.

Simon walked over to the desk and put the note down. "Why did you write this?"

Jarrett exhaled. "Can I be frank with you? Man to man?"

Simon said nothing.

"I have no interest in the child," he said matter-of-factly. "Or your cousin."

"Then why write this?" Simon asked.

"Because I wanted to talk to her," Jarrett said, shrugging. "And I thought using the child would be the best way."

Simon frowned.

"Look," Jarrett said, leaning forward in his chair. "Your cousin and I had a bit of fun one evening. I didn't even know about the baby until a couple of months ago—"

"She never told you?" Simon asked, his brow still furrowed.

"Why would she?" Jarrett asked, smirking. "It was just a bit of fun."

Simon gritted his teeth. He did *not* like how Jarrett kept using the phrase "a bit of fun."

"So you wrote the note as a way to talk with Jenna," Simon said. "What did you want to talk to her about?"

Jarrett said nothing for a moment as he traced the rim of his glass with his thumb.

"I don't need to tell you I'm an important man," Jarrett said. "And this child, well, if people found out, it would not be good for me or my business."

Simon could have guessed that his motivations were self-serving. Everything about Jarrett Davidson, from how he spoke to how he dressed his house in all his success, told Simon that he was a vain man with a seriously inflated sense of self. Yet he was not stupid, he was cold and calculating.

"But why not just deny it?" Simon asked. "Why admit that you are the boy's pa?"

"I don't expect someone like *you* to understand," Jarrett continued. "But I am my reputation; even the mere suggestion of impropriety on my part could have a significant impact on my business and my life. Which is why I wanted to make your cousin a proposal."

Simon raised his eyebrows.

"No," Jarrett said, smirking again. "Not that kind of proposal. I am already engaged to be married and, your cousin, well, let's just say I could never marry someone like her."

Simon balled his fists up at his sides. "My cousin is twice the person you are."

Jarrett smiled again, raising his eyebrows in disbelief. "I sincerely doubt that. But what I need is for her not to talk, to keep her mouth shut about the child and about my involvement."

Simon stared at Jarrett with loathing. He could hardly fathom what Jenna had seen in this man.

"So I propose to give her money," Jarrett said plainly. "For her silence."

"You want to buy her off?" Simon said, his tone disapproving.

"Let's not pretend you don't need the money," Jarrett said, looking him up and down with pity.

Simon's fists were now so tight, the whites of his knuckles were showing.

"I can tell you are a proud man," Jarrett said. "And I respect that. But think about the child. This money could make a difference in his life."

"You couldn't care less about the boy if it rained toads," Simon said.

"You're right," Jarrett agreed without hesitation. "I don't care about him. But how long can you really keep your ranch going on wool and jam?"

Simon frowned. He did not know how Jarrett knew so much about his ranch, but he found it unnerving. Had Jarrett been looking into them? Into their finances?

"You seem like a reasonable man," Jarrett continued, his cold eyes focused on Simon. "But one can never have enough money."

Simon did not deny they needed money, but he would not take it from this man. He was unwilling to give him the satisfaction of owning them, not after how he'd spoken about Jenna.

"We don't need your money," Simon said firmly.

Jarrett smiled mockingly, his eyes glimmering dangerously.

"Just think about it," he suggested.

There was an edge to his voice which told Simon that Jarrett wanted him to more than just think about it.

"I think I should be going," Simon said.

He turned around without another word, but as he reached the door, Jarrett cleared his throat and Simon hesitated, his hand on the brass door knob.

"I am a man who gets what he wants," Jarrett threatened. "And you'd do well to remember that."

Simon did not turn around but opened the study door and left the room. He kept his head down as he walked down the hallway and out of the front door. It was only when he was on the road back to the ranch that he relaxed his shoulders.

It was not often that Simon was intimidated by another person, but there was something dangerous about that man, something lingering beneath the surface of that well-groomed exterior. Simon could not quite put his finger on it, but he had the strongest sensation that he'd not seen the last of Jarrett Davidson.

Chapter Fifteen

Sophie looked out of the kitchen window, squinting as the last of the light faded behind the distant mountains. She had not seen Simon all afternoon and wondered where he was. Supper was almost ready and the sweet scent of the cornbread baking in the oven filled the kitchen.

Sophie had looked after Oliver all afternoon. Jenna had a migraine, so she'd been in her room with the blinds drawn. Oliver had fallen asleep a short while ago and Sophie had put him down in her bedroom so as not to disturb Jenna's rest.

Sophie heard the front door open and turned. She knew it was Simon by the heavy footsteps on the wooden floorboards. It was unusual for him to use the front door, and she frowned slightly.

"Hi," Sophie said as he stepped into the room.

"Hi," Simon echoed as he removed his hat, his dark hair tumbling over his forehead. His soft brown eyes looked troubled.

"I was wondering where you were," she said, trying to gauge his mood.

"Where's Jenna?" he asked, looking at the empty kitchen table.

"In her room," Sophie said. "She's been in there all afternoon."

Simon frowned but said nothing and Sophie wondered what was troubling him.

"Do you want to sit? Supper is almost ready."

Simon went and sat down, and a short while later, Sophie served them supper, but Simon hardly touched his food. Sophie watched as he pushed it around the plate.

"I can make you something else," Sophie said.

Simon looked across at her and frowned. "No. It's not the food."

"Then what is it?" she asked.

Simon exhaled deeply. "I went to see Oliver's pa this afternoon."

Sophie's jaw dropped as she stared at him. She hadn't even known that Simon knew who he was.

"You did what?" Jenna said.

Sophie looked over to see Jenna standing in the doorway, her auburn hair tied in a long plait down her back and dark rings under her eyes.

"Jenna," Simon said, getting up from his seat. "Just let me explain—"

"I asked you to stay out of it," Jenna said, shaking her head. "How could you do this?"

"I am sorry I didn't tell you," Simon said. "But I thought that if I just talked to him, then—"

"Then what?" Jenna asked, her green eyes glowering.

"Then maybe I could understand why he wrote that note. That it might be because he wanted to be in Oliver's life and you could all be a family."

"A family?" Jenna challenged, her voice shrill.

"Is that such a ridiculous notion?" Simon asked, although he would hate to be in some way related to that man. "After all, you two were together, there must have been strong feelings—"

Sophie caught Jenna's eye and Simon frowned, witnessing their silent exchange.

"What was that?" Simon asked.

Neither of them spoke for a moment.

"I think you need to tell him, Jenna," Sophie said.

Jenna shook her head. "I can't."

"You can," Sophie said.

All of Jenna's outrage had left her and she crumpled like a piece of paper.

"Is someone going to tell me what is going on?" Simon asked, looking from Sophie to Jenna.

Jenna sighed shakily. "I think you should sit down."

Simon took his seat at the table and Jenna joined them. No one spoke for a long moment.

"There were no strong feelings between Jarrett and myself," Jenna said, not looking at Simon but staring at her hands. "I only knew him from the saloon. He was a regular."

Sophie looked across at Simon, who was listening intently to Jenna.

"I was locking up one night when Jarrett came in for a drink. It was late, and no one else was there, just me—"

Jenna stopped and looked across at Sophie, who nodded encouragingly.

"He had a few drinks and we talked, but when I told him it was time to go, he wouldn't leave. He told me that he'd come for more than a few drinks and that I'd been flirting with him for weeks. He grabbed me by the wrist and I tried to fight him off, but he was too strong—"

Sophie looked across at Simon and she saw the muscles in his jaw tense as the realization of what had actually happened between Jenna and Jarrett started to sink in.

"Once he'd finished, he left," Jenna said as she blinked back tears. "And when he came in the next night, he pretended like nothing had happened."

Simon was pale now, and he trembled with rage. Sophie instinctively put a hand on his arm, but he stood up suddenly, his chair crashing to the floor.

"Why didn't you come to me?" he asked, his tone a mixture of anger and anguish.

"How could I?" Jenna implored. "I hadn't seen you since your parents' funeral—"

"So?" Simon said. "You should have come to me, and I could have done something. I can still do something—"

"No," Jenna said. "That's why I didn't tell you. I knew you'd try to do something honorable but at what cost? Your life? His?"

"You can't tell me that you care whether that monster lives or dies?" Simon asked incredulously.

"I thought about killing him myself," Jenna said. "But he'd already taken everything from me, so I chose to try and forget him, to move on rather than let him take my life."

Simon was pacing the kitchen floor. Sophie had never seen him like this before. It was as if he was fighting every instinct in his body.

"Did you ever think about going to the sheriff?" Simon asked.

"Do you think he would have believed me?" Jenna asked. "You know the reputation of saloon girls."

"So you said nothing?" Simon asked. "You just let him get away with it? To do what he did to you to another woman?"

Jenna inhaled sharply.

"Simon," Sophie cautioned.

Simon exhaled deeply as he ran a hand through his hair. "I'm sorry, Jenna."

"I told some of the other girls who worked in the saloon," Jenna said, her green eyes brimming with tears again. "I warned them to be careful, not to let themselves be alone with him."

"That woman, who was here yesterday, Rose, does she know?"

Jenna nodded and Simon sighed. "Why didn't you tell me?" he asked again. "After you came to stay here, you let me just think you'd be foolish enough to get yourself pregnant."

"It was better than the alternative," Jenna said. "Better than you knowing my shameful secret."

"Hey," Simon said, walking over to Jenna and kneeling down. "This is not your fault and if anyone should be ashamed, it's him, okay?"

"He's right, Jenna," Sophie said firmly. "You didn't do anything wrong."

Jenna smiled sadly. "I sometimes wonder what would have happened if I'd never left the ranch. Maybe I'd have met a young ranch hand and got married. I'd have a family and a home."

"You have a family and a home," Simon insisted.

Jenna reached over and placed her hand on Simon's cheek. "You're a good man. You deserve a better cousin than me."

Simon put his hand over hers. "Don't say that."

Jenna smiled sadly again. "I am tired. If it's all right, I will go to bed."

"Do you need anything?" Sophie offered. "Something to eat or drink?"

"No, thank you," Jenna said. "I think I just need to sleep."

She got up from her chair and walked toward the door, but before she stepped into the hallway, Jenna turned around.

"Promise me you won't do anything stupid?" she said, looking at Simon. "I couldn't bear it if something happened to you."

Simon said nothing for a moment and then he nodded. "I promise."

Neither Sophie nor Simon spoke until they heard the latch on Jenna's bedroom door click shut and then Simon rounded on her.

"You knew this entire time?" he accused.

"It wasn't my secret to tell," Sophie said with both defense and determination. "And until tonight, Jenna wasn't ready to tell you the truth."

Simon sighed as he shook his head. He sat down in the chair opposite Sophie.

"All this time she's been carrying it around with her and I didn't see it," Simon said. "How could I not have seen it?"

"Maybe it was because she wouldn't let you see it," Sophie said.

"No," Simon said. "It's always been there. When she arrived with Oliver, I saw it in her eyes, but I chose to ignore it. I never asked her about Oliver's father because I was selfish. I did not want to have to deal with any of it. For months I've let her deal with all this on her own."

Simon was disappointed in himself. It was written all over his face and in the tone of his voice. Without thinking, Sophie reached across the table and touched his fingers. Simon's face softened at her touch.

"There is only one person who should feel badly about all this," Sophie said. "And that's the man who attacked Jenna."

"I can't believe I was in the same room as him and had no idea of the truth. The way he talked about Jenna…"

Simon shook his head, the muscles in his jaw tensing again.

"What did he say to you?" Sophie asked.

"He has no interest in Oliver," Simon said in disgust. "He was only using him to get to Jenna. He knew she wouldn't meet with him otherwise."

Sophie shook her head.

"He wants to buy her silence," Simon continued. "He's worried if the truth gets out, it will hurt his reputation."

"And what of Jenna's reputation?" Sophie said, angry at the injustice.

"The man's an egomaniac," Simon said. "And he's dangerous. When I told him we wouldn't take his money, he threatened me."

Sophie frowned. "Are you going to tell Jenna?"

Simon sighed. "I don't know. I'm worried about her. She isn't eating and she's barely sleeping by the looks of it. What if I tell her and it pushes her over the edge?"

Sophie said nothing, but she agreed with Simon. Jenna was struggling, and knowing that Jarrett was making more threats would not help.

"We'll figure it all out," Sophie said. "Together."

Simon met her eye and for a long moment, they sat in silence. As much as Sophie wanted to be there for Jenna, she also wanted to be there for Simon. She wanted him to know that he could depend on her.

"I need to keep everyone safe," Simon said. "I won't let that man hurt this family again."

Sophie heard the conviction in Simon's voice and knew that he was right. He was the only one who could keep Jenna and Oliver safe. However, she would not let him do it alone. For what it was worth, she was his wife, and she'd help in any way she could. After all, she'd spent years fighting monsters.

Chapter Sixteen

Simon did not sleep well that night. He lay awake for hours, thinking of Jenna and all those months she'd kept her attack a secret from him. Simon had always known how strong and spirited she was, but Jarrett had tried to break her, which in turn broke his heart.

As he lay awake, he also thought about what his father would have done in his place. Simon's father had taught him the importance of family and how it was a man's responsibility to protect his family. Yet he'd failed to protect Jenna.

Before dawn, Simon got up and dressed. The house was still as he left his bedroom, closing the door behind him. He entered the kitchen and found Jenna seated at the table with Oliver.

His cousin did not notice him immediately, and Simon watched her for a moment, the tenderness in her face obvious as she looked down at her little boy. Motherhood was something Simon would never experience, but it was something that he deeply respected and admired. Oliver was the product of violence, yet Jenna loved him with her entire being.

Jenna looked up then, and she smiled. "Couldn't sleep either?"

Simon shook his head. "Would you like some coffee?"

"Yes, please," Jenna said. "The water should be boiled by now."

Simon walked over to the china hutch and took out two clean mugs before he fetched the coffee from the pantry.

"How's he doing?" Simon asked, turning to look at Oliver.

"Much better, I think," Jenna said. "He's coughing less."

"That's good," Simon said, carrying a mug of coffee over to the table and putting it down.

He then fetched his own mug and sat down opposite her. Neither of them spoke for a while. Outside, Simon heard the first sounds of dawn, the roosters crowing and the birds chirping; the whole world waking up to another day.

"How are things going with Sophie?" Jenna said, looking across the table at him.

Simon took a sip of coffee, nodding. "Fine, I think. We've got clean mugs."

Jenna smiled. "You know that's not what I meant."

Simon took another sip of coffee and then put his mug down on the table. "Did you know about Sophie's family when she applied for the post?"

Jenna shook her head. "No, she only wrote that the situation was urgent."

Simon nodded. "She's told me a bit about her family, the way they treated her, and I can't quite imagine what growing up in such a house must have been like. To be desperate enough to leave home in the middle of the night and marry a stranger."

"I think she's brave," Jenna said. "To not just accept her fate."

"I agree," Simon said quietly.

"She told me the other day that she worries her stepfather will come looking for her," Jenna revealed.

Simon frowned. "She's married now. What could her stepfather do?"

Jenna shrugged. "Powerful men have tools at their disposal, ways and means of getting what they want."

Simon said nothing, but he knew that Jenna was not just talking about Sophie and her stepfather. "You're worried about Jarrett?"

Jenna nodded as she hugged Oliver a little tighter.

"You know I won't let him hurt you," Simon said. "Either of you."

Jenna said nothing, but Simon saw the worry in her eyes, and he wished he could do something to help, something more than making promises.

"Can I tell you something?" Jenna asked.

Simon nodded.

"When I put the advertisement in the newspaper, it wasn't only because we needed help around the house."

Simon frowned but waited for her to continue.

"I was going to leave," Jenna confessed. "I thought that if you were married, I could just disappear, and you and Sophie could be his parents. That way, he'd never have to feel ashamed of me, or have people whispering about him behind his back because he didn't have a pa."

Simon stared at Jenna for a moment. Had she really been planning on leaving?

"I even had my bag packed," Jenna said. "But when I went to the crib to kiss Oliver goodbye, he looked up at me and smiled, and I just couldn't go through with it."

"Jenna," Simon said, leaning forward in his seat. "That little boy needs you. He needs his ma, so you have to promise me you won't think of leaving him again."

"I know," Jenna said as she blinked back tears. "But I am so scared he will hate me one day—"

"I won't let that happen," Simon said. "Okay?"

Jenna nodded, but something in Simon's gut told him that she would struggle with this for the rest of her life. It was hard being a parent under normal circumstances, and Jenna's situation was anything but ordinary.

In truth, Simon had imagined that Jenna and Oliver would one day leave the ranch. She'd move to a new town where she could pretend Oliver's father had passed away, and she would be a widow and not an outcast. A few months ago, Simon believed that would be the best thing for Jenna to do, to move on and start afresh, but now he wasn't so sure. Family needed to stick together.

"Sophie and I will help you," Simon promised. "We'll all raise him together."

Jenna half smiled at him before she frowned. "And what about Jarrett?"

"Don't worry about him," Simon said. "I'll figure something out."

***

Simon headed out to the barn after breakfast, but as he did, he spotted a group of six men coming up the driveway.

"Mornin'," said the man in the front with a ginger beard. "Name's Reuben, and this is my team. We saw your advertisement in town."

With everything that had happened, Simon had almost forgotten about the advertisement.

"You the shearers?" he asked.

"That's right," Reuben said. "Myself and David are the shearers, Jasper here is the handler. Harry does the bailing, and young Milton is our rouseabout."

Reuben indicated to each of the men as he spoke.

"You any good?" he asked.

"Yes, sir," Reuben said. "Best shearing team you are going to find."

"You got your own equipment?"

"The best money can buy," Reuben assured him.

Simon looked around at the group of men before he nodded again. "Well, all right then, come back first thing Monday morning, and we'll get started."

Reuben tipped his hat, and the men turned to leave. Simon was relieved to have found a team of shearers but had much to prepare for the morning.

Simon spent the morning getting the rest of the sheep into the paddock near the stables. Once they were all there, he began to inspect them to ensure they didn't have any injuries or diseases. After each inspection, he herded the sheep into a holding pen he'd erected beside the paddock. There they would stay until the shearing the next day.

He'd just started when Sophie arrived, with Mittens following a short distance behind.

"I came to ask what you'd like for lunch," she said, leaning against the wooden railing.

"No lunch today," Simon said. "Got too much work to do."

Sophie frowned. "Can I help?"

"You inspected a sheep before?"

Sophie shrugged. "It can't be that hard, right?"

Simon raised an eyebrow.

"What?" Sophie said, frowning. "You don't think I can do it?"

"Never said that," Simon replied.

Without another word, Sophie slipped between the wooden railings and walked over to Simon. "Show me what to do."

"All right," Simon agreed. "First, you got to check that they got clear eyes and normal breathing."

Sophie nodded.

"Then you got to check their coat, make sure there ain't any matted or soiled wool. Also, keep an eye out for any ticks or fleas."

Sophie wrinkled her nose.

"Once you've checked the wool, you run your hands up and down their backbone and ribcage, make sure they are carrying enough fat."

"Is that it?" Sophie asked.

"No," Simon said. "Then you got to check their legs and hooves, make sure there is no lameness or injuries."

"And you have to do this with each one?" Sophie said, looking around at the flock.

"Yup," Simon said. "So we'd better get to work."

Mittens, who was now sitting atop a wooden pole, watched with interest as Sophie tried, in vain, to catch her first sheep. When she finally caught one, it head-butted her, and she ended up on the ground, her skirts full of mud.

Simon could not help but smile in amusement.

"It's not funny," Sophie insisted as she struggled to her feet.

"It's a little funny," Simon said.

Sophie muttered under her breath, but a moment later, she lost her footing and almost fell again, but Simon caught her this time. He had his hands around her narrow waist as he looked into her eyes. She was panting slightly, her cheeks flushed, and she was close enough that Simon could feel the warmth of her breath on his face.

For a long moment, he found himself lost in her eyes. He'd never noticed how blue they were before, or the scattering of light freckles across her nose and cheekbones. He wondered if she could hear his heart beating, because that's all he heard.

Something suddenly spooked the flock, and they reacted quickly, almost knocking Simon and Sophie to the ground.

"Sorry," Simon said, dropping his arms to his sides.

Sophie's face was still flushed as Mittens streaked across the paddock, and Simon guessed she was the one who'd startled the flock.

"I guess this isn't as easy as it looks," Sophie said.

"It just takes practice," Simon said. "Look, I'll show you."

Simon showed Sophie how to catch a sheep and keep them still enough to do the examination. After watching for a time, Sophie managed to get the hang of it. As they worked, Sophie asked him questions about his parents and his childhood. It felt good to reminisce about the old days.

After a couple of hours, they'd gotten all the sheep checked and into the holding pen.

"Well, we'll make a cowboy out of you yet," Simon said.

"I am a mess," Sophie laughed.

She wasn't wrong—strands of ash-blonde hair hung around her face, and she had dirt on her chin and nose. Her clothes were full of mud, but Simon was sure she had never looked more beautiful.

It was late afternoon by the time they returned to the house. Jenna and Oliver were in the back garden; Jenna had laid out a blanket, and Oliver was lying on his back, cooing happily.

"What happened to you?" Jenna asked, her green eyes widening.

"I was helping Simon with the sheep," Sophie said as she tucked a strand of hair behind her ear.

"She did a good job," Simon said. "She'd make a good ranch hand."

Simon nudged Sophie playfully in the ribs, and she smiled. It had actually been nice having someone helping him that afternoon. He hadn't realized that he missed having someone to talk to. He and his father had some of their best conversations out working on the ranch.

"So everything is ready for the shearers then?" Jenna asked.

Simon nodded.

Then, out of the corner of his eye, Simon caught a movement and turned his head to see Rose, Jenna's dance hall friend, coming around the side of the house.

"Rose?" Jenna said in surprise. "What are you doing here?"

"I need to talk to you," Rose said grimly.

Simon frowned. "What is this about?"

"Can we go somewhere private?" Rose asked.

Jenna nodded as she got up from the blanket. "Will you keep an eye on Oliver?"

Simon nodded as Jenna and Rose disappeared inside.

"I wonder what that's about," Sophie said as she kneeled down next to Oliver on the blanket.

"I reckon it's not good news, by the look on her face," Simon said.

Sophie frowned in concern as Oliver continued staring at the sky, cooing to himself.

Simon stayed with Sophie and Oliver in the back garden until Jenna and Rose emerged from the house. Jenna was pale, and her eyes were full of concern.

"I'd better get back," Rose said. "My shift starts soon."

Jenna nodded. "Stay safe."

The two women embraced before Rose turned and headed back around the house. Jenna walked over to them, her arms folded around her body.

"What was that about?" Simon asked.

Jenna did not answer right away.

"Jenna?" he prompted. "What did she say?"

"She came to tell me that another girl was attacked," Jenna said, her bottom lip quivering. "Another dance hall girl."

"What?" Sophie said in disbelief.

Jenna nodded but, again, remained silent.

Simon's mind raced as he considered what Jenna had just told them. When he met Jenna's eye, he knew without asking who was responsible for attacking that girl.

"We can't let him get away with this," Simon said. "We have to do something."

Sophie nodded, but Jenna shook her head.

"She doesn't want anyone to know," Jenna said.

Simon gritted his teeth. Jarrett Davidson was ruining lives, and he couldn't just sit back and do nothing. He had to find a way to hold that monster accountable for his actions before anyone else got hurt.

Chapter Seventeen

"I think we should go to church," Sophie said as she stepped into the kitchen.

Both Simon and Jenna looked across at her in surprise. They were seated at the kitchen table. Oliver was on Jenna's lap, milky porridge dribbling down his chin.

"Church?" Simon asked, frowning slightly.

"Yes,"

She'd thought about it a lot in the night. A black cloud had been hanging above the house since learning that Jarrett Davidson had attacked another girl. Jenna had hardly left her room in days, and Simon walked around the place with a near-constant scowl on his face. She knew going to church wouldn't change what had happened, but it might be good for all of them. She was hopeful that the word and songs of God would boost their spirits.

"I can't remember the last time I went to church," Simon said.

"Neither can I," Jenna agreed.

"Well, then it's all the more reason to go," Sophie said. "I am certain it will make us all feel better."

Neither Simon nor Jenna said anything for a moment, but they both looked unconvinced.

"You two go," Jenna said. "He might be there, and I don't want to bump into him."

Sophie frowned. She was sure a man like Jarrett Davidson couldn't cross the threshold of a church without being smited by God's wrath. Still, she could not blame Jenna for not wanting to bump into him.

"Simon?" Sophie said, turning to him. "Will you go with me?"

Simon sighed heavily as he sat back in his chair. "Fine," he agreed. "If you really want to go. It'll be a good chance for Buck to stretch that leg, if nothing else."

"I do," Sophie said, smiling.

***

The next day was Sunday, and Sophie made a special effort with her appearance. She brushed her long ash-blonde hair until it shone and twisted it into an elegant knot rather than her usual long plait. She then dressed in her best dress, which was cornflower blue, and complemented her eyes.

The afternoon before, she'd shined her boots until she could see her reflection in them, and now she slipped her feet into them and fastened the buckles. She fetched a cream shawl from the dresser and draped it over her shoulders before fetching her bonnet from the nail behind the door.

When she was all dressed, Sophie stepped into the hallway, leaving her bonnet on the table near the front door. She then headed to the kitchen, and as she stepped inside, Simon looked across at her, and his eyes widened.

"What is it?" Sophie asked, wondering if she had a stain on her dress or if she'd put her boots on the wrong feet.

"It's nothing," Simon said, recovering himself. "You look nice, that's all."

"As opposed to how I usually look?" she challenged.

Simon sighed and shook his head but said nothing.

Once she'd fetched a helping of eggs and biscuits, Sophie took her seat at the kitchen table. Simon kept stealing glances at her and Sophie pretended not to notice. But she was secretly pleased that he'd noticed the special effort she'd made with her appearance.

"Have you seen Jenna this morning?" Sophie asked.

Simon shook his head.

"Did you make breakfast?" Sophie asked in surprise.

"Don't sound so surprised," Simon said. "I had a life before you and my cousin showed up."

Sophie raised her eyebrows but said nothing. Simon had also made a special effort with his appearance—his dark hair was combed back, and he'd trimmed his beard. He was also dressed in a crisp green shirt that complemented his coloring. Sophie thought he looked very handsome, although she felt too shy to say it out loud.

Once they'd finished breakfast, Simon left to hitch Buck to the buggy. This trip to town would be his first journey since the coyote attack. Sophie headed back down the hallway to fetch her bonnet off the table. As she did, she hesitated outside Jenna's bedroom door, but there was no sound from within. Sophie thought about knocking to tell her that they were leaving, but she did not want to wake Jenna or Oliver.

She walked back through the kitchen and out the back door. The buggy was parked alongside the barn, and Simon was just finished hitching Buck up.

"How's he doing?" Sophie asked as she ran a hand over the horse's sleek neck.

"Good," Simon said, nodding approvingly. "I think he's excited to get out."

A short while later, they were bumping down the road toward town. As the rooftops of the houses and shops came into view, Simon steered Buck down the main street. All of the stores were closed and would only open after church, and there was not a soul to be seen.

The small stone church soon came into view. Sophie had not been there since the day she married Simon. The street outside the church was packed with buggies and horses. As Simon brought the buggy to a halt, notes from the piano drifted out of the open doors, and inside, Sophie heard the hum of the congregation.

She climbed down from the buggy, careful not to get any dust on her dress. She and Simon crossed the road together toward the church. Sophie had gone to church every Sunday back home, and had always looked forward to it. Sundays were the only time Mr. Colton thought it appropriate for her to visit town, so her sentiments toward church were mixed in with a sense of freedom.

Simon pushed open the small gate, and Sophie stepped inside the churchyard. She led the way down the path toward the doors with Simon behind her. As they stepped inside the stone building, several members of the congregation turned to look at them. Some even went so far as to crane their necks to get a good view, while others frowned in disbelief.

"Let's find a seat," Simon mumbled, his jaw tense.

Sophie nodded and followed Simon to a bench near the back of the church.

As they sat down, the minister arrived at the front of the church, and the congregation fell silent.

"A warm welcome to you all," the minister said, smiling at the sea of faces. "In the presence of God, we gather this beautiful morning as a community of faith to offer our praise and seek guidance."

There were a few nods and murmurs of amen from the congregation.

"Let us begin our worship by joining our hearts and minds together in prayer."

Everyone bowed their heads, and the minister prayed. When the prayer was over, the minister adjusted his spectacles, which had slipped down his nose.

"Today, I want to share a message of hope and encouragement that reminds us of the unwavering light that shines even in the midst of life's storms," he said.

Sophie glanced at Simon, who was not looking at the minister but kept his head down.

"*'God is our refuge and strength, an -present help in trouble,'*" the minister quoted. "*'Therefore, we will not fear, though the earth gives way and the mountains fall into the heart of the sea, though its waters roar and foam and the mountains quake with their surging.'*"

Sophie listened carefully to the sermon, and as she did, she felt fortified by the minister's message. Undoubtedly they were going through a difficult time, but it was hope that must sustain them. For even in the darkest times, hope could be found.

***

After the service ended, the congregation left the church and broke into smaller groups. As Sophie and Simon stepped out, many people turned to them again, and Sophie did her best to smile politely while Simon's expression stayed stony.

"Let's go," Simon said.

But before they had the opportunity, a young woman with a very swollen stomach came waddling up to them. She had raven-colored hair and large brown eyes, like a doe.

"Simon?" she said. "Is that really you?"

"Rachel," Simon said somewhat stiffly. "How are you?"

"Well," she said as she tried to catch Simon's eye, but he seemed determined to avoid hers.

"Hello," Sophie said, raising a hand. "I am Sophie."

Rachel turned her head and met Sophie's eye. "So you are the woman who finally convinced Simon to come down from his mountain?"

There was something in her tone, a sharpness that Sophie did not quite understand. A short distance away, Sophie saw a short man with sandy-colored hair watching them, craning his neck to get a better view.

"Well, it was good seeing you," Simon said. "But we should get home."

Without another word, Simon steered Sophie away from the church and across the street.

"What was that all about?" Sophie asked as she climbed into her seat. "Who was that?"

Simon said nothing as he grasped the reins. He clicked his tongue softly, and Buck stepped forward, and Simon steered the buggy back onto the road.

"Simon?" Sophie pressed, her head turned to him. "Who was she?"

Simon exhaled deeply. "That was Rachel, my ex-fiancée."

"What?" Sophie said, her mouth popping open in surprise. "You had a fiancée?"

Simon nodded.

"What happened? Why didn't you marry her?"

"It's a long story," Simon said.

"Well, I am not going anywhere," Sophie insisted.

Simon sighed again, keeping his eyes on the road in front of them.

"We actually met at church," Simon said. "A year before my parents were killed."

"So what happened?"

"My parents died, and I changed," Simon said, shrugging. "I didn't even realize what was happening until it was already over. Rachel told me that she was lonely and that being with me made her feel lonely. She didn't want to live on an isolated ranch with a husband who was more shadow than man."

Sophie said nothing, but her heart hurt for him, for what must have been like to lose so many people.

"She was right," Simon said matter-of-factly. "I wasn't there for her, and I certainly didn't fight for her, so she broke it off. A few months later, she married a banker in town, and I hadn't seen her since, until this morning."

Sophie thought about the man with the sandy-colored hair who'd been watching them so intently. He must be Rachel's husband, the banker.

"Did you love her?" Sophie asked.

Simon frowned. "I don't know," he confessed. "Maybe if I had, I would have fought harder to make things work."

"How come you've never mentioned her?" Sophie asked.

Simon shrugged. "She's just another ghost now," he said. "A part of a future that was never meant to be."

They both fell silent for a while as the buggy bumped back up the road toward the ranch.

"What about you?" Simon asked.

"What about me?" she asked.

"You ever broken anyone's heart?"

Sophie shook her head. "No. Never."

Simon scoffed. "I struggle to believe that."

"It's true," Sophie insisted. "I told you about my stepfather, how controlling he was. The only time I was off the ranch was Sunday for church, and I was sworn from even talking to any of the young ranch hands."

"So you never had any friends in town? Never went out to socials or dances?" Simon asked, his tone disbelieving.

Sophie shook her head.

"Were you lonely?" Simon asked as he glanced over at her, his expression tender.

"I had Mittens," Sophie said, shrugging. "But as soon as my ma remarried, my home became my prison. I was only permitted to go where he told me to go and say what he told me to say."

Simon frowned and she could almost hear his mind working.

"You don't still feel trapped, do you?" he asked, his eyes now full of concern.

"No," Sophie said firmly, her brow creasing. "Why would you think that?"

Simon sighed. "Rachel said she felt trapped, isolated, up on the ranch, and I just wouldn't want you to feel that same way—"

"I don't," Sophie assured him. "I feel freer there than I've felt anywhere else in my entire life."

"Good," Simon said, dropping his shoulders in relief. "Because I want it to feel like home."

"It does," Sophie assured him.

They fell silent for a while, but Sophie was very aware of the warmth of Simon's arm, which was almost touching hers.

"I've been wondering," Sophie said thoughtfully. "What made you decide to agree to come with me to church? You must've known you might bump into Rachel."

"I didn't want you to have to go alone," Simon said thoughtfully.

Sophie had spent so much of her life surrounded by people but entirely alone, and Simon's words tugged at the strings of her heart. She wanted to tell him how much that meant but she could not find the right words, so instead she reached across and put her hand on his, hoping to convey, with this gesture, the gratitude in her heart.

Chapter Eighteen

Simon had hoped to get a good night's sleep. The shearing team would arrive the next morning, and he wanted to be in top form. However, as he tossed and turned that night, sleep continued to evade him. His mind bounced from one thing to another. When he finally managed to silence the intrusive thoughts about Jarrett Davidson, he thought about Sophie and how he could still feel the warmth of her hand on his.

Eventually, Simon gave up on the idea of sleep and got dressed. It was still an hour or so before dawn, and the house was still. Simon went into the kitchen and boiled a kettle of water. He drank his coffee alone before he headed out just as the dawn's first light was creeping over the horizon.

Simon set about doing the morning chores. He milked the cow, fed and watered Buck, and collected the eggs from the chicken coop. Usually, Sophie or Jenna did these things, but Simon had time to kill.

When he returned to the kitchen, he found Sophie at the stove. He stopped to watch her in the soft morning light, and his heart skipped a beat as she turned and smiled at him.

"Morning," she said brightly. "Did you sleep well?"

"I've slept better," Simon said as he handed the basket of fresh eggs to Sophie.

"What time are the shearers coming?" Sophie asked as she walked over to the sink and started to wash the eggs.

"Right after breakfast," Simon said as he stifled a yawn.

"I'd like to come and help," Sophie volunteered. "If you need an extra pair of hands? Jenna said she'd manage to get the lunch done on her own."

"Sure," Simon agreed, pleased that Sophie was showing such an interest. "We can always use the help."

Sophie smiled as she walked over to the stove and cracked an egg into the sizzling pan.

"Why don't you sit?" Sophie said, not turning her attention away from the egg. "Breakfast is just about ready."

Sophie and Simon ate together, and as they did, Sophie enquired more about the shearing and how the day would be structured. By the time they'd done eating, Jenna had emerged from her room with Oliver. Simon noticed the dark circles under her eyes were more prominent than they'd been the day before, and he wondered if she was getting any sleep at all.

"Are you sure you can manage the lunch for the shearers all on your own?" Sophie asked, her tone mirroring Simon's unspoken concerns. "I can stay and help."

"I can manage," Jenna said. "I've already baked the bread; it's in the pantry."

Sophie nodded, but before anyone had time to say anything else, Simon heard the shearers arriving outside.

"Let's go," Simon said, getting up from the table.

Sophie got up and followed Simon out of the back door. The shearers were gathered by the barn. Reuben and David were wearing their hand blades in belts around their waists while Harry was carrying an armful of burlap sacks he'd use to bail the wool when the time came.

"Mornin'," Simon said, tipping his hat.

"Morning," Reuben said. "Good day for it."

Simon nodded as he squinted up at the sun, which was already shining brightly above them, and there was not a cloud to be seen for miles.

"Shall we get started then?" Reuben asked.

"Yep," Simon agreed "By the way, this is my wife, Sophie. She's interested in watching the shearing."

The men all turned to Sophie, and her cheeks pinkened slightly.

"Nice to meet you," Reuben said. "I am Reuben; this is David, Jasper, Harry, and Milton."

The men all mumbled words of greeting, and Sophie smiled in response.

"All right," Simon said. "Let's get to it. I've set up some tables inside the barn for the skirting and sorting."

"Milton," Reuben said. "You'll be taking the sheared wool to Jasper and Harry in the barn then."

Milton nodded as Jasper and Harry turned and headed to the barn.

"Let's do this," Jasper said.

Simon led Reuben and Jasper to the pen where the sheep were waiting.

"I'll join you in a minute," Simon said. "I need to fetch my blades."

When Simon returned a few minutes later, he had his hand blades in his belt and a sharpening stone in his hand. Reuben and David were already shearing, and Simon watched them for a moment, satisfied with what he saw; their technique was quick but careful and clean.

"Come on," Simon said to Sophie. "I'll explain how we do it."

Sophie followed Simon to the pen and he grabbed a sheep, who bleated loudly as he laid it on its side, and secured it under his knee to stop it from moving too much.

"We remove the wool in sections," Simon said. "Starting from the stomach and moving up to the neck, then the back and finally the hindquarters and legs."

As he explained it to Sophie, Simon slid his hand shears carefully through the wool, close to the skin but not too close. He did not want to nick the skin.

"You want to try and get the fleece off in one piece," Simon explained.

"How long does it take?" Sophie asked. "To remove the whole fleece."

"Well, that's dependent on the shearer," Simon said as he cut through the wool on the sheep's back. "And how experienced they are."

"David claims he once sheared a sheep in under two minutes," Reuben said, from where he was now on to his second sheep. "Not that anyone was around to see it."

"It's true," David insisted.

Reuben rolled his eyes.

"An experienced shearer can usually get a fleece off in two to five minutes," Simon said as he cut the wool off the sheep's legs. "Got one here for you, Milton."

Milton, whose face was already pink with exertion, hurried over to Simon, who bundled the warm fleece into his arms, and the young man hurried to the barn.

Simon released the sheep, who now looked much less sheep-like, and it got up and raced into the paddock, where all the shorn sheep were grazing happily in the warm sunlight.

"How about a friendly competition?" David suggested. "First person to get to fifty is the winner."

Reuben glanced up at Simon. "What do you think?"

"Sure." Simon shrugged. "Why not?"

Despite all his big talk, David was seven sheep behind by the time Simon finished, with Reuben only two sheep behind.

"You should join our team," Reuben said to Simon. "You're good."

Simon laughed dryly as he ran the back of his hand across his brow, which was dripping with perspiration. "That's a nice offer but I have a ranch to run."

It was close to midday now and they'd sheared half the flock.

"Let's break for lunch," Simon said. "We can finish the rest this afternoon."

There was no argument from Reuben or David, who were all damp with sweat.

"I'll go and see how Jenna's getting on with the lunch," Sophie said.

"Thanks," Simon said.

Sophie smiled at him as she turned to go. She'd watched him shear every one of the fifty sheep and cheered him on.

"You're a lucky man," Reuben said as Simon watched Sophie go back toward the house. "How long have you two been married?"

"Not long," Simon said. "You got yourself a saddle pardner?"

"No," Reuben said, shaking his head. "Travel too much, but if I met a woman like your wife, I might reconsider."

"Pshh," David scoffed. "A woman like that wouldn't think twice about marrying you—"

"Oh yeah?" Reuben challenged. "Well, I don't see any gals lining up to marry you, either. Perhaps if you washed more often, you'd smell less like a sheep."

"Ha ha," David said sarcastically.

Simon shook his head and smiled.

"Shall we go and look in at the barn?" Reuben suggested. "See how Jasper and Harry are getting on?"

Simon, Reuben, and David headed to the barn to find Jasper standing behind the long, broad table. He was bent over, carefully examining the wool and removing any pieces that were mattered or soiled. He had two large piles, one a better grade and the other a lesser grade. Simon was both pleased and relieved to find that the better-grade pile of wool was taller.

"How's it going?" Simon asked.

"Good," Jasper said, not looking up from the wool he was examining. "The grade is good; you should fetch a decent price."

Simon nodded as he turned to see Harry carefully packing the sorted wool into large burlap sacks, making sure to compress the wool with his hand to maximize storage efficiency. Milton was helping him by holding the sack open for him.

"We're breaking for lunch," Reuben announced.

Just as he did, Sophie arrived in the barn carrying a large basket that Simon took from her and carried to the empty table.

"Lunch is ready," Simon announced, and everyone looked hungrily at the basket.

Simon and Sophie unpacked the basket containing fresh bread, boiled eggs, pickles, cheese, cold meats, and fresh biscuits. There were also three bottles of ginger beer and Jenna had packed enough enamel cups for them all.

"This is a feast," David said, nodding in approval as he looked around the table.

The others nodded in agreement and Simon took a step back.

"Tuck in," he said.

A short while later, they were all seated around the barn, their plates stacked with food. The room was quiet for a while as everyone ate.

"So?" Simon said, looking across at Sophie. "What do you think about your first shearing season?"

"It's impressive," Sophie said, her tone full of awe. "The way you handle the sheep—"

"He's got the touch," Reuben said, cutting into their conversation with half a pickle dangling from his mouth.

Simon frowned as he swallowed a bit of bread.

"The what?" Sophie enquired.

"The touch," David interjected. "It's what us shearers say when someone shears like your husband does."

Simon looked between the two men, frowning.

"It's all in the way you handle the sheep," Reuben expanded. "You have the kind of touch that calms them and makes it easier to shear."

"It's a gift," David added.

Simon took another bite of his sandwich, shaking his head, but Sophie was nodding, her eyes bright.

"What is it?" Simon asked incredulously. "You don't actually believe what they are saying?"

"I do," Sophie said firmly. "I saw it the other day when you were leading Buck. You have a gift with animals."

Simon had always loved animals, but he'd never considered that he might have a gift with them. Sophie had seen something in him that he did not know existed, and he liked how it made him feel, being truly seen by someone. It was like looking at yourself through someone else's eyes and discovering you were so much more than you believed yourself to be.

"My pa used to say that you can tell a lot about a man by the way an animal responds to him," Milton chimed in.

"It's true," Jasper agreed. "Animals sense things that people don't."

The other nodded in agreement and the barn fell silent for a while.

An Unexpected Family for the Rugged Mountain Man

"Well," Reuben said, slapping his thighs. "Shall we get back to it?"

Simon and the others got up from their seats and carried their plates and cups over to the table and Sophie packed them back into the basket.

Simon, Reuben, and David headed back outside to finish off the shearing while Sophie, Jasper, Harry, and Milton stayed in the barn. During lunch, Jasper had volunteered to teach Sophie how to skirt and sort.

It was late afternoon by the time the last sheep had been sheared. Simon's back and shoulders were aching, but it was a good ache. The shearing had been a success, and the team had done good work. Once they'd washed up, Simon paid them what was owed.

"So?" Reuben asked, pushing his damp hair back from his face. "Will you have us back again next year?"

They were all gathered around outside of the barn; the sun was starting to sink below the tree line.

"You did good work," Simon said, nodding in approval and appreciation.

All the wool had been sorted and bailed and was now ready to be sold in the coming weeks.

"Well," Reuben said. "We'd best get back to town."

He put out his hand to Simon, and he shook it.

"Goodbye, Sophie," Reuben said, tipping his hat to her. "It was good to meet you and if you'd consider joining our team, you'd find yourself most welcome."

Sophie smiled. "Thank you for the kind offer," she said. "But I think I'll leave the shearing up to my husband."

Simon smiled, liking the way it sounded when Sophie referred to him as her husband.

"Suit yourself," Reuben said with a grin.

They all said their farewells before the men turned and headed down the drive toward the ranch gate. Simon and Sophie stood by the barn until they disappeared out of sight.

"That went well," Sophie said.

"It did," Simon agreed. "And now it's done for another year."

Simon felt a great sense of relief. He'd been worried about the team and the quality of the wool, but it had all worked out and he was feeling good.

"Shall we go in?" Sophie said.

"You go," Simon said. "There are a few things I need to do, and then I'll be right in."

Sophie nodded as she turned and headed toward the kitchen. Simon returned to the barn and began to collect up the bits of discarded wool. However, he turned when he heard hurried footsteps.

Sophie appeared in the doorway, her cheeks flushed.

"What is it?" Simon asked, his tone urgent. "What's wrong?"

"I can't find Jenna," Sophie said. "I've searched the house but she's not there."

"And Oliver?"

"He's asleep in his crib," Sophie said.

Simon's head and heart began to race. "You're sure you searched the whole house?"

Sophie nodded. "Maybe she took a walk? She might be around the ranch somewhere."

Simon frowned, his brow furrowing in thought. There was always the chance she'd fallen or hurt herself.

"Let's split up," Simon said.

For the next while, he and Sophie searched, calling Jenna's name, but she was not there. As the minutes ticked by, Simon's stomach sunk lower and lower, until he felt it would drop out of his body altogether. What if she'd run away like she had planned to do? After everything that had happened, what if it had just become all too much for her?

"Simon!" Sophie cried loudly from inside the house.

Simon turned and ran. He found Sophie in Jenna's bedroom, holding a piece of paper in her hand.

"I found it on the dressing table... I didn't see it before—"

Simon grabbed the note from her, almost tearing the paper in his haste. Only three words were scribbled down in Jenna's handwriting.

I am sorry.

"You stay with Oliver," Simon said hastily. "I have to go and find her."

Without waiting for Sophie to reply, Simon dropped the paper and ran out of the room, throwing open the front door and racing toward the gate. He did not know if he would reach town before the last train left the station, but he knew that he had to try.

SALLY M. ROSS

Chapter Nineteen

Sophie returned to the house after Simon went to find Jenna. She checked on Oliver, but he was still sound asleep. Sophie looked around Jenna's room, frowning. Why would Jenna just leave that note? What had it meant?

Sophie sighed as she left the bedroom and headed to the kitchen. She decided to get started on the supper; she wasn't hungry but she needed to distract herself while she waited for everyone to return home.

After putting the potatoes on to boil, she heard Oliver crying from the bedroom and went to fetch him. She carried him into the kitchen and placed him down in his Moses basket. She gave him his wooden rattle, which he immediately put in his mouth.

Sophie checked on the potatoes, which were bubbling away, and then she turned and looked outside the kitchen window. The sun had almost sunk and the world outside was quiet.

Oliver gurgled from his basket, and Sophie walked over to him.

"Your ma is going to be home real soon," Sophie said.

Oliver stared up at her with his big blue eyes, and she brushed his smooth cheek with her thumb. She wasn't sure when Oliver had eaten last, so she went back to the stove to heat a saucepan of milk. As she did, Mittens appeared.

"This isn't for you," she said. "It's for the baby."

The cat looked up at her with her yellow eyes and Sophie sighed as she leaned down and filled the saucer at her feet with milk.

"There you go, greedy guts."

Mittens lapped up the milk happily while Sophie fetched the bottle from the sink. When the milk was warm, she poured it into the bottle. She sat down beside the Moses basket and fed Oliver, who ate hungrily. When the bottle was empty, she returned it to the sink, sighing softly. Where were they?

Sophie sat at the kitchen table with Oliver until long after the world had turned dark. The supper was cold, the gravy congealed in the pan. The small paraffin lamp glowered in the corner, casting long shadows across the room.

Oliver was now asleep in his basket.

Sophie wasn't sure how long Simon had been gone when she finally heard footsteps on the porch, and she got up from her seat and hurried out of the kitchen to the front door, just as Jenna stepped inside the hallway, followed by Simon.

"Jenna," Sophie said in relief, as she pulled her into her arms, but Jenna was cold and stiff. "Where have you been?"

Jenna did not answer, and Sophie looked over her shoulder at Simon, who shook his head grimly.

"You're so cold," Sophie said, rubbing Jenna's arms with her hands. "Come into the kitchen, and I'll make you something hot to drink."

"No," Jenna said, her voice thin and tired. "I just want to go to bed."

"Okay," Sophie agreed. "I'll just get Oliver—"

"Will you keep him?" Jenna asked. "Just for tonight."

Sophie frowned at her request but then nodded. "Yes, sure."

Without another word, Jenna walked past Sophie and into her room, closing the door behind her. Sophie looked at Simon, and it was only then that she saw he had a rifle swung over his shoulder.

"What happened?" Sophie asked, her voice wavering.

"Not here," Simon said. "Let's go into the kitchen."

Sophie followed Simon into the kitchen, unable to keep her eyes off the gun. Why did he have it?

"Tell me," Sophie said as soon as Simon turned around.

He shook his head and exhaled heavily. He took the gun from his shoulder and placed it against the wall behind the kitchen door, out of sight, although certainly not out of mind.

"I found Jenna on Jarrett Davidson's porch," Simon said. "She had my gun; she was waiting for him."

"What?" Sophie breathed, her eyes widening in horror.

"I know," Simon said, his tone strained.

"But I don't understand," Sophie said, shaking her head. "What was she planning to do?"

Simon did not answer right away, but Sophie knew from the troubled look in his eyes and the way the muscles in his jaw tensed that Jenna had not gone over there to talk.

"He wasn't home," Simon said. "No one was, but I hate to think what might have happened if he had been there..."

Simon's voice trailed off, and he dropped his head. Sophie crossed the room and put her hand on his back. Ever since the day before, when she'd touched his hand on the buggy ride home, she'd wanted to touch him again. It made her feel closer to him, more connected, as if they were attached by some invisible string

"Hey," she said soothingly. "Nothing happened, okay? Jenna is back home; nothing happened."

Simon exhaled, but Sophie did not remove her hand.

"Why don't you sit?" she suggested. "I'll make you something to drink."

Simon walked over to the table without a word and sat down. Sophie put the kettle on to boil, casting a glance at Simon every now and then. He was far away, though, lost in his thoughts.

"There you go," Sophie said as she placed a cup down in front of him.

"Thanks," Simon mumbled.

Sophie looked into the Moses basket but Oliver was still sleeping peacefully and so she sat down at the table.

"Will you tell me what happened?" Sophie asked. "How did you know where to find her?"

"I didn't," Simon said, taking a sip of coffee.

Sophie frowned, and Simon sighed, his large hands wrapped tightly around the mug on the table in front of him.

"Jenna told me the other morning that she'd been planning to run away," Simon explained.

"Run away?" Sophie repeated in disbelief.

"She thought that if she left, then we could adopt Oliver and raise him as our own son. That way, he'd never have to know the truth about his pa or where he'd come from—"

"So that's what you thought when you read her note," Sophie said, piecing it together. "That she was leaving town."

Simon nodded. "I raced to the train station, but she wasn't there; I searched the carriages, but she wasn't on board—"

"So, how did you know where she was?" Sophie asked, leaning forward in her chair.

"I don't know," Simon confessed. "Gut instinct, perhaps?"

"Well, thank goodness for your gut," Sophie said, relief in her voice. "And what happened when you found her?"

"She was just sitting on the edge of the porch with the rifle across her lap," Simon said, his tone still full of disbelief. "I never thought Jenna would be capable of hurting anyone—"

"We don't know that she would have done anything—"

"You didn't see her eyes," Simon argued as he shook his head. "She wasn't there, it was as if all the lights had been turned off."

Sophie frowned as she saw the fear and concern in Simon's eyes. Finding Jenna like that must have been terrifying.

"What did you say to her?" Sophie asked. "To get her to come home."

"I told her the truth," Simon said, looking up from his mug. "I told her that if she went through with shooting Jarrett, her life would be over. She would never see Oliver again and after everything, he would have won."

"And what did she say?"

"Nothing," Simon said. "She got up from the porch, handed me the gun, and turned in the direction of home."

Neither Sophie nor Simon spoke for a moment. Sophie was not convinced that Jenna would have gone through with it. Still, it was concerning.

"It was late," Simon said, more to himself than to Sophie. "The streets would have been largely empty by the time Jenna walked through town, so with any luck, no one saw her."

Sophie hoped he was right. The last thing they needed was more rumors circulating about Jenna.

"So what are we going to do?" Sophie asked as she met Simon's eye.

"I think we need to talk to the sheriff," Simon said.

"Do you think that will help?" Sophie asked, unconvinced.

Simon sighed as he pressed his thumb and index finger to his temples. "I don't know," he confessed. "But it's better than sitting around doing nothing."

Sophie was not sure that the sheriff would be able to help, but Simon was right, at least they'd be trying.

"It's worth a shot," Sophie agreed.

"I'll go first thing in the morning," Simon said.

***

The next morning, Simon set into town before breakfast. Sophie was in the kitchen, feeding Oliver, when Jenna came in. She was still dressed in her night clothes, her long auburn hair hanging down her back. She tried to smile as she stepped into the room, but it was more of a grimace.

"Hi," Sophie said, swiveling around in her chair. "How did you sleep? Would you like something to eat?"

"Just coffee, please," Jenna said.

Sophie nodded and got up from her chair, and handed Oliver to Jenna. She took the little boy and kissed him on the forehead. As Sophie made her coffee she heard Jenna whispering to Oliver, but it was too low to make out what she was saying.

"There you go," Sophie said, putting the coffee on the table.

"Thanks," Jenna said, not looking up at her.

Sophie sat back down and looked at Jenna, but she kept her eyes on Oliver.

"Where's Simon?" she asked, taking a sip of coffee.

"He went into town," Sophie said. "To talk to the sheriff."

Jenna stiffened. "He shouldn't have done that."

"Well, you didn't give him much choice," Sophie reasoned.

Jenna looked up at her, green meeting blue, but she remained silent.

"Why did you do it, Jenna?" Sophie asked. "You could have been in serious trouble."

Jenna sighed shakily. "Ever since Rose came by the other day to tell us that he'd attacked another girl, I haven't been able to sleep. I see him every time I close my eyes. I can feel his breath against my skin and the heat of his skin against mine—"

Jenna stopped, the last word sticking in her throat as she closed her eyes, and Sophie reached out and touched her hand.

"I just wanted it to stop," she said, shaking her head. "To know that he could never hurt anyone again."

A tear rolled down Jenna's cheek as she opened her eyes and looked at Sophie, and she could see how much pain she was in; she wore it in every line on her face.

"We will find a way to stop him," Sophie promised.

Jenna nodded but her eyes looked unconvinced.

"How about some eggs?" Sophie said. "You need to eat something."

Sophie got up and turned to the stove. As she fetched two eggs from the basket, she thought about Simon. He would be arriving in town about now, and Sophie hoped that he would really listen. If they could get the sheriff on their side, maybe there was a chance they could stop Jarrett Davidson once and for all.

Chapter Twenty

Simon brought Buckaroo to a halt outside the sheriff's office. He climbed down from the saddle and led his horse over to the rail, and tethered him to it. The town was only starting to wake up, and most stores were still shut. Simon had come early in the hopes of going unseen by anyone in town who might be inclined to gossip, which was nearly everyone.

"I won't be long, boy," he said, putting a hand on his neck.

Simon then turned and headed to the sheriff's office, which also served as the town jail. It was a small single-story wooden building with a narrow porch out front, which creaked under Simon's weight. He walked over to the door and pushed it open.

The building had two rooms; the front room was the sheriff's office, and the back room was the jail. Simon had only been here once, when his father had come to report some missing sheep. He hoped the sheriff would be more helpful now than he'd been then.

"Mr. Jones," the sheriff said, not bothering to hide his surprise.

He was seated, his feet casually resting on the desk. Sheriff Hugh Duncan was a tall man, with salt-and-pepper hair and a mustache. He was a smart man and not one who tolerated fools gladly.

"Sheriff," Simon said as he took off his hat. "I was wondering if you had a moment to talk?"

Sheriff Duncan nodded as he removed his feet and leaned forward in his chair. "This wouldn't have anything to do with your cousin walking through town with a rifle last night?"

Simon grimaced. "Actually, it does have something to do with that."

Sheriff Duncan raised his gray eyebrows as he waited for Simon to elaborate.

"Last year, my cousin was attacked in the saloon," Simon explained. "She was closing up one night and a man came in—"

Sheriff Duncan's eyebrows knitted together skeptically as Simon talked, but he did his best to ignore it.

"He attacked her, and as a result, she became with child," Simon explained, but as he did, he found it hard to say the words out loud.

"Do you know that man who allegedly assaulted her?" he asked.

"It was Jarrett Davidson," Simon said.

"Jarrett Davidson?" he said, frowning. "And you are certain this is the man?"

"I am," Simon said. "He's admitted to me that he had relations with my cousin, although he led me to believe that they were consensual."

Sheriff Duncan said nothing for a moment as he continued to frown, his peppery brow furrowing deeper. "Does she have any proof?"

"Is the baby not proof enough?" Simon asked.

"Any witnesses?"

Simon shook his head.

The sheriff sighed as he sat back in his chair. He did not speak for a long moment as he considered all that Simon had told him.

"Why report it now?" he asked. "It's been almost eighteen months."

"Because Jarrett Davidson attacked another girl at the saloon," Simon said.

"You're sure?" he asked.

Simon nodded. "My cousin hasn't been right since she found out..."

"Well, that explains the sighting of her in the street with a rifle last night," Sheriff Duncan sighed.

"I don't think she would have gone through with it," Simon said. "But she needs some kind of justice."

Sheriff Duncan frowned as he leaned forward again. He pressed his finger into a steeple and exhaled sharply. "Look, I don't need to tell you what people in this town think of your cousin, or the girls who work at the saloon. And without proof or a witness, there is really only so much that I can do—"

"Please, Sheriff," Simon said in desperation. "I am reaching the end of my tether. I don't know how else to help her."

Sheriff Duncan sighed.

"If you can convince your cousin and this other girl to come in and make a statement, then we might have something," he said. "But I'd keep it quiet. Jarrett Davidson is a powerful man with a lot of friends. I wouldn't recommend he catches wind of this."

Simon nodded, feeling a flicker of hope in his chest. He'd not had a high opinion of the sheriff coming into this, so he was pleasantly surprised that he was willing to help. Perhaps people could change after all.

"Also, you best keep an eye on that cousin of yours," Sheriff Duncan advised. "Make sure she doesn't walk into town with a rifle and scare half the people to death."

"I will," Simon promised. "Thank you, Sheriff."

Sheriff Duncan nodded, and Simon turned to go. He headed back out of the office and across the porch. Buck was grazing on a narrow strip of grass but lifted his head as Simon approached.

"All right, boy," Simon said. "We have one more stop to make."

Simon untethered his horse and placed his foot into the stirrup. He pulled himself up into the saddle before steering Buckaroo toward the old coroner's house.

The one-eyed ginger cat was seated on the porch in the exact same position it had been the last time Simon had visited the house.

It watched him as he crossed the porch and knocked on the door. However, this time, Simon did not need to knock a second time before Rose appeared in the doorway.

"You again?" she said, raising an unimpressed eyebrow.

She was not wearing night clothes this time, but a simple sage-green dress with a white apron. Her dark hair was tied in a simple plait down her back.

"I need to talk with you," Simon said. "It's urgent."

Rose looked around Simon, making sure the street was empty before she sighed.

"All right," she said. "Come in, quickly."

Simon stepped into the entrance hall; the curtains were all half-drawn, so it was difficult to make out all the details of the room. Rose led him through one of the doors into a brightly lit kitchen. A fire burned in the large fireplace, and a copper pot bubbled on the stove. Hung over the mantel piece were various items of women's clothing placed there to dry and Simon averted his gaze when he spotted a pair of drawers.

Upstairs, Simon heard women's voices talking and laughing.

"So?" Rose asked, folding her arms across her chest. "What is it?"

"Jenna's not doing well," Simon said.

Rose's hard expression softened and her tone grew concerned. "What happened?"

"She disappeared from the ranch last night," Simon explained. "I found her at Davidson's house with my rifle."

Rose's eyebrows shot up in shock.

"He wasn't home," Simon continued. "But if he had been, well..."

Simon did not need to spell it out for her.

"So what do you need me to do?" Rose asked.

"I need you to convince the girl who was attacked by Jarrett to make a statement," Simon said.

Rose frowned. "I can't. She's gone."

"Gone?" Simon asked, his heart sinking.

"She left, day before yesterday," Rose said. "Went back home—"

"Do you have an address for her?" Simon asked, clutching at straws. "I could write to her."

Rose shook her head.

"Nothing?" he sighed in frustration. "There must be some way to reach her?"

"Simon," Rose said levelly. "Maybe you should just go home and take care of Jenna—"

"That's what I am trying to do!" Simon said, his voice rising.

Rose sighed, her eyes softening. "You're a good man. And Jenna is lucky to have you."

Simon said nothing. What was there to say? He knew it wasn't Rose's fault, but the small flame of hope that the sheriff had ignited in him had been snuffed out by the knowledge that Jarrett Davidson would never be held accountable for his crimes.

"I'd better get back," Simon said.

Rose nodded. "I'll show you out."

***

As soon as Simon arrived back at the ranch, Sophie sought him out. He was feeding Buck in the stables when she came inside. Just being in her presence made Simon feel better, and his shoulders relaxed a little.

"So?" she asked. "What did the sheriff say?"

Simon turned to her and shook his head in discouragement. "He asked me to get a statement from the other girl that Jarrett attacked, so I went to the older coroner's house to speak with Rose, but the girl is gone."

Sophie's face fell. "So now what?"

Simon shrugged. "Without both of their statements, it's just Jenna's word against Jarrett's, and with my cousin's reputation..."

Sophie's mouth twisted angrily. "This is so unfair."

"I know," Simon agreed.

"And Rose gave no indication of where this girl was from?" Sophie asked.

Simon shook his head, and Sophie sighed.

"So what do we do now?" she asked.

"We keep an eye on Jenna," Simon said. "Try and help her through this as best we can. How was she this morning?"

"Not great," Sophie confessed. "She hardly touched her breakfast and went straight back to her room afterward."

Simon frowned, as he thought about what they could do to try and help Jenna.

"Her birthday is coming up," he said. "Maybe we could plan something to cheer her up?"

Sophie's eyes brightened. "That's a good idea. We could invite Rose and some of her other friends and have a little party."

Simon frowned. He had been thinking perhaps a nice dinner just the three of them, and maybe a game of cards afterward. "Do you think a party is a good idea? I mean, is Jenna up for it, given what happened last night?"

"I think being surrounded by the people she loves is exactly what she needs," Sophie said. "It will remind her that life is full of good moments to celebrate."

"All right," Simon agreed, unable to argue with that thinking. "Her birthday is this Saturday, so we will have to work quickly. I have the wool merchant coming tomorrow—"

"Don't worry," Sophie said enthusiastically. "I'll take care of all the details."

"Are you sure?" Simon asked.

Sophie nodded. "I'll go into town this afternoon and get what we need. I'll also stop in at the old coroner's place and invite Rose and some of her other friends."

"We'll have to have it early," Simon reasoned. "Because the girls all work in the evening."

Sophie nodded, looking thoughtful again.

"I'd better get inside and make a list," she said as she turned to go.

"Sophie—"

She turned back to him and tilted her head expectantly.

"Try and keep it small," he said. "Jenna's in a delicate state; we don't want to overwhelm her."

Sophie nodded. "I promise it will be perfect," she assured him.

Without another word, Sophie left the barn, and Simon turned back to Buck. In the back of his mind, Simon wondered if this was really the right thing, throwing a party. If they were wrong about this, if it all went south, then things with Jenna would just get a whole lot worse.

Chapter Twenty-One

That afternoon, Sophie went into town to get everything they would need for Jenna's party. She was excited about it, and she hoped that it would cheer her up. Sophie could not remember the last time she'd seen Jenna smile as if she meant it.

Sophie went to the old coroner's house first, but Rose was not there, so she left word about the party with another girl.

After that, she went into town and straight to the general store. Sophie consulted her list to see what she would need. She'd never planned a party herself, but she'd lost count of the number of parties she'd watched her mother plan. Her mother's parties were always grand and over the top because Mr. Colton liked to show off to his rich friends.

Sophie could remember how stressed her mother would get, worried some small, forgotten detail might embarrass her stepfather and cause a scene. Sophie didn't want this party to be like the ones her mother had planned. She wanted it to be simple and fun, and to be all about Jenna.

Sophie's idea was to have a lunch party with a mixture of savory and sweet foods. There would be a cake with a cream frosting, and she'd decorate the room with ribbons and fresh flowers. Sophie was mindful of Simon's words and would not go too over the top; it would be a simple birthday celebration with lunch, cake, and some friends.

She'd only been in the general store a couple of times and was not very familiar with the layout. For most people, it probably would not have been hard to navigate their way around, as most general stores took on the same layout, but Sophie had never been allowed in town before coming to Shadow's Ridge.

With her list in hand, Sophie made her way down the well-worn floors of the aisles, collecting what she needed and placing it carefully in the basket on her arm. In the dry goods section, she found flour, sugar, icing sugar, and cocoa, all the ingredients she needed for the birthday cake. She bought extra flour to make bread for the sandwiches as well as for the biscuits.

In the canned food aisle, she bought strawberry jam, tinned corn beef, and baked beans. She also found horseradish and whole-grain mustard for the sandwiches. There were still a few bottles of ginger beer in the pantry, which would do for drinks.

By the time Sophie was finished shopping, the basket weighed a great deal more than it had on the way down to town.

"Find everything you need?" the clerk asked as Sophie approached the counter.

"I think so," Sophie said, looking down at the items in her basket. "Although I've been gone a lot longer than I planned."

The clerk ran up all the items and Sophie put it on Simon's account as she'd been instructed to do.

"Thank you," Sophie said as she took her receipt and tucked it carefully into her basket.

The clerk smiled in reply and Sophie turned and left the store, but as she stepped outside, she accidentally bumped into someone and almost dropped her basket.

"Sorry," Sophie apologized, not looking up.

"It's fine," the woman said.

Sophie thought the voice sounded familiar and looked up to see Rachel, Simon's ex- fiancée, smiling at her.

"Fancy bumping into you twice in one week," Rachel said.

"It's a small town, I suppose," Sophie said awkwardly.

"I was actually hoping I might see you again," Rachel said, the smile on her face just a bit too bright.

"You were?" Sophie asked, surprised.

"Yes," Rachel said. "I wanted to ask you how Simon is, really?"

Sophie looked into the woman's face, but she was hard to read, and she could not tell if she was being sincere or simply nosey.

"He's well," Sophie said shortly.

Rachel nodded. "That's good, I am glad to hear that. After we broke up, I was worried that he'd turn into some odd loner—"

Sophie pursed her lips.

"And I suppose things worked out for the better," Rachel said. "My family did not approve of me marrying Simon."

"Why?" Sophie asked, frowning again.

"I suppose the Joneses have always had a reputation in this town for being outcasts," Rachel said. "Although I think they've always preferred it that way, living all alone on that ranch miles from town. My ma was so relieved when we called off the engagement that she actually cried with relief—"

Sophie's dislike for Rachel grew with each passing word she spoke.

"And when they learned about what had become of his cousin, well, even I had to admit that ending it with Simon was or the best, imagine being part of such a scandalous family—"

Sophie's cheeks were now burning as she stared at Rachel.

"Well, if you ask me, I think it was Simon who made the lucky escape," Sophie said. "I'd hate to think of him living his life married to a revolting woman like you."

"What did you say?" Rachel demanded, her face flushing.

For all her fashionable clothes and elegant hair style, Rachel was rotten to the core on the inside. Sophie could see that now.

"What's more, I'd rather spend every year of my life up on that ranch than risk bumping into you again."

With that, Sophie pushed past Rachel and headed down the main street, her chin held high. She could feel Rachel's eyes boring into the back of her head, but she did not turn around.

She was halfway back to the ranch when Sophie's heart rate began to slow down. She could not believe that Simon had almost married that woman. She did not have a sincere or compassionate bone in her body. She deserved to have married some boring banker.

The house was quiet when Sophie arrived back. She quickly stashed all her shopping in the pantry, out of sight from where Jenna might find it. When she emerged from the pantry, she found Jenna in the hallway.

"Where have you been?" Jenna asked.

"I popped into town to mail a letter," Sophie lied.

Jenna nodded, but she was frowning slightly.

SALLY M. ROSS

"You won't believe who I bumped into," Sophie said, in a bid to distract Jenna from asking who she might be writing to.

"Who?"

"Rachel."

Jenna raised her eyebrows. "What did she want?"

"To tell me all about her lucky escape," Sophie said, shaking her head. "She is not a very nice woman, is she?"

"No," Jenna agreed. "Simon and her got together after I left, but from what I've learned, she always treated him as if she were doing him a favor by marrying him."

Sophie frowned. "The way Simon told the story, it's like he blames himself for what happened between them."

"Of course he does," Jenna said, rolling her eyes. "Simon's hard on himself about the whole situation, that it was his fault for changing so much after his parents died. He's never considered how selfish Rachel was to make so many demands on him. He'd just lost the two most important people in his life, and she should have been there for him, not made him feel bad for grieving."

Sophie knew how it felt to be changed by death. She was only a girl when her father died, but it had been one of the most significant events of her whole life because it marked the beginning of the end. She lost her mother a few months later—though she was not gone, she was lost to Sophie.

So she understood how Simon must have felt, and Sophie knew Jenna was right. Someone who truly loved you would never make you feel guilty for being different or for changing. They'd be there for you, for better or worse.

218

"Well, I told her what I thought of her," Sophie said matter-of-factly, not feeling the least bit bad.

"I wish I'd been there to see that," Jenna said, her lips twitching.

Sophie grinned. "How are you feeling, by the way?"

"A bit better today," Jenna said. "Less like I have a boulder resting on my chest."

"That's good," Sophie said.

Jenna smiled but it did not reach her eyes. "I think I am going to take Oliver for a walk in the carriage."

"That's a good idea," Sophie agreed. "It's a beautiful afternoon."

Jenna nodded and as she turned to go, Sophie glanced at the pantry. She really prayed this party would be a good thing for Jenna and remind her that she could still be happy.

***

Sophie worked hard over the next few days in preparation for Jenna's birthday party. It was not easy, keeping it all secret for her, but for the most part, Sophie had done well.

After dinner on the Friday night before the party, Jenna had gone to bed with Oliver. Sophie and Simon were still up, and icing the double-layered cake. Simon, who had been busy with the wool merchant the past couple of days, had felt bad about not contributing more, which was why he'd volunteered to help with the icing.

"Oi," Sophie said, playfully slapping Simon's hand. "I swear you've put more frosting in your mouth than on the cake."

Simon grinned cheekily.

"I didn't know that you had such a sweet tooth," Sophie commented.

"I don't usually," Simon confessed. "But this is so good."

Sophie smiled, pleased that at least it tasted good. The structure of the cake was a bit dodgy and it was slanting a little to the left. Still, it was not a bad effort for her very first birthday cake.

"My pa had a sweet tooth," Simon said, smiling at the memory. "Sometimes my ma would come downstairs in the middle of the night and find him eating strawberry jam out of the jar with a spoon."

Sophie laughed. "I wish I had met them."

"They would have liked you," Simon said confidently.

"What were they like?" Sophie asked as she looked up from the cake at Simon.

"Pa was a hard worker but he never took anything too seriously; he had a great sense of humor and you could often hear his booming laugh from all across the other side of the ranch."

Sophie smiled, imagining that laugh. "And your ma?"

"She was a lot like you, actually," Simon said, his face softening. "She was kind and compassionate but also fiercely loyal and protective when the time called for it."

Sophie said nothing for a moment as Simon's words sunk in. He really thought she was all those things?

"She wouldn't be afraid to call anyone out—"

Simon's eyes were shining as if he knew a secret, and Sophie's cheeks flushed under his gaze.

"Jenna told you, didn't she? About Rachel?"

Simon nodded, but he did not look upset. "Thank you for defending me," he said, his brown eyes full of warmth.

"Of course," Sophie said as if it were the most obvious thing in the world. "You are my husband."

Neither of them spoke for a moment, but Simon leaned in closer to Sophie and she felt the warmth of his body. Her heart was beating so quickly that she worried it might beat right out of her chest and into her lap.

"You've got some frosting on your nose," Simon said softly.

Before Sophie could react, he reached up and brushed her nose gently with his thumb, and Sophie's breath caught in her chest. He ran his thumb across her cheek, his eyes tracing the details of her lips.

Sophie did not move as Simon drew closer still, and she could now feel the warmth of his breath on her cheek and she closed her eyes, parting her lips so slightly as Simon leaned in closer. Then, just as he was about to kiss her, Mittens jumped into her lap. Sophie's eyes popped open and she jumped, startled.

"Mittens," she said crossly as Simon leaned back in his chair.

Sophie met his eyes, her face flushed and her heart still racing, but the moment was over. Sophie could not help but feel disappointed, and she could tell by the way Simon's shoulders sloped that he was disappointed too.

"I'd better get up to bed," Simon said, clearing his throat. "Big day tomorrow."

"Yes," Sophie agreed, nodding a bit too vigorously. "Thank you for all your help."

"You're welcome," Simon said as he stood up.

Sophie turned back to the cake, but as Simon reached the doorway, he turned back to her.

"I think this party is going to be really great," Simon said, smiling. "You should be proud of yourself."

Sophie smiled back at him, grateful for the encouragement. Then, without another word, Simon turned and left the kitchen.

***

"I need an hour," Sophie said softly, her eyes intent on Simon's.

"I've got it," Simon said in an equally low voice. "Keep Jenna out of the house for an hour—"

Just then Jenna came into the kitchen with Oliver and frowned slightly as Sophie and Simon stopped whispering and turned to her, smiles plastered on their faces.

"Happy birthday!" Sophie and Simon said in unison.

Jenna sighed. "Don't remind me."

"Do you want something for breakfast?" Sophie said. "I've made pancakes to celebrate."

Jenna did her best to smile as she took her seat, Oliver squirming on her lap.

"Here," Simon said as he stretched out his arms. "Give him to me."

Jenna passed Oliver on to Simon, and the little boy smiled as he reached up and touched Simon's face. Sophie watched them for a moment, her heart swelling as Simon smiled down at the little boy, whose blue eyes were bright with adoration.

Sophie finished cooking the pancakes and placed a steamy plate of them right in the center of the table, along with some maple syrup.

"Let's eat," Sophie said, smiling around the table.

Simon put Oliver down in his Moses basket with his rattle, and they sat down to breakfast.

A short while later, the pancake stack had greatly diminished. Jenna had only eaten one, but at least it was something.

"So," Simon said, leaning back in his chair and looking across at Jenna. "I was thinking we might go on a walk around the ranch, just like old times."

Sophie looked at Jenna, who was pursing her lips

"I am actually a bit tired," Jenna said.

Sophie's heart sank a little, but she was determined not to spoil the surprise.

"I am sure a brisk walk will be just the thing," Sophie said, her voice full of determination. "Besides, you haven't been out of the house for days."

"What about Oliver?"

"Don't worry about him," Sophie said. "I'll put him down for his morning nap and keep an eye on him."

Jenna was silent for a moment as Sophie made eyes at Simon.

"Come on, Jen," Simon said encouragingly. "We haven't gone on one of our walks for ages."

Jenna sighed. "All right," she agreed. "Maybe a walk will be good for me."

Sophie smiled triumphantly. "I'll get your bonnet," she volunteered, getting up and heading to the bedroom quickly before Jenna changed her mind.

A few minutes later, Sophie waved from the kitchen door as Simon and Jenna disappeared over the rise past the stables. As soon as they were out of sight, she jetted into action. Oliver was asleep in his Moses basket, so she picked him up and carried him to the bedroom, laying him down gently in his crib.

She left the door slightly ajar as she exited the bedroom and then headed straight for the sitting room.

Sophie had prepped all the food the day before, so all there was to do was decorate. Because it was a lunch party, she'd decided to host it in the sitting room; that way, it would be more casual and also more comfortable. The party guests could move around at their leisure and mingle with each other.

As Sophie stepped into the sitting room, the first thing she did was pull the drapes open and unlatch the windows. She pushed up the thick wooden frames, filling the room with bright sunlight and fresh morning air.

She then fetched a white tablecloth for the long sideboard and then went back to the kitchen and out the back door. In the gardens out back, she picked bunches of bright orange California poppies. She took them into the kitchen and filled three vases, which she carefully carried to the sitting room.

She placed the vases around the room and then smiled, pleased with the effect the flowers had on brightening up the room.

Sophie had bought bright yellow ribbons from the general store, which she used to tie the drapes back with the ribbons, finishing them off with yellow bows. The decorations were simple, but Sophie was happy with the overall effect.

As she headed back to the kitchen, Sophie heard Oliver niggling in his crib, so she went to check on him. She placed a soothing hand on his chest and a moment or two later, he was asleep again. She left the room and headed back into the kitchen, but just as she did, she heard voices; the guests had arrived.

Sophie stepped out of the back door just as Rose and four other girls came around the side of the house. They were all dressed simply, but their array of colors made them look like a walking rainbow.

"Welcome," Sophie said brightly. "I am so glad you could all come."

"We appreciate the invitation," Rose said. "Don't we, girls?"

The group of young women nodded and smiled.

"This is Sophie," Rose said. "Sophie, this is Ava, Olivia, Mary, and Bella."

Rose indicated to each of the young women as she spoke, and Sophie smiled at each one of them in turn.

"It's lovely to meet you all," Sophie said. "Why don't you come inside?"

Sophie showed the group of women into the house and down the hallway to the sitting room. As they stepped inside, the women looked around the bright, cheerful space with admiration and appreciation.

"How pretty," Ava said, lightly caressing the petal of a poppy.

"It all looks wonderful," Mary said, smiling at Sophie.

Sophie beamed, pleased that the room was so well-received by the party guests.

"Jenna should be back soon," Sophie said. "Why don't you all sit down and relax?"

Just then, Oliver woke from his nap and started crying, Sophie turned to go, but Rose put a hand on her arm.

"I'll get him," she volunteered.

"Thank you," Sophie said gratefully.

She showed Rose to Jenna's bedroom and left her to care for Oliver while she returned to the kitchen. She counted out plates, glasses, and cutlery for eight people. Just as she was finishing, she spotted Simon and Jenna walking across the garden, and she turned and raced back down the hall. She found all the women oohing and ahhing over baby Oliver.

"She's coming," Jenna said, her voice high with excitement.

The chatter died down as Sophie returned to the kitchen just as Jenna and Simon stepped in through the back door.

"How was your walk?" Sophie said brightly.

"It was good," Jenna said, her pale face flushed with exertion. " I think you were right; the fresh air made me feel better."

Jenna's green eyes were brighter than they'd been an hour ago.

"Where's Oliver?" Jenna asked as she peered into the Moses basket. "Still sleeping?"

Sophie shook her head, trying not to smile. "No," she said, catching Simon's eye. "He's in the sitting room."

"The sitting room?" Jenna said, frowning.

"Come on," Sophie said. "Let's go and get him."

Without another word, Sophie turned and led Jenna down the hallway to the sitting room. She pushed open the door, and Jenna stepped in behind her.

"Surprise!" the voices chorused in unison.

Jenna looked around at all the smiling faces, her eyes wide with surprise, and then, to Sophie's relief, she smiled.

"Happy birthday," Sophie said, pulling Jenna into a tight hug.

"Thank you," Jenna said as she blinked back tears.

Sophie let Jenna go, and she was instantly surrounded by all her friends, who were all talking excitedly over one another. Simon stood in the doorway as Sophie met his eyes, and she smiled at him.

"You did it," he said proudly.

"*We* did it," Sophie said.

The rest of the party went better than Sophie could have hoped. Oliver was passed around from guest to guest, enjoying all the attention. The food was eaten and praised, and when it came time for cake, everyone sang at the top of their lungs. Sophie kept a close eye on Jenna, hoping she would not feel overwhelmed, but she seemed to be having a good time as she smiled, chatted, and laughed.

"I've never seen Jenna like this before," Sophie said to Simon as Jenna and Rose laughed together.

"This is how she used to be," Simon said. "Smiling, carefree."

Sophie said nothing. She hated the fact that man had taken so much from Jenna, but she was glad that, even just for an afternoon, Jenna could feel like her old self again.

It was late afternoon by the time the party came to an end, and everyone was sad that it must be so.

"We'd stay all night if we could," Rose said. "But we are all going to be late for work as it is."

"Let me give you a ride back into town on the buggy," Simon volunteered.

Rose and the others gratefully accepted, and while Simon went out to hitch up the buggy, everyone helped to carry the empty plates and glasses to the kitchen.

As Sophie came down the hallway carrying two empty platters, she heard Jenna and Rose talking in the kitchen.

"Is everyone being careful?" Jenna asked.

"We are," Rose said. "No one is locking up on their own anymore, but he hasn't been in since he attacked Laura. We think he's keeping a low profile."

"Good," Jenna said, her tone strained. "That's good."

Sophie came into the kitchen and smiled at the two women as she walked over to the sink. She looked out the window to see Simon finishing up with the buggy.

"Well," Rose said. "We'd best be going. Thank you, Sophie, for a wonderful afternoon."

"Thank you all for coming," Sophie said.

A short while later, Sophie and Jenna were waving goodbye as the buggy bumped down the drive. Once it disappeared out of sight, Jenna put her arm around Sophie's waist.

"I really needed that," she sighed.

"I am glad you had a good time," Sophie said.

The two women headed back inside and started on the dishes. As they washed and dried, they chatted about the party.

Just then, they were interrupted by a loud knocking at the door.

"Who could that be?" Sophie asked as she looked at Jenna.

"Maybe one of the girls forgot something," Jenna said as she dried her hands on her apron. "I'll go see."

Jenna turned and left the kitchen, and a moment later, Sophie heard her gasp loudly; she dropped the plate she was holding back in the sink and rushed out of the kitchen.

Sophie had only seen the man once before, weeks ago, when she'd first arrived in Shadow's Ridge. Yet she would never forget those cold, blue eyes, not until the day that she died. Time stood still for a moment as Sophie's gaze traveled from the blue-eyed man to Jenna's rigid body, and everything fell into place. This was him—this was Jarrett Davidson.

"W-w-what are you doing here?" Jenna stuttered.

Jarrett did not answer her right away; his mouth was twisted into a sneer.

"I think you should leave," Sophie said as she came down the hallway toward the door. Jarrett turned his gaze on her, and she saw a flash of recognition.

"I have no plans of staying," he said coolly.

"Then go," Sophie said, trying to stop her voice from trembling.

Jarrett looked at Jenna again, and Sophie could see her whole body shaking.

"You made a grave mistake sending your cousin to speak with the sheriff," Jarrett said, his threatening tone contradicting the almost perfect symmetry of his face.

Jenna inhaled sharply.

"That's right," Jarrett said, his tone dangerous. "I have eyes and ears everywhere. There is nothing you can do or say in this town without me knowing about it."

Sophie put a hand on Jenna's arm as she glared at Jarrett.

"Leave," she said, with as much force as she could muster.

Jarrett's eyes, however, stayed fixed on Jenna. "I've come to warn you to keep your mouth closed. And to keep that cousin of yours away from town—"

From the bedroom, Oliver began to cry loudly, and for a moment, no one moved. Sophie looked into Jarrett's face, but there was nothing, not a trace of emotion at hearing his son cry for the first time.

"I have to go," Jenna said, but as she turned to leave, Jarrett reached out and grabbed her wrist, making her cry out.

"Let her go!" Sophie shouted.

Jarrett's grip was so tight that Sophie could see the skin twisted behind his hand, and she was worried he might break Jenna's arm.

"If you continue to try and ruin my life, I will come for you," Jarrett said in a menacing tone. "And I will take everything from you—*everything*."

Without another word, Jarrett let go of Jenna's arm. As he did, her knees gave way, and Sophie caught her. Jarrett gave them one last threatening look before he turned and walked back across the porch.

Sophie held Jenna tightly as she trembled and sobbed in her arms. In the background, Oliver continued to scream, but all Sophie could hear was Jarrett's promise, echoing in her ears.

Chapter Twenty-Two

After dropping off Rose and the other women back in town, Simon turned the buggy around and made his way home. As he did, he thought about the afternoon. He'd never been a great lover of parties, but Sophie's party for Jenna had changed his mind. He'd really enjoyed it, and it was a relief to see that part of Jenna, the part he thought was extinguished forever, was still there.

Despite his concerns, Sophie had made it work, and he could not help but admire her efforts. She'd been determined to make Jenna smile and she'd done even more; she'd made her laugh.

As Buck pulled the buggy up the steep hill, Simon's thoughts lingered on Sophie. He'd hardly been able to take his eyes off her during the party. He loved to see her smiling and to hear her laughter. He'd caught her eye a few times that afternoon and each time his heart had skipped a beat. Simon was not sure Sophie knew the effect she had on him; he was only just discovering it himself.

When Simon arrived back at the ranch, he found Sophie waiting at the stables for him. He could tell by the stiffness of her back and shoulders that something was wrong. So he brought Buck to a dead halt and jumped from the buggy seat.

"What is it?" he asked as he rushed over to her.

Sophie was shaking so badly that she could not speak for a moment, and Simon put his hands on her arms to try and steady her.

"Tell me," he said, his heart racing.

"Jarrett was here," Sophie said, her voice barely a whisper.

"What?" Simon said, the muscles in his jaw tightening.

Sophie nodded. "Right after you left, he was at the front door, he, he..."

Sophie's voice trailed off, and she bent her head.

"Hey," Simon said firmly. "I need you to tell me what happened. Where are Jenna and Oliver?"

"They're in the bedroom," Sophie said. "She's locked herself inside; she won't come out."

"Okay," Simon said, trying to think clearly. "Let's go inside, okay?"

Simon led Sophie back into the house, not taking his hands off her arms. It was a warm night, but she was still shivering. Simon and Sophie walked over to the table, and Sophie sat down. Simon crouched on one knee and looked up into her face.

"Did he hurt you?"

Sophie shook her head.

"And Jenna?"

"He grabbed her arm," Sophie said. "I thought he was going to break it—"

The rage built in Simon's chest grew, licking at his throat.

"But then he let her go."

"What did he want?" Simon asked, trying to resist the urge to get onto the back of Buck and hunt Jarrett Davidson down.

"To tell us to stop," Sophie said, her voice wavering. "He knows that we spoke to the sheriff."

Simon closed his eyes and exhaled sharply. He should have known that someone would see him. He had only been trying to help, but it was clear that he'd just made things so much worse.

"He threatened to take everything," Sophie said, shaking her head.

Simon reached up and put his arms around Sophie, enclosing her in a tight hug. As he held her, he felt her body relax, and her shivering eased. He held her for a long time, using the warmth of her body to distract himself from his rage, which was bubbling just below the surface.

"I need to talk to Jenna," Simon said, his heart as heavy as lead.

He let Sophie go and as he did, he heard Jenna's bedroom door open, and she stepped into the kitchen. She was carrying Oliver and the threadbare carpetbag she'd arrived with all those months ago.

Simon knew what it meant—she was leaving.

"Jenna—"

Jenna met his eyes, and he saw that her mind was made up.

"I am sorry," she said, her voice thin. "But I have to go. *We* have to go."

"No," Sophie said, shaking her head as she stood up. "You can't—"

Jenna looked at Sophie, and the look they shared broke Simon's heart.

"I don't want to go," Jenna said. "But everyone will be safer this way."

"We can figure this out," Sophie insisted. "But we can't if you leave, we have to stick together—"

Sophie's voice broke, but Jenna's resolve did not weaken.

"Simon," Sophie said, looking at him now. "Say something!"

Simon looked back at Jenna and sighed. "Will you not at least stay until the morning? Sleep on it?"

Jenna shook her head. "I can't live like this any longer. I can barely sleep anymore; he is all I can think about."

Simon saw the desperation in her eyes, and he knew she was right. All the good that had come from the party had been ruined in an instant. She was not free of him, and it was slowly eating her alive from within.

"Nothing you say will change my mind," Jenna said firmly. "So if you can give us a ride into town, I will stay with Rose tonight, and catch the first train tomorrow."

The room was silent for a long moment. Simon knew his cousin well enough to know that when her mind was made up, nothing would change it. He did not want her or Oliver to go but understood that she needed to protect her son.

"All right," he sighed. "I'll take you into town."

"Thank you," Jenna said as she made a start toward the door.

"No," Sophie said as she rushed over to block the exit. "You can't go! Families need to stick together."

Jenna sighed as she put her carpetbag down on the floor, and for a brief moment, Sophie's eyes flooded with relief.

"Just because we aren't together doesn't mean we aren't a family," Jenna said softly as she reached out and brushed a strand of hair behind Sophie's ear.

Sophie said nothing as a tear rolled down her cheek.

"This is not goodbye forever," Jenna said.

Sophie shook her head as Jenna hugged her tightly, with Oliver pressed between them.

"Look after our boy," Jenna said softly as she tilted her head back toward Simon.

"And you do the same," Sophie whispered, looking down at Oliver.

Jenna gave her one last smile as she reached down for the carpetbag.

"Here," Simon said, putting out his hand. "Let me take that."

Jenna handed him the carpetbag as Sophie stepped out of the way. It was dusk now; the sun had fallen behind the hills, creating a dark, jagged outline across the red sky.

"Will you be all right here on your own?" Simon asked, turning back to Sophie.

"I don't think Jarrett will come back tonight," Sophie said. "And I think you and Jenna need to say your goodbyes."

Simon nodded, his throat raw.

He turned and walked over to the buggy, where Jenna was waiting with Oliver asleep in her arms. Simon helped Jenna into her seat before walking around the other side of the buggy and climbing up. Simon could sense Sophie watching them from the doorway, but he did not turn around. He took the reins in his hands, holding them tighter than necessary as they set off down the drive.

Neither he nor Jenna spoke for a long while. When the first star appeared in the sky, Simon glanced over at Jenna, and saw her gazing up at it. They'd always been in competition as children to see who would be the first to spot the first star because whoever was fortunate to do so got to make a wish.

"Why don't you make a wish?" he suggested. "For old time's sake."

Jenna said nothing, but she closed her eyes for a moment.

They fell silent again as the buggy crunched stones.

"Where will you go?" Simon asked.

"Rose's parents. They live in a small town up north and have offered to take us in," Jenna said. "Until I can find a job."

Simon nodded but said nothing more.

As the town came into view, Simon's stomach dropped. All those months ago, he hadn't wanted Jenna and Oliver in his life, but now that they were going, his house would feel less like a home.

Simon brought the buggy to a stop in front of the old coroner's house, and for a long moment, neither of them moved.

"So I guess this is it," Simon said, turning to Jenna. "You know you don't have to go—"

"I think we both know that I do," Jenna said sadly. "I need to keep Oliver safe, which means getting as far away as possible."

Simon exhaled shakily as he looked at the sleeping baby in his cousin's arms, and the knowledge that he'd grow and forget about him was almost too much to bear.

"I know this is not what any of us wanted," Jenna said, reaching out to touch Simon's cheek.

"I don't want you to go," Simon said, the words falling out of him.

"I know," Jenna said. "But you've got Sophie, and she's got you, and when I'm missing home, I will remember that you are not alone. Sometimes I think that the only good thing I've done these past few years is put that advertisement in the paper."

Jenna smiled sadly, and Simon's heart felt as if it were being ripped from his chest one artery at a time.

The front door to the house suddenly opened, and Rose's silhouette came into view. She walked across the porch toward them.

"I'd better go," Jenna said.

Simon nodded, his throat too swollen to speak. He leaned over and kissed Oliver on the forehead.

"You be good for your ma," he whispered.

Rose appeared at the buggy's side and took Oliver so Jenna could climb down. Simon reached over and handed her the carpetbag.

"Promise me that you'll write when you get there," Simon said. "So that I know you are safe."

"I promise," Jenna said.

She looked up at him and smiled, and Simon tried his best to smile back, but it hurt.

He waited until Jenna and Rose had disappeared into the house before he turned the buggy around. Part of him, a big part, wanted to drive to Jarrett Davidson's house and make him feel the same pain he felt now. But it was the thoughts of Sophie that stopped him. She would be waiting for him to get back, and they were all each other had now.

***

It was dark by the time Simon arrived back at the ranch. He unhitched Buck from the buggy and led him to the stables. Once he was in his stall, Simon fed and watered the horse, then headed back to the house.

As he stepped inside, the place felt so much emptier. Sophie was not in the kitchen or in her bedroom. As he passed by Jenna's room, he peered inside, and the empty crib made his throat swell again. Simon finally found Sophie sitting on the edge of the front porch. She had her back to him, a shawl wrapped tightly around her shoulders.

As he walked across to her, she did not turn around.

"Hey," Simon said as he sat down next to her.

Sophie's hands were clasped in her lap, and as he cast a sideways glance at her, he saw the tearstains running down her cheeks.

"How could you just let them go?" Sophie asked, her voice cracking.

Simon did not reply immediately because he did not know exactly what to say. He'd promised Jenna that he would protect her and Oliver, but had failed on more than one occasion. So who was he to make this promise again?

"If I convinced her to stay, and something happened to her and Oliver, I could never live with myself," Simon confessed.

"But we are a family," Sophie insisted, another tear running down her face.

Simon put his arm around her shoulder and pulled her into his body.

"We will get them back," he said.

"How?" Sophie asked.

Simon shook his head. He did not have an answer yet, but he would find one, no matter what it took.

Chapter Twenty-Three

Sophie woke up the next morning and lay in bed for a while, staring up at the ceiling. When she'd first woken up, she'd forgotten that Jenna and Oliver were gone. She'd expected to hear Oliver through the wall, like she had every morning since she first arrived. But the house was silent.

Eventually, Sophie got out of bed and dressed. She left her room and headed into the sitting room. There were still remnants of yesterday's party, the yellow ribbons tied around the drapes and the Californian poppies now drooping in their vases. How had things gone so wrong in the space of a single evening?

Sophie collected the vases and carried them through to the kitchen. She then opened the window and threw the poppies outside, scattering them on the ground underneath the window. As she was emptying the last vase, Simon came in through the back door.

"Mornin'," he said, removing his hat.

"Mornin'," Sophie echoed.

Sophie knew that it wasn't Simon's fault that Jenna and Oliver had gone, but a small part of her resented him for not trying harder to make them stay.

"What would you like for breakfast?" Sophie asked, not turning to look at him.

"Anything is fine," Simon said.

Sophie nodded as she walked into the pantry and collected eggs, beans, and some of the leftover biscuits from the day before.

As Sophie fried them up, she could sense Simon's eyes on her but busied herself with preparing breakfast. When she'd finished, she plated the eggs, beans, and biscuits and carried them over to the table where Simon was waiting.

"You not eating?" he asked, looking up at her with a furrowed brow.

"Not hungry," Sophie said, still not meeting his eye.

She turned to go, but as she did, Simon caught her hand.

"Hey," he said, tugging her arm gently. "Sit with me."

Sophie met Simon's eyes, which were full of tenderness, and she sighed.

"All right," she agreed as she sat down in her seat at the table.

Neither of them said anything for a while. Simon's breakfast lay untouched as he kept his gaze fixed on Sophie.

"I know this isn't how it should be," he said. "I miss them too, but I will find a way to bring them home—"

"How?" Sophie challenged.

Simon sighed as he sat back in his chair. "I don't know how yet, but I will find a way."

Sophie said nothing. What was there to say?

After breakfast, Simon headed back out onto the ranch, leaving Sophie alone. She went about her morning chores, but her heart was not in it. She missed Jenna and Oliver and the family they'd become.

At around midday, Sophie found herself sitting on the edge of Jenna's bed, staring into the empty crib. Simon had told her the night before that Jenna had traveled north to stay with Rose's parents. She wondered if they'd gotten there yet; she was desperate to know they were safe.

Simon did not come in for lunch, and Sophie could not blame him. She'd been too frosty with him that morning. Jenna was her own person, and she'd done what she felt was necessary to keep Oliver safe. As bitter as a pill that was to swallow, Sophie could not blame her, or Simon.

Sophie knew she owed Simon an apology for her behavior that morning. He'd lost his family too, after all, and he probably felt partly responsible for Jenna's decision to go, as he was the one who'd gone to speak with Sheriff Duncan.

By midafternoon, Sophie had finished her chores, but there was still no sign of Simon, and so she took off her apron, hung it on the hook behind the back door, and headed outside.

She first searched the barn, but Simon was not there. She went into the stables and, to her surprise, found that Buckaroo was gone too.

Sophie headed back outside, thinking that perhaps Simon was out checking the fences or tending to the flock, but just as these thoughts crossed her mind, a horse whinnied, and she turned to see Simon coming up the driveway on Buck. However, he was not alone—beside him was a beautiful bay mare with a mane and tail of silver, like the color of lightning. Sophie had never seen a horse with such coloring before.

As Simon rode up, he dismounted and walked over to Sophie, leading the mare behind him.

Sophie furrowed her brow as she waited for an explanation.

"This was not exactly how I'd planned it," Simon admitted, grimacing slightly.

"I don't understand," Sophie said, looking from the horse to Simon.

"She's yours," Simon said. "I bought her for you."

Sophie's eyes widened in surprise. "You bought me a horse?"

"As I said, the timing could have been better, but I made the deal about a week ago and had promised to pick her up today."

Sophie looked at the horse again, not knowing what to say.

"Do you like her?" Simon asked tentatively.

"She's beautiful," she said without hesitation.

Simon smiled. "She's a Morgan," he explained. "Four years old."

Sophie approached the mare, who bent her head, and ran her hand over the bridge of her nose. "I've never seen coloring like this before."

"It's unusual to be sure," Simon agreed. "She's what they call a silver."

Sophie reached over and touched the mare's mane, which was not coarse as she had expected, but soft, like silk.

"But how did you afford her?" Sophie asked, looking over the ridge of the silver mare's back at Simon.

He sucked his teeth, looking slightly abashed. "I traded her for that broach you gave me."

"Simon," she said disapprovingly. "That was a gift intended for you to use for the ranch, not to buy me a horse."

"It's an investment," he said defensively. "Now we have two horses."

Sophie frowned but did not argue. It was hard to be mad when he'd gone and bought her a horse.

Simon sighed, his expression softening. "I know how much it hurt you when your stepfather sold your horse. So I just thought, well, I don't know what I thought..."

"I love her, Simon," Sophie said sincerely.

"You do?" Simon said, his expression brightening.

"I really do," Sophie said.

Simon smiled in relief. "You'll have to give her a name."

"I think with this mane, there can only be one choice," Sophie said, hardly able to tear her eyes away from the horse. "Her name is Silver."

Simon nodded in approval. "So? How about we go for a ride?"

Sophie had not ridden a horse since she was a girl, yet as she climbed up into the saddle, she remembered everything. She'd been just four years old when her father put her on the back of a pony and taught her to ride. Now it was like muscle memory; her body knew exactly what to do without her brain having to think about it. It was a wonderful feeling, like coming home again after a long time away.

Sophie and Simon set off across the ranch together. As they rode, Silver's mane danced across her neck. Every now and then, Sophie caught Simon's eye, and she could not help but smile. This was by far the greatest thing anyone had done for her, and it proved to Sophie how far she and Simon had come in a short time.

As they reached the boundary of the ranch, Sophie and Simon slowed down and allowed the horses to graze on the sweet grasses beneath their feet. Sophie's face was flushed with exertion and excitement, and strands of her long ash-blonde hair had come loose from her plait and now hung around her face. Her blue eyes were bright, as bright as they'd been all those years ago when she was just a little girl on top of a pony.

"So?" Simon said, turning to her. "How's it being back in the saddle?"

Sophie shook her head and laughed. "I feel like a girl again," she confessed.

Simon smiled at her, and Sophie met his gaze, wanting to express how much this all meant to her, but words fell short. She'd never forget that day, all those years ago when she'd gone down to the stables and found her horse's stall empty. Something inside of her broke that day, and she never thought it would be fixed. Yet as she sat there, on the back of Silver, the memory did not feel as painful anymore. It was Simon who had given her that and she loved him for it.

"I've always loved it here," Simon said as he looked out at the distant mountains that stretched as far as the eye could see.

Sophie sighed as she took a deep breath.

"What are you thinking?" Simon asked, turning to look back at her.

"That with everything going on, I feel bad for feeling happy," Sophie confessed.

Simon sighed. "There should be a word for it. Feeling happy and sad all at once."

Sophie nodded as she looked back out at the scene that lay before them. This place had become home to her in such a short time. From the majestic mountains right down to the delicate dandelions that grew between the paving stones behind the house, she loved every part of it, and she loved the way they co-existed with nature.

It was so unlike where she'd come from; where men tried to control everything, from how tall the grass grew to the direction of the wind. Here, things were different. They existed together, and being a part of that had instilled a peacefulness in Sophie that she hadn't realized she'd been missing.

In that moment, she wanted to freeze time, for the world to fall away and leave just her and Simon out there on horseback.

"Simon," she said. "I am sorry about earlier for being so cold toward you. I know it's not your fault that Jenna left."

"You don't need to apologize," he said. "I still don't know if letting them go was the right decision."

"But it was Jenna's choice," she reasoned. "I shouldn't have put that on you."

Simon smiled a little sadly, and they fell silent, lost in their thoughts for a moment.

"I've been thinking," Simon said. "About how to get Jenna and Oliver back."

Sophie turned to him. "How?"

"I am going to go and see Rose," he said. "I am going to ask her about the other woman who was attacked and find out where she went after leaving Shadow's Ridge. Once I know where she is, I can go and speak with her."

Sophie said nothing for a moment. She did not know if Rose would tell them what they wanted to know, but it was a better plan than doing nothing.

"Let me go and speak with Rose," Sophie said. "Woman to woman."

Simon frowned but then nodded. "Okay."

"I'll go this afternoon," Sophie said, a new sense of determination coming over her.

"Maybe I should go with you," Simon suggested.

"No," Sophie said firmly. "I need to go alone."

Simon did not argue, and she was glad. Jarrett had his eye on Simon, and the town was probably full of his spies. The last thing they needed was for someone to see Simon visiting the old coroner's house.

"We should head back," Sophie said.

She turned Silver back toward home with Simon at her side. When they got back to the ranch, Sophie dismounted.

"Are you not going to ride to town?" Simon asked, his brow furrowed.

"She'll draw too much attention," Sophie said, looking at the mare's silver mane shining in the afternoon sun. "And we don't know who Jarrett has watching us. It's better if I walk."

Simon hesitated, and Sophie could see the concern in his brown eyes.

She reached over and placed a hand on his hand. "I'll be fine."

Simon nodded, but the worry in his eyes did not diminish.

"I'll be back as soon as I can," Sophie promised.

She handed Simon the reins and then hurried inside to fix her hair and fetch her bonnet.

A short while later, Sophie was making her way down the hillside toward town. She was walking briskly and by the time she got to town, she was out of breath.

Sophie took the back road to the old coroner's house and spotted Rose out in the front garden with another girl she'd never met. As she approached the house, both women turned to look at her, and Rose frowned.

"Sophie," she said as she walked over to the small gate. "What a surprise—"

"I need to talk with you, Rose," Sophie said, her tone urgent.

Rose frowned. "Why don't you come inside?"

Sophie nodded as Rose pushed open the small gate and led her indoors. The fire in the kitchen was burning brightly, and the afternoon sun streamed in through the windows. The room was uncomfortably warm.

"So what is it?" Rose asked.

"I need to speak with you about the other woman who was attacked," Sophie said. "Do you know where she is?"

Rose said nothing for a moment as Sophie kept her eyes fixed on her face.

"Do you know where she is, Rose?" Sophie repeated.

Rose sighed as she shook her head. "She left for a reason, Sophie. And she won't thank me for sending you to her door to dredge everything up again."

"I know you want to protect her," Sophie said, softening her tone. "But Jarrett Davidson isn't going to stop. If I can just talk with her, get her to write down what happened to her, then maybe we might have a chance to stop him once and for all."

Rose bit her bottom lip.

"That man is a monster," Sophie said with disgust. "He attacked Jenna and Laura, and who knows how many women before them, and he won't stop, Rose. Not unless we do something to stop him."

Rose exhaled shakily. "I know," she said, shaking her head. "I am terrified every time the saloon door opens that he's going to walk in."

"So you know that we have to try, right? Before he destroys someone else's life."

"Okay," Rose said. "I'll tell you where she is."

After they talked, Sophie made her way up the hill back toward home, a fire burning within her. The family she'd once had was destroyed by one monster, and she was not going to let this family be destroyed by another man. She would do whatever she could to see him brought down and her family put back together.

Simon was waiting for her on the porch when she arrived, and as soon as Sophie saw him, she broke into a run.

"I know where she is," Sophie cried, running into Simon's arms. "I know where we can find her."

Simon held her tightly for a moment before he let her go. "We'll leave at first light."

Chapter Twenty-Four

"Are you sure you don't want to take the buggy?" Simon asked.

Sophie shook her head as she swallowed a mouthful of scrambled eggs.

It was just before dawn; Simon had gotten up early to do all the chores before they left for Willow's Creek, a town about ten miles east of Shadow's Ridge.

"It will be quicker on horseback," Sophie said, taking a sip of coffee.

"It's a long journey for someone who hasn't ridden since they were eight," Simon reasoned.

"I'll be fine," Sophie assured him.

Simon did not argue as he finished up his coffee and carried their dishes to the sink.

"I'll just go and saddle up," Simon said.

Sophie nodded as Simon left the kitchen. The plan was to arrive in Willow's Creek in the midmorning, find Laura, and hopefully be back on the road again in the afternoon.

A short while later, Simon had saddled up the two horses, and Sophie joined him. She'd made them sandwiches for lunch, which she put into the saddlebag.

"You ready to go?" Simon asked.

Sophie nodded as she put a foot into the stirrup and pulled herself up into her saddle. "Let's go."

They set off on their journey, and as the sun rose, Simon prayed that it would prove to be fruitful. Sophie had told him all about her conversation with Rose the afternoon before. The young woman, whose name was Laura Perry, had left town to escape what had happened to her. She'd returned to her family's ranch in Willow's Creek and Rose had not heard from her since.

They'd ridden almost two miles when Simon caught Sophie shifting uncomfortably in her saddle, and he raised his eyebrows.

"What?" Sophie said, her tone bristling with annoyance.

"Nothing," Simon said, stifling a smile.

Sophie grumbled something under her breath, and Simon turned his head so she would not see the amusement in his eyes.

It was a good day for riding—the sky was clear, and there was just a hint of a breeze to cool the rising temperature of the morning.

Willow's Creek was named such because the town had been built around a wide creek lined with weeping willow trees. Simon had been to the town only once with his father, many years ago, but he remembered the way.

As he'd hoped, the town came into view around midmorning. Willow's Creek was smaller than Shadow's Ridge and he hoped they could easily locate Laura. As they rode into town, they spotted the sign for the general store on the main street.

"Let's stop and ask in there," Simon suggested. "They will probably know where we can find Laura's family home."

They brought their horses to a stop outside the store, and Simon climbed down; he watched Sophie wince in discomfort as she got off her horse.

"You go and ask," she said. "I'll wait here."

"You sure?"

Sophie nodded, wincing again.

Simon headed into the store, and the little bell above the door tinkled merrily as he stepped inside. He walked right up to the counter where the store clerk was busy filling in a ledger.

"Mornin'," Simon said, tipping his hat to the man. "I was wondering if you had directions to the Perry ranch?"

The clerk looked up and frowned. "You not from around here?"

Simon shook his head.

"What business you got with the Perrys?" he asked.

Simon frowned at the clerk's busybody question, but he knew he'd better be polite if he was going to get the directions.

"Just a family friend," he said. "I was passing through town and thought I'd look them up."

The clerk frowned slightly but then shrugged. "Perry's place is a half a mile south. Sign is up on the gate."

"Thank you," Simon said as he turned to go.

He stepped back outside and found Sophie standing in the same place. She looked expectantly across at him as he approached.

"Perry's ranch is half a mile south," Simon said. "Man said that there's a sign on the gate."

He slid his foot into the stirrup, but as he did, he saw Sophie had not moved.

"You all right?" he asked.

"I don't think I can get back in that saddle," Sophie confessed.

Simon had had his fair share of saddle sores in the past, and he knew how uncomfortable it could be.

"Why don't we walk the half a mile?" Simon suggested, climbing back down. "Stretch our legs?"

"Okay," Sophie agreed.

They set off south, leading their horses, and Sophie winced with almost every step she took. But as they walked out of town, her discomfort eased a bit.

"In hindsight, we probably should have taken the buggy," Sophie said, wincing slightly.

Simon turned and smiled at her sympathetically. "You've got the spirit of a cowboy."

"And look where that's got me," she said dryly.

He chuckled. "I can remember the first time I drove a flock of sheep out west with my pa. I had such bad saddle sores by the end of it that I couldn't sit down for a week."

Simon shook his head, smiling at the memory.

"I am not looking forward to the trip home," Sophie said, grimacing.

"I have some ointment in my saddlebag," Simon said. Just then, he spotted the sign for the Perry's ranch. "We're here."

Simon and Sophie walked up the drive toward the ranch. It was a small holding, with an old barn and farmhouse. A few chickens roamed about, pecking the ground, hoping to find something to eat. Simon looked around, but there was no one about.

"Let's go up to the house," Simon said.

He and Sophie tethered their horses to a nearby wooden rail to graze and then headed to the house.

The old farmhouse was a single-story building with a small porch out the front. As they approached it, Simon could not help but notice that the paint was peeling off the walls, and large patches of orange rust were visible on the tin roof.

As they crossed the small porch, the wood bent under his weight, and he saw that some of the slates had almost completely rotted.

Sophie knocked on the front door, and they both waited. A few moments later, the door opened, and a small woman with graying hair appeared.

"Hello," she said apprehensively. "Can I help you?"

"Good morning," Sophie said politely. "We are looking for Laura."

The older woman frowned.

"We are friends," Sophie said. "From Shadow's Ridge."

The woman did not appear any more reassured by this and continued to frown at them, not saying a word.

"We were traveling through town," Simon said, his tone casual. "And thought we might pop in and say hello."

"Laura's not here," the woman said stiffly.

Simon's stomach dropped.

"Do you know where we can find her?" Sophie asked.

"Laura's not been the same since she came back from that place," the woman said, her pale eyes full of worry. "I think it's best if you go now."

Without another word, the older woman closed the front door, and Simon turned to Sophie.

"What should we do now?" he asked.

She shook her head. "I don't know."

Simon knocked again, but the older woman did not answer.

"Please," Sophie called through the door. "We just want to talk to her."

But there was no reply from within.

Simon and Sophie walked back across the porch. Simon's stomach sank further with every step they took away from the house. Had they really come all this way for nothing?"

"Maybe she works in town," Sophie said. "We could go and ask around."

Simon nodded; it was worth a try.

Just as they headed back toward their horses, Simon spotted a lone figure in the distance. From where they were standing, he knew it was a woman by the way her skirt was blowing in the breeze.

"Could that be her?" he said, turning to Sophie.

Sophie squinted as she looked at the woman. "Let's go and see."

Simon and Sophie walked across the ranch toward the woman, who had her back to them. It was only when they got close enough that she turned around.

Laura Perry was a thin girl with dark hair that hung loose down her back. Like Jenna, she had large purplish rings under her eyes, and the skin across her cheekbones was taut.

"Who are you?" she asked, taking a step back and pulling her shawl tightly across her body, as if she were using it to hold herself together.

"We don't mean any harm," Sophie said soothingly.

"Are you Laura?" Simon asked.

She nodded and Simon felt his heart lift.

"My name is Simon Jones, and this is my wife, Sophie."

Laura, whose brow was still furrowed, looked between them. "Do I know you?"

"No," Sophie said. "But we've come from Shadow's Ridge."

At the mention of the town, Laura's face grew even paler, and Simon saw her shiver beneath her woolen shawl.

"We're friends of Rose's," Sophie said. "And we just wanted to talk to you—"

"No," Laura said, shaking her head. "Rose should never—you both need to leave now."

"Please, Laura," Simon said, taking a step forward. "The same thing happened to my cousin, Jenna. If you'll just make a statement—"

"I can't," Laura said, her bottom lip trembling. "Don't ask me to do this."

"If we don't stop him, he's going to keep hurting women the way that he hurt you and Jenna," Sophie said.

"I can't do it," Laura said, her tone pleading. "You are going to have to find someone else."

"There is no one else," Simon said, meeting Laura's eye.

Laura said nothing, but Simon could see by the fear in her eyes that she could not help them. She was still clutching her shawl tightly around her body so tightly that her knuckles had turned white. As Simon watched her, her dark eyes darted right and then left, as if she were looking for a some way to escape, like a cornered animal.

"I think you should go," Laura said, dropping her gaze. "Now."

Without another word, Laura turned her back on them, and Simon looked at Sophie.

"Laura," Sophie said softly, "I know how scary it can be to face the person who hurt you. I wasn't brave enough to face the man who hurt me, so I ran, but the problem with running away is that you'll never be able to stop."

Laura turned her head slightly to Sophie.

"I'll never stop running," Sophie said. "But you can. All you have to do is find the courage to speak out and face the man who hurt you."

Simon looked at Sophie and then at Laura, but she did not turn around. After a minute, Sophie looked at Simon, and he nodded.

He and Sophie turned and walked back across the ranch toward their horses. They'd failed at what they'd come to Willow's Creek to do, and this disappointment weighed on Simon's shoulders, making every step he took an effort.

***

Simon and Sophie did not talk much on the ride home. What was there left to say? Their plan to bring Jenna and Oliver home had failed.

Halfway home, they stopped to eat their sandwiches, but as Simon bit into his, he realized he wasn't hungry.

"Do you think she'll be all right?" Simon asked, picturing Laura's face in his mind.

"I don't know," Sophie confessed.

Laura had reminded Simon so much of his cousin; they had that same look in their eyes, a silent pain that could not be spoken.

"Did you mean what you said?" Simon asked. "That you will always be running?"

Sophie nodded. "I think I'll always be looking over my shoulder. Wondering if he'll find me and what he will do, when and if he does."

"I won't let him do anything," Simon said firmly.

"I know," Sophie said, but there was an edge to her voice, as if she did not completely believe it.

"Should we get back on the road?" Simon said.

Sophie packed the sandwiches away, and they set off home. As they did, Simon thought about all the ways he'd failed to protect Jenna, and he would not let it happen with Sophie. If her greatest fear turned out to come true, he would do everything in his power to protect her.

***

It was late afternoon by the time they arrived back at the ranch. Simon had been lost in his thoughts on most of the ride.

"I'll get inside and put supper on," Sophie said as she climbed down from Silver.

Simon took both the horses to the stables and removed the saddles. After he'd finished feeding them, he got on with the other chores. As he did, he could not help but feel disappointed. Had they really tried hard enough with Laura? But then again, how far could you push someone who was already teetering on the edge?

Simon headed inside just as the sun disappeared behind the mountains. Sophie was in the kitchen when Simon came inside. She had changed her clothes and was boiling peas on the stove.

"How are the saddle sores?" he asked.

"The ointment is helping," Sophie said.

"Good," Simon said, nodding.

He walked over to the sink to wash up and when he was done, he sat down and waited for supper.

Just like the ride home, they ate supper in relative silence. They were both disappointed with how the day had turned out. What was more was that they'd lost their chance to bring

Jenna and Oliver home. Simon looked over at Jenna's chair and sighed.

"I am glad we tried," Sophie said, looking across the table at the empty seat. "At least we can tell Jenna that we tried."

Simon nodded, but the day had left a bitter taste in his mouth, and he wasn't sure he was quite ready to see the bright side.

"I think that I am going to go up to bed," Simon said. "It's been a long day."

Sophie nodded as Simon got up. "Thank you for supper," he said.

Sophie smiled at him, and he did his best to smile back before he turned and left the kitchen.

In his bedroom, Simon changed his clothes and climbed into bed, looking forward to the sweet release of sleep. He fell asleep easily that night, thanks to the day's physical exertions, and when he woke in the morning, he felt a little better than he had the night before.

Simon got dressed and went out to do the morning chores. However, as he was right in the middle of milking the cow, Sophie appeared in the barn doorway. Her cheeks were flushed.

"You need to come inside now," she said urgently.

Before Simon could say anything, Sophie turned and left.

Slightly annoyed with her abruptness, Simon abandoned the half-pail of milk and followed her back toward the house. As he stepped into the kitchen doorway, he stopped dead in his tracks, unable to take his eyes off the person now sitting at their kitchen table.

Chapter Twenty-Five

Laura Perry clasped her pale hands in her lap as Sophie placed a hot cup of tea on the table next to her.

"There you go," Sophie said, smiling.

"Thank you," Laura said, but she did not return Sophie's smile.

Simon was sitting across from her. He was obviously still in disbelief that she was really there. Sophie had the same reaction when she'd opened the door ten minutes earlier to find Laura on the porch.

"How did you get here?" Simon asked.

"My pa brought me," Laura said.

"What reason did you give?" Sophie asked curiously.

"I just told him I was visiting some friends," Laura said. "He's coming back for me in two days."

"So you are staying?" Simon asked, raising his eyebrows in surprise.

Laura nodded.

Sophie caught Simon's eye, and she raised her eyebrows in response. She knew they were thinking the same thing: why had Laura come all this way? Why had she returned to Shadow's Ridge?

Laura took a sip of tea, her hand trembling slightly as she put the cup down. She then looked across at Sophie.

"I thought a lot about what you said yesterday about running away," Laura said, her voice wavering slightly. "Ever since that night, I can't close my eyes without seeing him, and I am so tired of being afraid..."

Sophie and Simon remained silent as they waited for Laura to continue.

"I didn't say anything yesterday, but I know Jenna," Laura said. "I didn't know her well before she left, but she was always kind to me, and she treated me like a sister."

Sophie knew how it felt to be treated that way by Jenna; it was a special feeling.

"So," Laura said shakily. "I've decided that I want to make a statement."

Sophie had not realized she was holding her breath until that moment, and she exhaled deeply. As she did, she looked at Simon again.

"Are you sure?" Sophie asked. "We don't want to pressure you—"

Laura nodded. "I am sure. You were right when you said he'd do it to someone else, and if Jenna is willing to come forward and tell her story, then I am too. Maybe together, we can try to stop this from happening to another woman."

Sophie reached across the table and put her hand gently on Laura's.

"Thank you," she said kindly.

Laura tried to smile, and as she did, Sophie saw that she had dimples.

"So what do we do now?" Laura asked.

"We need to talk with Sheriff Duncan," Simon said. "But I don't think it's a good idea for you to be seen in town. If Jarrett learns that you are back, he could cause trouble."

As the mention of Jarrett's name, Laura paled.

"I'll go into town and ask him to come here," Simon said, nodding to himself.

"Are you sure it's a good idea for you to be seen at Sheriff Duncan's office again?" Sophie asked, her brow furrowed in concern.

"No," Simon sighed. "It's probably not."

Simon looked thoughtful for a moment. "I am expecting a delivery today from the farm store in town. I could send a note back to Sheriff Duncan."

Sophie nodded slowly. They could not be sure who in town they could trust, but they needed a way to get a message to the sheriff.

"Maybe don't write what we really want him for," she suggested. "Maybe think of another reason we might want Sheriff Duncan to come to the ranch."

Simon nodded as he got up from the table. "I'll go and write the note now."

He headed to the study, leaving Sophie and Laura alone.

"Would you like something to eat?" Sophie offered.

"No, thanks," Laura declined, her face still drawn and pale.

"Well, you can stay in Jenna's bedroom for the next couple of days," Sophie said. "Would you like me to show you? Perhaps you'd like to lie down after the journey."

Laura nodded, and Sophie got up and led her down the hallway to Jenna's bedroom. Laura sat down on the end of the bed and glanced out of the window.

"Just call me if you need anything," Sophie said before she turned to go.

"Sophie," Laura said.

She turned back to the young woman.

"Where is Jenna?" Laura asked.

"She left town," Sophie said. "But we are trying to make it so that she can come home again."

Laura nodded but said nothing, and Sophie left the bedroom, closing the door behind her. She then returned to the kitchen, where she found Simon with the note in his hand.

"What have you written?" Sophie asked.

"I've said that some of the flock are missing and asked Sheriff Duncan to come to the ranch to open an investigation," Simon said.

"Good thinking," Sophie said.

"Where's Laura?" he asked.

"Lying down," Sophie said.

"Well, I'd better get out there in case the delivery arrives," Simon said. "And the cow's only been half-milked."

Sophie smiled, and to her surprise, Simon leaned over and kissed her on the cheek.

"I have a feeling Jenna and Oliver are coming back home soon," he said, smiling.

"I hope so," Sophie said, her cheeks flushed.

***

It was midmorning when the delivery arrived, and from the kitchen window, Sophie saw Simon hand them the note to deliver.

Laura did not come out of the bedroom until lunchtime and then only ate a bit of bread and cheese.

That afternoon, Sophie did her sewing on the front porch in the sun. Mittens was sleeping soundlessly at her feet. Sophie kept an eye on the road, hoping to see Sheriff Duncan, but as the hours passed by, there was no sign of him.

"Nothing?" Simon asked as he stepped from inside the house out onto the porch.

Sophie shook her head as she returned the mended shirt to her sewing basket. "Maybe they forgot to give him the note?"

Simon sighed. "Maybe they did."

Just as the words left his mouth, a rider appeared at the bottom of the driveway.

"It's Sheriff Duncan," Simon said in relief as he crossed the porch.

"I'll put the kettle on," Sophie said as she headed into the house, followed by Mittens.

A few minutes later, Simon came into the kitchen with the sheriff, introducing him to her. "This is my wife, Sophie."

"It's a pleasure, ma'am," Sheriff Duncan said, taking off his hat. "Sorry that it took me so long to get here. There were a few matters in town that needed my attention."

"Well, you are here now," Simon said.

"So what is this matter about missing sheep?" Sheriff Duncan asked, frowning. "You think stock thieves may be about?"

Simon looked at Sophie, a sheepish expression on his face.

"Actually, Sheriff—"

A movement by the door caught their attention, and Sophie turned to see Laura in the doorway.

"Sheriff, this is Laura Perry," Simon said. "She's the young woman I told you about. The one who left town after the attack."

Sheriff Duncan raised his eyebrows. "So I take it I am not here on a matter of stock theft."

"No," Simon said, his tone apologetic. "Miss Perry has come back to town to make a statement about what happened to her."

He nodded, looking at her kindly. "Is that right, Miss Perry?"

"Y-yes, sir," Laura stuttered.

"Is there a quiet place where we can talk?" Sheriff Duncan asked, looking from Simon to Sophie.

"You can use the study," Simon said. "It's right this way."

Sophie stayed behind as Simon showed the sheriff and Laura to the small study at the back of the house. He returned a few moments later.

"Do you want some tea?" Sophie offered.

Sophie and Simon finished two cups of tea before Laura and Sheriff Duncan emerged again. Laura's cheeks were wet with tears. Sophie walked over to Laura and put an arm around her shoulders.

"I have Miss Perry's statement," the sheriff said, his expression grim. "But before I can take this matter further, I need the statement from Jenna. Where is she?"

Sophie looked at Simon, frowning.

"She left town," Simon said. "A couple of days ago."

"Where did she go?" he asked.

"William's Town," Simon said. "She is staying with a friend's parents."

Sheriff Duncan furrowed his eyebrows. "I know the sheriff there. I'll send a telegram explaining the situation and ask him to take your cousin's statement."

"Thank you," Simon said gratefully as he looked at Sophie in relief.

"I will come back when I have Jenna's statement and update you," Sheriff Duncan promised, turning to look at Laura. "You look after yourself, Miss Perry."

Laura smiled faintly.

"Thank you, Sheriff," Sophie said. "For coming all the way out here."

"I have three daughters myself," he said, looking at Laura again. "And if anything happened to them, well, I'd stop at nothing to see that man brought to justice."

"That's all I want," Laura said quietly.

The room fell silent for a moment.

Sheriff Duncan then put his hat back on and turned to Sophie. "It was a pleasure meeting you, Mrs. Jones, although I wish it could have been under different circumstances."

"I am sure that happens a lot in your line of work," Sophie said grimly.

He sighed. "Unfortunately it comes with the territory."

"I'll show you out, Sheriff," Simon said.

"Good evening to you both," Sheriff Duncan said before he followed Simon out.

Sophie, who still had her arm around Laura's shoulders, dropped it and looked at her. "Are you all right?"

"It was harder than I thought," Laura confessed. "But I think I feel a bit better now that I've spoken about it."

Sophie smiled softly. "I think you are extremely brave."

Laura gave her a watery smile, and Sophie guided her to the table and poured her a strong cup of sweet tea.

A short while later, Simon returned.

"I will drive you back home tomorrow," he told Laura. "Sheriff Duncan said he will follow up if he has any more questions."

"Thank you," Laura said as she sipped her tea.

Simon looked across at Sophie, and she could see the relief in his eyes. All they needed was to wait for the statement from Jenna, and then this nightmare would finally be over.

***

The next morning, Simon drove Laura home in the buggy, and Sophie stayed behind to catch up on the house chores. With everything that had happened, she'd fallen behind on the washing, but despite having plenty to keep her occupied, Sophie could not focus. All she could think about was Jenna and whether the telegram had reached her yet.

Around midmorning, Sophie was out hanging the sheets on the line when the wind suddenly picked up. She looked over to the west to see a large, dark storm cloud gathering. The sky had a pinkish hue which Sophie knew meant that a bad storm was on the way.

She unpegged the sheets she'd just hung up and returned inside, carrying the heavy basket on her hip. She put the basket down on the kitchen floor and looked back out at the storm, which was fast approaching.

As she went back outside to shut up the barn and stables, Sophie prayed that Simon would not be caught up in the storm. Surely he would see it and stay at the Perry ranch until it was over.

Sophie fed Silver and refilled her water trough before she left the stables, securing the latch firmly just as the first drops of rain started to fall. Sophie hurried back to the kitchen just as there was a loud crack of thunder, and Mittens dashed in from outside, between her legs and under the kitchen table.

Against the howling wind, Sophie slammed the back door shut and bolted it securely. She walked over to the window as another rumble of thunder shook the glass in their panes. The world outside was white as sheets of rain fell, instantly soaking the ground. Sophie could not stop thinking about Simon, her worry gnawing away at her insides.

After an hour, the rain finally let up, and Sophie opened the door and stepped back outside. Large puddles had formed all around the barn and stables; the wind had ripped leaves from the trees, and they lay like a carpet of green all over the ground.

Sophie checked on Silver first. The horse was agitated by the storm, and as Sophie came into the barn, she stomped her back legs and whinnied loudly. Sophie walked over to her and placed a hand on her nose, and she immediately quieted down.

Sophie stayed with Silver a while before she checked on the chickens, who were wet and indignant but also unharmed. Sophie opened up the barn doors again, and the dairy cow, who was in her stall, turned her head and looked lazily at Sophie as she chewed her cud.

Sophie was glad that the storm had not caused any major damage, but she could not ignore the sinking feeling in the pit of her stomach. As she walked back to the house, she suddenly heard a whinny and turned to see Buck racing up the driveway, but he was not pulling the buggy, and there was no rider atop him—he'd come back alone.

"Whoa, boy!" Sophie cried, putting her arms up.

The horse came to a halt in front of her, but his eyes were wild, rolling back in his head. He was still wearing the harness from the buggy; the traces were dragging behind him, covered in mud.

"Where's Simon?" Sophie asked as she put her hands on the horse's neck, trying to soothe him like she'd done with Silver only minutes before.

Sophie's eyes traveled across the horse, and she could not see any signs of injury. He was wet, his mane matted to his body, and it was clear that they'd been caught off guard by the storm.

"Stay here," Sophie instructed as she turned and raced toward the stables. She hurried inside and fetched the saddle and reins from the wall before heading back to Buck.

Sophie removed the harness from Buck, her heart racing. Once the harness was removed, she lifted the heavy saddle and put it on his back. She had not saddled a horse for a long time, but she remembered what her father had taught her, and although she struggled, Sophie finally managed to secure the saddle and reins.

"Buck," Sophie said, looking him in the eyes. "I need you to take me to Simon."

The horse whinnied as Sophie put her boot firmly in the stirrup, and she pulled herself into the saddle.

Sophie took hold of the reins tightly as Buck started to trot, and although she knew the way to go, she did not need to direct the horse. He was taking her to Simon; she knew that in her bones.

As they rode, Sophie was blind to the world around her, the damage caused by the storm. Her mind was focused on finding Simon, and nothing else mattered.

They'd gone almost four miles when Sophie spotted the buggy overturned on the road. Her heart caught in her throat as she tucked her knees into Buck's side, and he broke into a canter.

"Simon!" Sophie cried as she slid off the moving horse, her feet hitting the ground with a heavy thud.

Simon was on the ground, his eyes closed. For a second, Sophie did not move. The only thought in her head was that he might be dead, and the idea of that, of losing him, terrified her.

Then she was running and she fell to her knees at his side.

"Simon?" She touched his face with her hands, and he was cold.

"Please no," she whispered, her throat raw.

Sophie leaned over his chest, her ear pressed to his wet shirt, searching for a heartbeat, and when she finally found the rhythmic thump, thump, thump, she whimpered, every muscle in her body softening. He was alive.

Sophie looked around, searching for help, but there was no one for miles. Her heart was pounding and she couldn't think what to do next. Sophie took a deep breath as she tried to calm herself down. Simon needed her.

"Simon," Sophie said, patting his cheek with her hand. "You need to wake up; I can't lift you on my own."

But Simon did not open his eyes.

Chapter Twenty-Six

"Simon?" Sophie said firmly. "Open your eyes."

In the darkness, Simon heard Sophie's voice calling to him, and suddenly, he became aware of his body again. He could feel the ache in his back, the warm hands on his face, and a second later, he was looking up at the blue sky, his eyes adjusting to the brightness of the world, and then there she was—Sophie.

"Hey," Sophie said gently, her hands on his face. "Can you hear me?"

Simon tried to nod, but as he did, he winced.

"What happened?" he asked, his voice not sounding like his own.

"I was hoping you could tell me that," Sophie said.

Simon frowned, trying to get up, but he suddenly felt nauseous and lay down again. His thoughts were all disordered, and his mind cloudy.

"Buck—" Simon said urgently, suddenly remembering his horse.

"He's fine," Sophie said. "He came to find me."

The sharp ache in Simon's lower back grew more pronounced as he concentrated on wiggling his toes, first the right foot and then the left.

"Are you hurt?" Sophie asked, her face and voice full of concern.

"Not badly, I don't think," Simon said, gritting his teeth. "Help me up."

With Sophie's help, he managed to sit up, but the world was spinning, and he stumbled; Sophie caught him on her shoulder. They managed to stagger over to the overturned buggy, and Sophie helped Simon into a sitting position, his back leaning against the large wooden wheel.

Sophie crouched down beside him. "What happened?" she asked as she peered into his face.

"I was stupid," he said, shaking his head. "I thought I could outrace the storm—"

Simon closed his eyes for a moment, shaking his head. He'd been foolish to challenge nature; he should have taken shelter until the worst had passed.

"It was a lightning strike," Simon said. "A branch came down in front of us, just missing Buck, and he reared up, taking the buggy with him. I guess the traces were worn because they just snapped, and I remember hitting the ground and then nothing until just now when I heard your voice."

Sophie's face was pale as she listened to Simon's account. He had, in fact, been fortunate; had the buggy fallen on him, he would have been crushed.

As Simon looked into Sophie's face, her expression suddenly hardened.

"How could you be so stupid?" she chided, her brow furrowing. "You so easily could have killed yourself—"

"I know," Simon agreed. "It was foolish."

Sophie shook her head, her expression softening again.

"What would I have done if I'd lost you?" she said tenderly.

Simon looked into her eyes as she reached over and brushed his cheek with her fingertips, and he closed his eyes again, leaning into her touch.

In the distance, there was another rumble of thunder, and Simon opened his eyes again, looking up at the sky.

"We should get home," Sophie said.

Simon nodded as Sophie helped him to his feet. The dizziness and nausea had subsided for the most part, but the pain in his back was worse.

"Lean on me," Sophie said.

Simon leaned on Sophie's shoulders, both surprised and impressed by her ability to walk under their weight.

"Hey, boy," Simon said as they approached Buckaroo. The horse nuzzled into Simon's chest, and he held his head for a moment.

"Can you get up into the saddle?" Sophie asked.

Simon grimaced as he put one foot up into the stirrup. With Sophie's help, he managed to pull himself into the saddle, but was panting in pain by the time he got up.

Sophie climbed on behind him, and the warmth of her body helped to soothe his aching back.

"Lean on me," Sophie said.

Simon took the reins and softly clicked his tongue, and Buck set off home.

***

"Come on," Sophie said as she helped Simon into his bedroom. "Straight to bed with you."

"But there are things, chores—"

"You are in no state to be running around the place," Sophie said, cutting him off mid-sentence. "You can barely walk."

"I am fine," Simon argued. "It's just a bruised back."

"No more arguing, Simon Jones," Sophie said firmly as she steered him to the bed.

Simon sighed, giving in, as Sophie helped him to the bed, and he sat down. She helped him take off his boots, and then he lifted his legs onto the bed. Sophie adjusted his pillows as he lay back and the pain lessened. She then leaned over him, tucking the blanket tightly around his body, and Simon had to admit that, despite feeling slightly annoyed by her bossiness, he quite liked being taken care of by Sophie.

"I'm going to go and feed the horses," Sophie said. "Then I'll be back to check on you."

Simon mumbled his thanks as he drifted off to sleep.

When he woke again, the room was dark and the house still. He looked around the room and found Sophie asleep in a chair at the side of the bed. Her face was illuminated by a sliver of moonlight that streamed in through a gap in the curtains.

Simon watched her sleeping for a while; she looked so peaceful, her long, dark lashes resting against the pale, smooth skin of her cheeks. He thought back to that afternoon, how it had been the sound of her voice, the touch of her skin, that had brought him back, and he knew now, in his heart, that he was in love with her.

A coyote howled in the distance, and Sophie stirred from sleep, her blue eyes opening as she looked down at Simon.

"Hey," she said softly. "You're awake. How are you feeling?"

Simon rolled over, and the pain in his back was less pronounced.

"Better," he said.

Sophie smiled in relief as she leaned forward in her chair. "Are you hungry? I can make you something."

At the mention of food, Simon's stomach rumbled, and Sophie smiled again.

"I'll make you something," she said as she got up.

Sophie disappeared from the room, and Simon heard her in the kitchen, lighting the stove and the clang of the copper kettle as she filled it with water.

Simon pulled himself into a sitting position, then he swung his legs over the side of the bed and stood up. He held onto the bed rail for a moment, steadying himself before walking across the bedroom and into the hallway, turning toward the kitchen.

"What are you doing up?" Sophie said disapprovingly.

"I don't like eating in bed. Gets crumbs in the sheets."

Sophie raised an eyebrow but said nothing as Simon made his way across the room to the table, and he sat down.

"What time is it?" he asked.

"About an hour before dawn. You slept for a long time."

"You didn't have to sit up with me," he said as Sophie placed long strips of bacon into the pan to fry.

"I wanted to," she said, not turning away from the task at hand. "In case you needed something."

"Did you get any sleep?"

"Some."

The smell of sizzling bacon made Simon's mouth water, and for a while, neither of them spoke. Simon watched Sophie make breakfast; he liked watching her, the way her brow creased in concentration, and how she kept forgetting where she'd put the spatula down.

How had he not seen it before? Everything she did, all the little details that made her who she was—Simon was in love with her.

A little while later, Sophie brought a loaded plate of bacon, eggs, beans, and biscuits over to him and placed it down on the table.

Simon ate hungrily as Sophie watched, smiling.

"You know that you talk in your sleep?" she said, her blue eyes lit up in amusement.

"I do?" Simon said, a little horrified.

Sophie nodded, her lips twitching.

"What did I say?" he asked. "Or don't I want to know?"

"You said my name a few times," she said, holding his gaze.

"Really?" Simon said, sitting back in his chair.

Sophie smiled but said nothing, and Simon could see, by the light in her eyes, that she was pleased he'd been dreaming about her.

"Why don't you go back to bed?" Sophie suggested when Simon had finished eating.

Simon shook his head. "Too much work to be done."

Sophie frowned. "You're not very good at being sick, are you?"

"Nope," Simon agreed. "Never have been, even as a boy."

Sophie did not push the matter any further, and Simon got up from the table and returned to the bedroom, where he changed into a fresh shirt and put on his boots.

When he returned to the kitchen, Sophie was standing at the window. As he came into the room, she turned, the first rays of the morning sun catching her face, and he stopped, his heart skipping a beat.

"What is it?" Sophie asked. "Is it your back?"

Simon did not answer right away. It wasn't his back; it was her.

"Simon?" Sophie said, her voice full of concern.

"Sorry," he said, clearing his throat. "It's nothing. I'd better get to work, I'll see you later."

Simon headed out the back door, his head bent. Why hadn't he just said it? Why hadn't he told her that he loved her?

***

Simon thought about Sophie all morning. He wanted to tell her how he felt, but he was afraid that she might not feel the same about him. It was scary to be so vulnerable. The more Simon thought about his feelings, the more he came to know that he had never been in love, not even with Rachel. He'd always been so happy on his own, enjoyed his own company, but now he craved Sophie; he wanted to be with her always.

Simon came in for lunch, and he and Sophie ate together. As they did, he wondered if she could sense the change in him. He wondered if she could tell that his heart was now hers. If she could, she did not let on.

After lunch, Simon went back out to work. Sophie joined him in the late afternoon, and they groomed the horses together.

Simon could not stop looking over at Sophie, and every time he did, he smiled.

"Do I have dirt on my face?" Sophie asked.

Simon frowned. "No. Why?"

"Because you keep looking at me and smiling."

"Can't a man smile at his wife?" Simon said lamely.

"It's just you aren't usually this smiley," Sophie said, her tone curious.

"Well, I almost died yesterday, and now I am alive," Simon replied. "Isn't that a reason to be happy?"

Sophie said nothing, and the crease between her brows remained in place, indicating to Simon that she did not believe him.

However, before Sophie could push the matter any further, they heard a horse arrive outside, and they left the stables to find Sheriff Duncan dismounting his horse.

"Afternoon," he said as he took off his hat.

"Afternoon, Sheriff," Simon said.

"I promised you an update as soon as I had one," he said, but there was something in his tone that told Simon it was not the news they were hoping for.

"What happened?" Simon asked.

Sheriff Duncan sighed. "We got Jenna's statement," he said. "But it looks as if Jarrett Davidson got word of what was happening."

Simon's heart sank as she glanced at Sophie; she had her arms across her body, each hand gripping tightly to an opposite elbow.

"He's hired a fancy lawyer who's arguing that both women are lying, that they made attempts to get money out of him—"

"But it's not true," Sophie insisted in outrage.

"Of course not," he agreed. "But there is no proof, no witnesses to come forward and support their accusations. All we have is purely circumstantial."

Simon gritted his teeth. After everything they'd done, Jarrett Davidson was still going to walk away.

"Is there anything else we can do?" Sophie asked, her tone desperate.

"I am going to keep my eye on him," Sheriff Duncan promised. "Make sure if he does try anything else that we catch him."

"That's it?" Simon asked, frowning. "That's all we can do?"

The sheriff exhaled through his pursed lips. "I know it's not the outcome we wanted."

Simon shook his head, his stomach tight with disappointment.

"I am sorry," he apologized.

"It's not your fault," Sophie said.

"No," Simon agreed. "There is only one man to blame."

They fell silent for a few moments before Sheriff Duncan put his hat back on his head.

"I'll let you know if anything changes," he said.

Sophie and Simon nodded as he turned to go. They watched him until he disappeared into the distance.

Sophie turned to Simon. "What do we do now?"

Simon shook his head but said nothing. What could he say? After all of it, they'd lost. Jenna and Oliver were not coming home.

Chapter Twenty-Seven

The reality that Jenna and Oliver would not be coming home hung over them, casting a shadow on everything. Simon stopped smiling and buried himself in ranch work, and Sophie felt alone again for the first time since she'd left her home and come to Shadow's Ridge.

A week passed, and nothing improved. They woke up, did their chores, and went to bed, and to Sophie, they'd become shadows themselves, going through the motions but not really living. With Sheriff Duncan keeping a close eye on Jarrett, Simon did not think he would try to get revenge on them, but the thought still kept Sophie awake at night.

Then one morning, Simon announced that he was going into town.

"I want to see if there is a letter from Jenna," he said.

Sophie nodded but said nothing.

Simon left right after breakfast, leaving her home alone.

The morning passed by, and Sophie did her chores; when noon arrived, she went into the kitchen to prepare lunch. As she searched the pantry for what she needed, she heard heavy footsteps in the room.

"Sophie?" Simon said loudly.

She came out of the pantry to find him in the doorway, his expression bright and his eyes wide with excitement. He had a newspaper in his hands.

"What is it?" she asked.

You won't believe it," Simon said, shaking his head.

"Believe what?" Sophie asked, frowning slightly.

"Come and see for yourself," he said.

Sophie put down the tin of beans she was holding and walked across the kitchen. Simon handed her the newspaper.

"Read it," he said excitedly.

"Prominent Businessman Accused of Assault," Sophie read out loud.

She looked up from the headline, her eyes wide with disbelief.

"Keep reading," Simon encouraged her.

Sophie looked down at the paper again.

"Prominent businessman Mr. Jarrett Davidson has been accused of the assault of more than half a dozen women," she continued. *"After two women from Shadow's Ridge came forward with their stories, more and more women have been coming out of the woodwork to talk about their attacks. According to their reports, these women are from vastly different backgrounds and are from several different states. While Davidson has yet to comment on these allegations, the sheriff of Shadow's Ridge, Hugh Duncan, is already building a strong case against him. Currently, the sheriff has eight written testimonies for the women, revealing startlingly similar details of their attacks. Whether more stories will come to the surface remains to be seen."*

Sophie looked up at Simon, her mind racing. "But how?"

Simon shook his head. "I don't know. But can you believe this? More than half a dozen women?"

Sophie shook her head, her heart sinking to her stomach with the knowledge that Jarrett had hurt so many women.

"Everyone in town is talking about it," Simon said.

"I am sure they are," she said. "But what does this mean?"

Simon's face cracked into a smile. "I think it means Jenna and Oliver can finally come home."

Sophie looked down at the paper again and then up at Simon, realizing that he was right. Without thinking, she dropped the paper and threw herself into Simon's arms. He lifted her off her feet and spun her around, laughing.

When he put her down, the room spun a little. She was still in his arms, and Sophie looked up into Simon's eyes, her own eyes bright with excitement. She felt his warm breath on her face as he reached down and brushed her cheek with his thumb. He leaned in closer, so close that Sophie could count each of his dark eyelashes. Her heart was pounding with anticipation, and she realized in that moment just how much she wanted this kiss.

But just as their lips were about to meet, there was a knock at the back door, and Sheriff Duncan stepped inside the kitchen. Sophie and Simon broke apart, looking at him in surprise.

He took his hat off, and as he did, he caught sight of the paper on the floor between Sophie and Simon.

"I was just coming to tell you the news," he said. "But it looks as if you already know."

"How did this happen?" Simon asked.

"Well, it's the result of a lot of elbow grease and a little bit of luck," Sheriff Duncan said wryly.

"Why don't you sit down?" Sophie said. "I'll put the kettle on."

He took up the invitation and sat down as Sophie filled the copper kettle and put it on the stove to boil. She took her seat, and they both looked expectantly at Sheriff Duncan.

"Last week, after I left the ranch, I didn't feel right about the whole thing," Sheriff Duncan explained. "So I sent telegrams to a few of the sheriffs I know in the neighboring towns, asking if they'd had any assault cases involving Jarrett Davidson. I knew it was a long shot, but I also knew Davidson had stayed in a lot of towns building his railroads. A few days later, I got some replies, and as it turns out, Laura wasn't the first woman to accuse Jarrett of assault."

Sophie shook her head in disbelief.

"I wrote back asking for copies of their statements," he continued. "And this is where things got interesting. A man arrived at my office in town, a newspaper man, claiming his daughter had been engaged to Jarrett a year earlier. However, she broke it off after there was some kind of incident, a violent incident. The man said he'd tried to have Jarrett arrested, but he'd skipped town before the authorities could question him."

"So this man, the newspaper man, had heard about the assault allegations?" Simon confirmed.

"Yes, he'd heard about these women's stories from a number of his sources and came to me to find out if they were true. I told him what I knew, and he left."

"So you didn't know he was going to print an article?" Sophie asked.

"No," Sheriff Duncan said gingerly. "And I wished he had waited until I'd had Jarrett in custody before he did, because he's gone and skipped town."

"Jarrett's gone?" Simon said, his brow creasing.

"I was surprised too," the sheriff confessed. "That he didn't stay and have lawyers fight. But the article did a lot of damage. It's a lot of women, and not just dance hall girls. From what I've heard, Jarrett's reputation is shot. His *fiancée's family have cut off all ties and my guess is no businessman worth his salt will get involved with him now.*"

"Where do you think he's gone?" Sophie asked.

"I don't know," Sheriff Duncan said. "But I have men out looking for him and we'll check with his relatives. But if he's smart, he'll be on a boat to England."

Sophie looked at Simon, and she could see from the look in his eyes that he was also concerned by this news.

"Everyone is on high alert," Sheriff Duncan added. "I don't think Jarrett will risk getting caught now."

Sophie hoped that he was right.

"So what happens when you catch him?" Simon asked.

"He'll go to trial, but with eight assault cases against him, he hasn't got a chance. My guess is that he'll leave the country as soon as possible."

Neither Sophie nor Simon spoke for a moment. Jarrett leaving the country would mean they were safe, but what about other women, women in England and France and Italy? He was a bad man who deserved to pay for his crimes.

"He shouldn't be allowed to escape," Sophie said.

"We are going to use every resource at our disposal to find him and bring him to justice," he said, his voice firm with determination.

"So, can Jenna come home?" Simon asked.

"I'd wait a few more days," Sheriff Duncan advised. "Until we've caught Jarrett or are certain he's left the country. He doesn't know where she and Oliver are, and it is better that way until we can say definitively that they are no longer in danger."

Sheriff Duncan left a while later, and Sophie and Simon stood at the door, watching him go. Sophie still couldn't believe that so many women had told the truth and been ignored. But finally, they were being heard.

"Do you really think they'll catch him?" Sophie asked, looking up at Simon.

Simon sighed, shaking his head. "Only if Jarrett slips up and does something stupid. But he has money, connections, so if he means to leave America, no doubt he will."

Sophie nodded as she rubbed her neck with her hand. She felt conflicted about the prospect. If Jarrett wanted to disappear, he would, but then just like Sophie's stepfather, he would become the shadow walking behind Jenna, the one she could never escape.

***

Sheriff Duncan came by the next day to tell Sophie and Simon that there had been no reports or sightings of Jarrett Davidson. Sophie was not sure if this news was good or bad.

For three days, the sheriff rode up to the ranch with the same news, and soon Sophie started to believe that he'd fled the country.

"So, can Jenna come home yet?" Sophie asked, placing Simon's lunch on the table in front of him.

"Not yet," Simon said. "The sheriff wants us to wait a few more days just to be safe."

Sophie sighed. She couldn't wait to have Jenna and Oliver back and for things to get back to normal. Their family would be whole again.

"I need to go into town after lunch," Simon said. "But I was thinking, when I get back, maybe we could go for a ride along the creek?"

"Sure," Sophie said.

So after lunch, Simon headed into town, leaving Sophie alone. She worked quickly to finish all the chores in time for their ride that afternoon.

As Sophie swept the front porch, she suddenly heard a horse and looked up. She squinted in the bright sunlight, struggling to make out the rider. Suddenly, she caught sight of a bay-green Stetson and she dropped the broom, her blood turning cold. She'd recognize that hat anywhere—Mr. Colton had given it to his son on his eighteenth birthday. Riding up toward the house was her stepbrother, Frank.

Chapter Twenty-Eight

Simon left the farm supply store with a smile on his face. On their ride this afternoon, he planned to tell Sophie how he felt about her, that he was in love with her.

As Simon climbed up into the saddle, he felt a mixture of emotions. The past few days had been a whirlwind, but things were finally coming right. Jarrett was gone, Jenna and Oliver would be home in the next week, and he was very much in love with his wife.

On the ride back up to the ranch, Simon had butterflies in his stomach, and the reins beneath his enclosed hands were sweaty. He could not recall the last time he had felt so nervous or if, in fact, he'd ever felt this nervous before.

It felt impossible to Simon that a few short weeks ago, he had not wanted to be Sophie's friend, and now he could not imagine his life without her. Still, that was the thing with love—it came when you least expected it.

As Simon rode through the ranch gate and up the driveway, he spotted a horse grazing near the barn. Simon had never seen a horse such as this one in Shadow's Ridge. It was a thoroughbred, to be sure, with his well-chiseled head, high withers, and lean body. Simon looked around for its rider, but there was no one by the barn. As Simon steered Buck to the stables, the stallion looked up at him for a moment, then bowed his head again and continued to graze.

Simon dismounted by the stables and left Buck outside. He headed into the kitchen, but it was empty, so he walked down the hallway and heard a stranger's voice coming from the front porch. Frowning, Simon stepped out to find Sophie alone with a man. They were standing on opposite sides of the porch, and a broom lay on the ground between them.

Simon looked from Sophie to the man. Whoever this stranger was, he certainly was not from around here. He was impeccably dressed in a green linen suit, and his copper-colored mustache was fashionably trimmed.

No one spoke for a moment. Sophie's face was pale, and her posture rigid. She was clutching the skirts of her dress with both hands, and Simon knew that something was wrong.

"Who are you?" Simon said, his tone hard.

"My name is Frank Colton," the man said, his voice nasally.

Simon frowned. He knew the name; Sophie had spoken about her stepbrother on occasion. Sophie had described him as a bully, a younger version of his father. She had detailed the trauma he'd inflicted on her over the years. As children, he would pinch and kick her whenever their parents weren't watching. As they grew older, Frank became more subtle in his forms of torment. When he wasn't whispering cruel words in her ear, he would also spy on her and report everything she did to his father.

"What are you doing here?" Simon demanded, his brown eyes flashing with anger.

"I've come to fetch my sister home," Frank said, looking away from Simon back to Sophie.

"I am not your sister," Sophie said, her voice wavering slightly. "And I am never going back to that place."

Simon walked over to Sophie, placing a hand on her lower back protectively. "Sophie is my wife," he said firmly. "Her place is here."

"Have you consummated the marriage?" he asked with an unabashed sneer.

"That's none of your business," Simon said as he gritted his teeth.

Frank smirked. "By the color of my sister's face, I would say not."

Simon looked down to see Sophie's pale face was now flushed,

"Look," Frank said as he took a step toward them, and Sophie flinched. "I don't know who you are, and I don't particularly care, but Sophie was already promised to marry someone else, and our father has spent a great deal of time and money looking for her."

Sophie was shaking now, and Simon secured his arm around her waist.

"Sophie is my wife, and this is my house, so I think you should leave," Simon said, his voice dangerously low.

Frank sighed loudly as he reached into his jacket and removed a leather pocketbook.

"How much?" he asked, looking up at Simon.

Simon said nothing as he bit the inside of his cheek, struggling to keep his anger under control.

"You must have a price," Frank said. "Looking around this dump, you could certainly use the money."

Simon took a step forward, his fists now in tight balls at his sides, but Sophie put a hand on his arm. "Don't," she said softly. "He's not worth it."

Frank smirked again.

"Get out now," Simon said, his voice shaking with anger. "Before I throw you out."

Frank did not move as he returned his pocketbook to his jacket.

"Fine," he agreed. "I'll go, but this isn't over; our father always gets what he wants."

"He isn't my father," Sophie said as she met Frank's gaze.

"Go," Simon ordered. "Now."

Frank left the porch without another word, and it was only when they heard the hooves of his thoroughbred disappearing into the distance that Sophie turned to Simon and placed her head on his chest, exhaling shakily. Simon put his arms around her.

Simon held Sophie until she stopped trembling and then took her into the kitchen. He sat her down at the table while he made some tea. She was still as white as a sheet when Simon placed the pot between them and sat down.

"How are you feeling?" he asked, his voice full of concern.

"I-I don't know," Sophie confessed as she looked across at him. "I never expected to have to see Frank again, and then all of a sudden, he was standing on the porch..."

Simon frowned as he took a sip of tea. "What did he say to you? Before I got back."

Sophie did not answer right away, as if she were trying to remember it word for word.

"I asked him how he had found me," Sophie said shakily.

"And what did he say?" Simon gently prompted.

"He smiled and told me that I'd led him right to my door."

Simon frowned, not understanding.

"It was the brooch," Sophie said, shaking her head.

"The brooch?" Simon said, his eyes widening in disbelief. "But how?"

Sophie sighed. "Even since I left, he's been traveling through the state looking for me," she said, her voice strained. "He was in a town not far from here when a woman passed him by in the street; she was wearing the brooch."

Simon listened to Sophie's explanation with a mixture of dread and disbelief. It wasn't her who'd led the wolf to the door—it was *him*.

"He recognized it," Sophie said. "When we were younger, Frank used to sneak into my bedroom and steal that brooch. He would hide it somewhere in the house just to torture me."

Simon's stomach tightened at the injustice of it.

"So when he saw the woman wearing it, he stopped and asked her where she'd gotten such an unusual piece of jewelry. When the woman explained her husband had traded it for a horse, Frank got your name from the horse seller and came straight to the ranch."

Simon looked at Sophie, unsure what to say. The unlikeliness of it all was astonishing, and yet it had happened.

"This is all my fault," Simon said, shaking his head. "I should have never traded the brooch."

"It's not your fault," Sophie assured him. "If my stepfather was as determined to find me as Frank said, then it was only a matter of time."

Simon exhaled heavily as he looked at Sophie, the corners of her mouth turned down.

"What do you think Frank is going to do?" Simon asked.

"I don't know," Sophie confessed. "But now that they've found me, they won't let me go until they've done everything in their power to bring me home."

"I won't let them," Simon said firmly.

Sophie said nothing, and without thinking, Simon got up from his seat and kneeled on the floor beside Sophie's chair. He took her hands in his and looked up at her.

"This isn't how I wanted to tell you," Simon confessed, holding Sophie's gaze. "But I've fallen in love with you, Sophie."

Sophie's eyes widened slightly, but she stayed silent, waiting for Simon to continue.

"I want us to have a proper marriage," Simon continued. "For us to be man and wife in every way possible, and I want children, a whole house full of children."

Simon knew he was gushing, and it was quite unlike him, but he meant every word, and now that he had gotten started, he was struggling to stop. He kept his eyes on Sophie as he spoke, his heart racing but when he was finished speaking, she dropped her gaze.

"So?" Simon said, his heart pounding. "What do you think?"

Sophie opened her mouth and then closed it again, and Simon's heart beat even louder, but as the seconds passed and Sophie said nothing, he lowered his gaze, his stomach sinking to his feet as he released her hands.

"I'm sorry," Simon said, getting up from the floor. "Just forget I said anything."

Then without another word, he turned away and headed out to the back door to the stables.

As Simon led Buckaroo into his stall, he wished he could take it all back, every word, but it was too late. He'd spilled his heart at Sophie's feet, and she'd said nothing in return. Simon had been terrified that this would happen, and now it had, and he just didn't see how their relationship could move past it.

Chapter Twenty-Nine

Sophie sat very still in her chair, her mind racing. What had just happened? Ever since the storm, finding Simon like that, Sophie had known she was in love with him. She wasn't exactly sure when it had started, but almost losing him like that had confirmed it. She had fallen in love with Simon.

Outside, Sophie heard Simon unlatch the stable doors, but she still did not move. Why had she not said anything when he confessed his feelings? Instead, she'd been frozen, unable to speak, to react. She'd seen the hurt in his eyes, the embarrassment, and still, she'd said nothing? She knew she had to make this right.

Sophie got up from the chair and walked out of the back door to the stables. As she approached, she could hear Simon inside, and she stopped in the doorway.

"Simon?" she said. "Can we talk?"

Simon said nothing as he continued to return the tack to their nails on the stable wall.

"Simon—"

"I've got a lot of work to do," Simon said coolly, still not turning around. "Can it wait?"

"No," Sophie said firmly. "It can't. I am sorry that I didn't say anything in the kitchen—"

"We don't have to talk about it," Simon said, cutting her off. "I should never have said anything—"

"I am glad you did," Sophie said. "Because I want all those things too, Simon. I want to be your wife and to carry your children. I want us to be a family."

Simon still had his back to her, but suddenly he turned to face her, and she could see the confusion in his eyes.

"You want to have a family?" he asked, his brow creasing.

"Yes," Sophie said tenderly.

"But earlier, in the kitchen, you said nothing?" Simon said.

Sophie sighed. "I know, and I am sorry. You were saying everything that I wanted to hear, and all I could think about was how it could all be taken away from me. I want us to have a life together, but Frank turning up today, it just feels like every time we find a modicum of happiness, it gets taken away. I was scared to tell you how I feel because I'm worried I could lose you at any moment."

Simon said nothing for a moment, his eyes on Sophie.

"You're in love with me?" he asked, holding her gaze.

"I'm in love with you," she confirmed, putting as much feeling as she could into every word.

In an instant, Simon was there. He wrapped his arms around Sophie's waist, and as he did, he leaned in and kissed her. She closed her eyes as the whole world dropped away at that moment; nothing existed except the two of them.

Simon's lips were warm and soft against hers, and Sophie's heart raced like the wings of a hummingbird beating against her rib cage.

When the kiss dissolved into memory, Sophie met Simon's eyes, and she smiled, the color high in her cheeks. Simon returned her smile, and for a moment, neither of them spoke, not ready for the moment to end.

"I could get used to this," Simon said softly, his eyes twinkling.

Sophie smiled again as she placed her head on his chest and listened to the beat of his heart. Without realizing it, she sighed.

"You okay?" Simon asked, looking down at her.

"I just wish we could stop time and stay like this forever."

"Hey," Simon said as Sophie lifted her head and looked up into his eyes. "This is just the beginning for us, okay? I won't let them take you away."

Sophie nodded, and she silently prayed that Simon was right.

***

The days that followed were some of the happiest of Sophie's whole life. She and Simon could hardly keep their hands off one another and spent as much time as they could in each other's company. Sophie moved into Simon's bedroom and they lay awake at night snuggled together, talking until dawn. Sophie did all her chores in the morning and then helped Simon out on the ranch in the afternoon. When all the work was done, they went on long rides, returning home only when the first stars began to twinkle in the sky above.

Yet despite this love bubble they were in, a shadow loomed, and as much as Sophie wanted to pretend it wasn't there, she couldn't. The knowledge that Frank was just a few miles away in town gnawed at her insides, making it impossible for her to be truly happy. It also made her resentful; after all this time, could they not just leave her be?

"Sophie?" Simon said, coming into the kitchen. "I've got good news."

Sophie turned from where she was washing windows just as Simon stepped in from the hallway.

"What is it?" Sophie asked.

"I stopped in to speak with Sheriff Duncan, and he says we can write to Jenna and tell her to come home?"

"Really?" Sophie said in excitement.

Simon grinned and nodded. "He reckons Jarrett is long gone, so it is safe for them to return."

Sophie walked over to Simon and put her arms around his waist. She stood on her tippy-toes and kissed him on the lips. Simon smiled.

"I am going to write to Jenna now and take the letter into town this afternoon," Simon said. "I want to get it to her as soon as possible."

"Good idea," Sophie agreed.

Simon leaned down and kissed her again, and Sophie dropped her arms, letting him go. She then turned back to the windows. As she cleaned, she caught her reflection in the glass, and she was smiling. Jenna and Oliver were finally coming home, and their family would be together again.

After lunch, Simon left for town again to deliver the letter to the post office. Sophie had promised to do the ranch chores while he was out.

Sophie stood by the chicken coop as she did; she reached into the pail and removed a handful of kitchen scraps to scatter on the ground. From all corners of the ranch, the chickens came running, fighting over the vegetable peels, old pieces of bread, and bits of grit. Sophie watched them for a moment before she turned back to the barn, but as she did, she heard carriage wheels coming up the drive, and her heart stopped.

Sophie would know her stepfather's carriage anywhere. It had a low-slung body with a curved roof and open sides. The sides were covered with ornate carvings, and the interior was done up in the finest upholstery. Like everything Mr. Colton had, the carriage was a status symbol, something he could use to show off to his friends.

Sophie stood frozen on the spot for a moment, wondering if she should run, but as she considered it, she realized that she didn't want to keep running. So she stood her ground.

The carriage came to a stop outside the barn, and the door opened. Sophie's heart raced as Mr. Colton stepped out, followed by her mother. Frank was not with them. Her stepfather was dressed in a well-tailored, dark blue linen suit and her mother wore a white, high-necked dress of the finest silk. Against the backdrop of the old barn, they looked entirely out of place.

"Sophie!" her mother said, walking over to her. "Thank goodness you are all right."

She pulled Sophie into an awkward hug.

"We've been worried sick about you," she said, her tone slightly disapproving. "How could you just take off like that in the middle of the night?"

Up until that point, Mr. Colton had said nothing, but his hard eyes were unblinking as he looked at Sophie.

"I had to go, Ma," Sophie said. "So I could finally be free—"

Mr. Colton scoffed rudely, his eyes glinting dangerously. "We gave you everything. Your whole life, you have wanted for nothing, and this is how you repay us? By sneaking away in the middle of the night and marrying some poor rancher with nothing to his name? Do you have any idea how much shame you've brought on me? On your mother?"

Sophie glared at her stepfather. "Well, it's a good thing I am not your daughter, then."

Without hesitating, her stepfather slapped her hard across the cheek, and the sharp sound lingered for a moment. Sophie brought a hand up to her cheek before dropping it again. Her mother averted her eyes and she said nothing in Sophie's defense.

"Go and pack your things," he said, pointing at the house. "We are taking you home."

"No," Sophie said, shaking her head, her cheek burning. "This is my home now."

"Sophie," her mother implored. "This is not your home."

"This *is* my home," Sophie insisted.

"Do not make me ask again," Mr. Colton said, his voice dangerously low.

"My husband will be home soon," Sophie said, trying to keep her voice from wavering. "So I think you should go."

Sophie was about to turn and walk away, but as she did, her stepfather grabbed her wrist tightly.

"Let me go," Sophie said as she struggled to free herself from his grip.

But Mr. Colton only gripped her harder, twisting and pinching the skin as he did. Sophie looked at her mother for help, but she stood back, wordlessly biting her bottom lip.

"You're an ungrateful little witch," he said between gritted teeth. "I should whip you for your insolence."

Sophie stared into his eyes, which were burning with fury. She continued to struggle against his iron-clad grip when she heard a horse whinny, and she turned to see Simon galloping up to them, dust rising in his wake.

"I'll thank you to take your hands off my wife," Simon said as he leapt from his horse and marched straight up to Mr. Colton.

He grabbed him by the collar of the shirt, pushing him against the side of the carriage. Simon easily lifted him off his feet, his thumbs pressing into Mr. Colton's neck.

Sophie watched the anger in her stepfather's eyes melt into fear, proving that, when all was said and done, bullies were just cowards.

"I've heard all about you," Simon said, his hands still gripping Mr. Colton's collar, his fingers pressing even harder into his throat. "And I've often thought about what I'd do to you if I ever got the chance."

"Let go of me," Mr. Colton gasped.

But Simon tightened his grip.

"Over the years, people have gone missing in these mountains," he said, his voice low. "Never to be seen again, no bodies found to tell their stories. Just gone, without a trace."

Mr. Colton's puce face paled slightly. He was gasping for air now.

"Please," Sophie's mother said, her eyes wide. "He can't breathe."

Still, Simon did not let him go; his whole body shook with rage.

"Simon," Sophie said, placing a hand on his back. "It's okay, I am all right."

Simon stopped trembling, and after a moment, he let Mr. Colton go. Her stepfather fell to his knees, spluttering and gasping as he tried to catch his breath.

"If you, or your son, *ever* come back here or try to take Sophie from me, I will make sure they never find your bodies," Simon growled as he looked down at Mr. Colton in disgust.

He turned to Sophie and took her in his arms.

"You've made a grave mistake," Mr. Colton said as he pulled himself to his feet, his voice hoarse. "Do you have any idea who I am?"

"I know exactly who you are," Simon said, his eyes glowering. "And I know that you've spent years torturing Sophie, but she is my family now, and if you try anything, I will come for you, and there won't be enough money in the world to save you when I do."

Sophie looked at her stepfather and she saw the look in his eyes. He was afraid of Simon.

Mr. Colton turned to her mother. "Are you just going to stand there? Say something to her."

Sophie looked at her mother, who was pale and trembling.

"Sophie," she said. "Come home, please—"

"No," Sophie said firmly. "That place hasn't been my home for a long time, and you know that. You saw what was happening, and you said nothing. So you have no right to stand here now and ask me to go back."

"Sophie," her mother said, her eyes pleading. "I did what I had to do to make sure you had everything you could want. That you could have a better life than I had—"

"I didn't want everything," Sophie interjected, her voice thick with emotion. "I just wanted you, but you were never there for me; you never fought for me."

Sophie shook her head, blinking back tears. She'd wanted to tell her mother for years how she felt, but she'd always been too afraid. Telling her the truth, how she felt, it was hard, but it was also liberating.

"If you want to do something for me, then go," Sophie said. "Go and never come back."

Her mother continued to plead silently with her eyes as she took a step toward Sophie, but she took a step back, shaking her head.

"I've finally found a place that feels like home, and a family who wants me," Sophie said. "And I'll never give it up."

"They are welcome to you," Mr. Colton spat, brushing dust off his jacket sleeves. "You were always trouble, and after your little disappearing act, Mr. Beaumont called off the engagement, so you are no longer of any value to us. If your mother hadn't insisted we look for you, I wouldn't have bothered."

Sophie gritted her teeth but said nothing.

"I think you should go now," Simon said.

Mr. Colton puffed out his chest as he looked up at Simon. "I hope she brings you as much misery and trouble as she brought us."

"A life of misery and trouble sounds perfect to me," Simon said, tightening his grip on Sophie.

"Goodbye, Ma," Sophie said, looking across at her mother.

Sophie's mother opened her mouth but then closed it again, and Sophie's heart sank. Her mother had never been able to speak up, not even now, when it was the last thing she'd ever say to her.

"Get in the carriage, Lauren," Mr. Colton barked.

Without another word, Sophie's mother turned and walked back to the carriage. Mr. Colton gave Sophie and Simon a hard look before he turned and left, slamming the carriage door loudly.

Sophie and Simon did not talk as they watched the carriage drive down toward the gate.

These last few days, Sophie had been so afraid of facing them again, but now she was glad, because she wasn't scared anymore. Her stepfather had always seemed so big and untouchable, but he wasn't. He was just a man, a cowardly man who took pleasure in belittling and intimidating women.

While Sophie did not know if she'd ever see her mother again, she hoped she found the courage to stand up for herself. She wished that for her—that, even after everything, she might break free and find happiness, just as Sophie had managed to do.

"Are you all right?" Simon asked, looking down at her.

Sophie nodded, allowing the relief to finally flood through her. "I feel better, actually. Like I can finally stop looking over my shoulder."

Simon kissed her on the top of the head as the carriage disappeared into the distance. He'd promised to protect her and he had. He'd stood up for her against her stepfather, something no one had ever done, and she loved him even more for it.

SALLY M. ROSS

Sophie sighed softly as she looked up at Simon, and he leaned down and kissed her. With Simon's help, she'd closed a terrible chapter in her life. She could finally move on and be happy with Simon. She was free.

Chapter Thirty

Simon and Sophie stood on the front porch, staring out at the road. They were holding hands, their fingers intertwined, like branches of two trees growing together. It was late afternoon, and the ranch was bathed in golden sunlight. This was Simon's favorite time of day; it always felt like there was magic in the air. Today was all the more special because Jenna and Oliver were finally coming home.

"I bet Oliver's grown," Sophie said affectionately as she glanced up at Simon.

"Oh yes," Simon agreed, his lips quivering. "He'll be about six feet tall now."

Sophie rolled her eyes as she playfully poked Simon in the ribs with her elbow.

Three days had passed since Sophie's family had come to fetch her, and since then, they'd not seen or heard from them again. Simon greatly hoped it would stay like that. While Simon was not sure one could ever entirely escape their past, he'd noticed a change in Sophie these past few days.

She was lighter somehow, and she smiled more easily. Sophie had once told Simon how afraid she was that one day her past would one day catch up with her, and yet when her greatest fear had come true, they'd stood together and won. Simon did not believe there was anything that they could not overcome together, and it was a great feeling, the best feeling in the world, to know that no matter what hardships lay ahead, he was not alone.

"What's taking them so long?" Sophie said impatiently.

Simon smiled. Ever since they'd learned Jenna was on her way home, Sophie had been counting down the minutes. He couldn't blame her; he couldn't wait to have them home, either.

In the distance, Simon heard the crunch of rock and stone, and Sophie squeezed his hand in excitement as the wagon came into view.

"Come on," Sophie said, laughing as she dragged Simon off the porch. She broke into a run, pulling Simon along behind her. They reached the entrance to the ranch just as the wagon did, and it came to a stop. Jenna was seated beside the wagon driver with Oliver on her lap, and when she saw them, she smiled brightly.

"Jenna!" Sophie panted, her face flushed with exertion and her eyes wide with excitement. "You're home."

"You two are a sight for sore eyes," Jenna said, beaming at them.

Simon smiled, pleased to see how well his cousin looked. The dark circles under her eyes were gone, and her skin complexion was brighter.

"Would you take Oliver?" Jenna asked as she handed the little boy to Sophie.

Sophie took the little boy and hugged him tightly; as she had predicted, he had grown.

"I missed you, Ollie," Sophie said, planting little kisses all over the boy's face, and he giggled.

Simon helped Jenna to the ground and as he did, she put her arms around him and hugged him tightly. "I missed you, cousin," she said.

"I missed you too," Simon said, his heart swelling.

The driver of the wagon cleared his throat loudly, and Jenna pulled out of Simon's arms.

"Sorry," she apologized as she reached into her skirt pocket and gave the driver his payment.

The wagon driver tipped his hat to them before turning the wagon around and heading back toward town.

"How's my boy?" Simon said as Sophie handed Oliver to him.

The little boy placed his tiny hands on Simon's face, and he closed his eyes in joy. He hadn't realized how much he'd missed him.

"Oh!" Jenna said suddenly. "My bag!"

Without another word, she turned tail and raced after the wagon driver, waving her arms above her head. He came to a halt, and Jenna climbed onto the back of the wagon to retrieve her bag. She then hurried back to the gate.

"It is so good to have you home," Sophie said as she slipped her arm around Jenna's waist.

"It's so good to be home," Jenna said, sliding her around Sophie's shoulders.

"Should we get back up to the house?" Simon said. "Put on a pot of tea?"

Jenna nodded enthusiastically, and they all walked back up to the house. When they reached it, Jenna came to a stop, looking up at the house.

"What's wrong?" Sophie asked her.

"It's nothing," Jenna said, shaking her head. "It's just that... when I left this place, I didn't think I'd ever be coming home again."

Simon smiled at his cousin. "Well, you are back now."

They continued up to the house and went around to the back door. Sophie had spent all afternoon baking, and the kitchen smelled like warm apples and spicy cinnamon.

"You made an apple pie?" Jenna said, not bothering to hide her surprise.

"Sophie's become quite the cook in your absence," Simon said as he smiled lovingly at Sophie, who flushed.

Jenna tilted her head as she looked between them. "I see that's not the only thing that's changed around here."

Simon grinned sheepishly.

"I am going to put Ollie down for his nap," Jenna said as she took him from Simon. "And then I expect to hear all the news."

While Jenna was putting Oliver down, Simon helped Sophie make the tea. He stood close behind her as the copper kettle boiled, basking in her warmth and her smell. He would never grow tired of being near her. He leaned forward and kissed the back of her neck, and Sophie sighed softly, melting into him.

Jenna returned just as they put the teapot and mugs down on the table. She smiled at them as she took her seat.

"He go down okay?" Sophie asked as she poured the tea.

Jenna nodded. "I think he was exhausted from the trip."

Sophie passed Simon a mug, and as he reached for it, their hands touched, and he gently brushed her hand with his thumb.

"Okay," Jenna said firmly as she sat back in her chair. "What's going on with you two? Spill!"

Sophie looked at Simon, her cheeks flushing.

"I knew it," Jenna said as she beamed at them. "I knew that eventually you two would see what I see."

"And what is that?" Simon asked curiously.

"That you're perfect for each other," Jenna said, shrugging.

Simon caught Sophie's eye again, and she was smiling.

"So now that I know you two are madly in love, what else has happened?" Jenna asked as she took a sip of tea and leaned forward.

"Sophie's family show up," Simon said, raising his eyebrows.

"What?" Jenna said, coughing as tea nearly came out of her nose. "What happened?"

Simon and Sophie told Jenna the whole story, not sparing any of the details, and by the time they were finished, Jenna was on the edge of her seat.

"So they are gone?" she asked. "For good?"

"I think so," Sophie said. "I've never seen my stepfather like that before—afraid."

"He's a coward," Simon said plainly. "But he's not stupid. I meant what I said, and he knew it. Men like Mr. Colton always put self-preservation before pride."

Jenna sat back in her chair and crossed her arms. "I guess I missed all the fun."

Simon grimaced. "Fun" was not what he would've called it.

"How have you been?" Sophie asked as she looked across at Jenna. "How was William's Town?"

Jenna did not answer right away as she reached for the teapot and filled her cup again.

"Rose's parents were very kind to us," Jenna said, smiling fondly. "They treated Oliver like their grandson."

Simon smiled, glad that they'd been safe.

"They have a small house in town, and Rose's pa is a gardener, so on some days, Rose's ma cared for Oliver, and I helped in the gardens—"

Jenna smiled at the memory, but her eyes were sad.

"Being away from home and from you both was hard, but I also think now that I needed to be somewhere else. It felt like, for the first time, as if I was breathing air that he wasn't breathing, and I needed that to finally start healing."

Simon looked at his cousin and his heart swelled with pride.

"When I left here, I thought that one day I'd be able to come home," Jenna continued. "But the more time I spent in William's Town, the more I realized that I could never come back here, not while he was still in Shadow's Ridge."

Jenna shook her head sadly. "I couldn't reconcile the idea of Oliver growing up not knowing you both, and then I got a visit from Sheriff Fields, and he told me that Laura had made a statement."

Sophie nodded. "We went to see her in Willow's Creek."

"She wrote to me a few days ago," Jenna said, smiling at them. "She told me what you two did, how you wouldn't give up until we were a family again."

"We tried," Simon said, nodding. "But it was Sheriff Duncan who came through for us in the end. If he hadn't reached out to his contacts, spoken with the newspaper man..."

"I still can't believe it," Jenna said, shaking her head. "All those women, all those lives."

Sophie reached across the table and squeezed Jenna's hand.

"He's gone now," she said. "He's not coming back."

Jenna closed her eyes for a moment and exhaled. "I know," she said, opening her eyes again. "And I am glad I never have to see him again, but there is no justice in it. How can he do so much harm and just get away with it?"

Simon nodded. His cousin was right; there was no justice in it.

"Sheriff Duncan is not giving up," Sophie said. "He'll keep looking for him."

The room fell silent for a moment, and Simon looked over at Jenna, who was staring into her cup, her brow creased. Jarrett was gone, but if they never found him, if there was no justice, then the reality of him returning one day would always be a possibility.

"I think I might go and lie down with Ollie for a bit," Jenna said. "It was a long trip."

"Of course," Sophie said, smiling. "I'll wake you up when dinner is ready."

Jenna smiled gratefully as she got up from her chair and left the kitchen. Sophie got up, too, and carried the mugs to the sink. As she washed them, Simon slipped his arms around her waist, resting his chin on her shoulder.

"Do you think Jenna will be all right?" Simon asked.

"It'll take time, I think," Sophie said. "If they don't catch Jarrett, she'll have to learn to live with the possibility that he might come back."

Simon sighed. He wished the sheriff could find Jarrett and lock him away. The women deserved to move on with their lives and never have to look him in the eyes ever again.

"Do you fancy a walk?" Simon asked.

"Sure," Sophie agreed. "There is still a bit of time before supper."

Sophie dried her hands on her apron and then untied it, hanging it on the hook behind the door. Simon took her hand and led her out the back door. They walked past the barn and stables as the sun started sinking below the tree line. As they walked, they talked about Jenna and Oliver, and how good it was to all be together again.

Dusk came quickly, and by the time they returned to the house, they'd lost track of time. Simon hurried to the stables to feed the horses while Sophie went inside to start the supper. The last rays of light were beginning to fade when Simon returned to the kitchen. He found Sophie at the stove.

"Supper is almost done," Sophie said. "Would you please call Jenna?"

Simon nodded as he walked through the kitchen and down the hallway. He stopped outside Jenna's bedroom and rapped on the door with his knuckles.

"Jenna?" he said. "Supper is almost ready."

There was no reply, and Simon frowned. He reached down and turned the doorknob. As he pushed the door open, he saw Oliver asleep in his crib. But when he turned his head toward the bed, he froze. In the fading light from the open window, he found Jenna. However, she was not alone— behind her stood Jarrett Davidson, brandishing a silver blade at her throat.

Chapter Thirty-One

Sophie took the peas off the stove and carried them to the sink, pouring them out into the colander.

"Simon?" she called over her shoulder. "Did you call Jenna?"

Sophie waited for a reply, but there was none, and she frowned. She hung the kitchen cloth over her shoulder and turned from the sink, but as she did, Simon appeared in the doorway.

"Where's Jenna?"

Simon said nothing, but his pale face and locked jaw told her something was terribly wrong.

"Simon?"

He stepped into the kitchen, and it was only then that Sophie saw Jenna, with a knife to her throat, being shoved forward by Jarrett Davidson.

"Sit down," Jarrett commanded.

Sophie did not move.

"I said sit down!" he yelled, his voice cracking.

Simon walked over to her, took her hand, and led her to the table. They sat down and then looked over at Jarrett. He'd always been a terrifying man, but he was scarier now. His once-fine suit was disheveled, torn, and dirty. Stubble covered his chin, and his hair was matted and scruffy. From his appearance, he'd been living rough, and it was clear that it was not something he was used to, nor did it suit him. Sophie saw a wildness in his blue eyes that had not been there before.

"Jarrett, please," Simon said, keeping his voice level.

Jarrett pressed the knife harder, and Jenna whimpered.

"I should slit her throat and let her bleed out on the floor," Jarrett said.

Jenna whimpered again as Sophie's heart raced.

"We can talk about this, Jarrett," Simon said, holding his gaze.

"Talk?" Jarrett said, his voice now dangerously low. "I think you've all done enough talking."

"Please," Sophie implored. "Just let Jenna go, and we can figure this out—"

"You've ruined my life," Jarrett snapped, his blue eyes hardening like steel. "I have nothing left. No business, no fiancée, no friends. You've taken everything from me—"

"And don't you think any of it was your own fault?" Simon challenged.

Sophie frowned at him, but he tilted his head slightly, indicating to her that he had a plan.

"My fault?" Jarrett said, his eyes flashing.

"You attacked my cousin and those other women," Simon said, not breaking eye contact. "You destroyed their lives—"

"They wanted it," Jarrett said. "Each and every one of them."

"No," Simon said firmly. "None of them wanted it. You attacked them."

Jarrett smiled, and it sent shivers down Sophie's back. "My father always said that a woman's worth is all under her skirts."

Simon frowned, shaking his head. "Your father was wrong, and so are you. Why don't you be a real man and take responsibility for what you've done? Stop being such a coward—"

Jarrett's grip tightened on the knife, and Sophie glanced at Simon, trying to figure out what he was trying to achieve by riling up the man with a knife to Jenna's throat.

"What did you call me?" Jarrett said, his voice near a whisper.

"You're a coward," Simon repeated. "You prey on women because you think that life owes you something. But the truth is that you are a weak man who takes what doesn't belong to him because he isn't man enough to earn the love and respect of a woman."

Jenna was trembling as a crimson hairline appeared along her throat.

"Simon," Sophie warned.

No one spoke for a moment; Sophie could not take her eyes off Jenna. Her heart was racing so quickly that she could hear the blood rushing in her ears.

"If you want to punish someone, then punish me," Simon said.

Sophie looked at Simon, but his gaze was fixed on Jarrett.

"Maybe you are right," Jarrett said, his eyes glowering. "But what better way to punish you than take away the people you love the most? Starting with Jenna, then your wife, and then the baby—"

Up until this point, Jenna had not moved or uttered a single word but at the mention of Oliver, something snapped, and she struggled, for the first time, her eyes wild, primal.

"No," she said, her voice a strangled cry. "Not my baby, please—"

Jarrett sneered nastily as he tightened his grip on Jenna.

"You're a monster," Sophie said, her eyes flashing with anger and fear.

"Perhaps I am," Jarrett said, turning his cold gaze on her. "And perhaps *you* are the fools for thinking you could win."

All her life, Sophie had known monsters existed, but they did not live in cupboards or under the bed; they were flesh and blood, humans twisted out of shape by life. In her experience, it was prosperity that turned men into monsters, and adversity that made men.

"You don't have to do this, Jarrett," Simon said, his tone turning desperate. "Everyone thinks you're gone, so just go."

Jarrett frowned, and for the first time, Sophie saw a hint of vulnerability in his face; it was slight, but it was there.

"Go?" he said, his dark brows furrowing. "Go where? I have no home, no family. You've taken it all from me—"

"I have some money," Simon said. "It's not much, but you can have it all if you just drop the knife."

Jarrett smiled, amused by Simon's suggestion. "I didn't come here for money."

Sophie looked at Simon, and she knew they were clutching at straws. It was only a matter of time before Jarrett grew tired of talking.

"We have horses," Sophie said, thinking of Silver. "You can take them."

Simon nodded, but Jarrett shook his head.

"No," he said simply. "I came here for one thing only, and when you are all dead, I will set this house alight, and once it is burned to the ground, I will dance on your ashes—"

"And then what?" Simon challenged. "You're a wanted man."

But Jarrett did not answer and Sophie guessed he did not have a plan after they were all dead. All he cared about was getting his revenge.

Suddenly, a loud wail came from the bedroom, and Jarrett was distracted for a moment. It was just a moment, but Simon took the opportunity and leaped out of his chair, which clattered to the ground. He threw himself at Jarrett, who pushed Jenna away as he raised his hands in defense. Jenna fell to the floor in a heap. As Simon wrestled Jarrett to the ground, the men rolled and grunted as they fought, the knife still in Jarrett's hand.

"Jenna," Sophie said as she rushed over to her. She dropped to the floor, placing her hands on Jenna's back. "Are you all right?"

Jenna nodded as Sophie helped her up. Her throat was bleeding, and her face was as white as a sheet.

"You're hurt," Sophie said in concern.

"I need to go to Oliver," Jenna said, rushing past Sophie.

The clatter of the knife on the floor caught Sophie's attention. With her heart in her throat, she turned and was relieved to see Simon sitting on Jarrett's back; he had his hands bent behind him. Jarrett struggled loudly as Simon removed his belt and used it to secure his wrists together.

"Let me go," he demanded as he wriggled.

"You're too much of a narcissist to see who you really are," Simon said as he roughly tightened the belt, its silver buckle winking in the lamp light as he moved. "But in the end, we are all a result of the choices we make, and I don't doubt that very soon you are going to wish that you had made *many* different choices."

Once he'd secured Jarrett's hands, Simon lifted him up and into a sitting position in a chair. As he did, Jenna stepped into the room alone.

"Is Oliver okay?" Sophie asked.

Jenna nodded but said nothing. She was not looking at Sophie but at something behind her. Sophie turned to see what Jenna was looking at and saw Jarrett's knife. It was on the floor by the table, glinting in the light of the small paraffin lamp. Sophie turned back to Jenna, and before she could stop her, Jenna rushed across the room and picked it up. She marched right up to Jarrett and pointed the knife at him, her hand trembling.

"You don't have the guts," Jarrett said, his bravado wavering.

"Jenna," Simon cautioned. "What are you doing?"

"He deserves to die," Jenna said, her voice full of anger. She pushed the knife to his throat as he had to hers only moments ago. "And no one would miss him or come looking."

Sophie looked at Jarrett. Fear and apprehension filled his blue eyes now. He knew as well as they did that no one would look for him. No one outside of that kitchen would ever learn the truth. Sophie could not argue with Jenna that Jarrett deserved to be punished, but if they let her kill him, then he'd always be there, hanging over all of them like a ghost.

"Jenna," Sophie said. "If you do this, you will never be free of him."

"I'll never be free of him if I don't," Jenna said, her voice trembling now.

"Sophie is right," Simon said. "You are not like him, and the price of taking his life will stay with you for the rest of your life."

Jenna's hand shook, and no one spoke for a long moment. Then Jenna exhaled heavily, dropping the knife at her feet.

Simon walked over and picked up the knife. Without another word, Jenna turned away from Jarrett and left the kitchen.

Simon turned to Sophie, his face pale. "Can you ride into town and fetch the sheriff?"

Sophie nodded, hesitating only a moment before she turned and left the kitchen. She rushed to the stables in the dark. Once inside, she lit the small lamp and managed to saddle Silver in the dim light.

Sophie was in a hurry to get into town, but Silver did not know the road well, especially in the dark, and the trip took longer than she'd hoped. She did not like the idea of her family being alone with Jarrett. She wanted him arrested as soon as possible and for them all to be safe at last.

When she got to the sheriff's office, it was all shut up, and Sophie frowned. She had no idea where the sheriff lived, so she turned Silver toward the saloon. When the old stone building came into view, Rose appeared in the doorway; she must have seen her coming from the window.

"Sophie?" Rose said, frowning. "What are you doing here? Is everything all right?"

"I need to get the sheriff," Sophie said urgently. "Do you know where he lives?"

"I can show you," Rose said, crossing the narrow porch. "What's happened?"

"Jarrett was at the house tonight," Sophie explained.

"What?" Rose said, stopping dead in her tracks.

"He tried to kill Jenna—"

Rose's eyes widened in shock and horror.

"But she's safe. Simon managed to save her; he's got him tied up in the kitchen at the house, which is why I need to fetch the sheriff."

Rose walked out to the street and directed Sophie to the sheriff's house, one street over at the end.

"I'll come up to the ranch as soon as work is over," Rose promised.

Sophie nodded as she set off down the street.

As Rose had said, the sheriff's house was the last one, and she dismounted Silver and rushed up to the front door. She rapped loudly on the wood with her knuckles, and a moment later, Sheriff Duncan appeared in the doorway.

"Sophie?" he said, frowning.

"We've got him, Sheriff," Sophie gushed. "We've got Jarrett."

Sheriff Duncan's eyebrows shot up toward his hairline. "Let's go."

Together she and the sheriff set off back up the steep hill toward the ranch; as they rode, Sophie told him all had transpired that evening.

As they came up the drive, however, they found Simon on the back of Buckaroo, and from his expression, Sophie knew something was wrong.

"He's gone," Simon said grimly.

"What?" Sophie gasped.

"I turned my back for a second to check on Jenna," Simon said. "But he can't have gone far—"

"Let's go," Sheriff Duncan said, gripping tighter to the reins.

"I'm coming too," Sophie insisted.

"No," Simon said, his face softening. "You need to stay here with Jenna."

Sophie knew he was right, but that did not quell the fear gnawing at her insides.

"Be careful," she said.

"Don't worry," Simon said. "I know these mountains like the back of my hand."

Sophie tried to smile.

"We need to go," the sheriff said with urgency. "Now."

The two men set off into the darkness without another word, and Sophie watched them go with a hollow stomach.

She did not like Simon being out there in the dark, and even less so with Jarrett Davidson out in the wild.

Epilogue

Simon and the sheriff rode east, through the pastures and out into the mountainous terrain. It was difficult to navigate in the dark; the new moon was pale in the sky above them, and so all they had to guide them were the stars.

"You certain he went this way?" Sheriff Duncan asked.

Simon nodded as he steered Buck down the rocky path. He and the sheriff fell silent, listening for any sounds that might give Jarrett's location away, but the night was quiet.

Simon was angry with himself for letting Jarrett escape, but he could not think about that now. He needed to focus.

"Let's head to the top of that hill," Simon suggested. "It should give us a clear view for a mile or so."

Sheriff Duncan nodded and Simon steered Buck up toward the hill. Simon brought Buck to a stop just before the land fell away into a slope. Down below was a bed of jagged rocks. Simon turned to see the sheriff several feet behind, his horse struggling to navigate the steep hill in the dark.

Simon turned back, squinting out into the darkness for any sign of movement. From the top of the hill he had a good view, but the land was still. He was about to turn away when he saw it, a flash of silver, and he glanced down the slope. In the dim light, he saw Jarrett's body lying among the rocks. He wasn't moving. His hands were still tied with Simon's leather belt and his legs jutted out at strange angles. From where he was, Simon could not tell if his eyes were open.

"See anything?" Sheriff Duncan asked as he brought his horse up beside Simon's.

"I think we can stop searching now," Simon said gingerly.

***

As Simon expected, Sophie was waiting for him at the back door when he arrived home.

"What happened?" she asked, hurrying up to him. "Where's the sheriff?"

Simon climbed down from the horse and turned to her. Sophie's blue eyes were wide with concern.

"Jarrett's dead," Simon said as Sophie raised a hand to her mouth in shock. "He fell down the side of a hill and broke his neck. Sheriff's taking the body back to town as we speak."

"He's dead?" Sophie repeated in disbelief.

Simon nodded. He could not pretend that he had not imagined that fate for Jarrett a million times, yet there was something sad about it. He'd never get the chance to find redemption now, or try to make up for his behavior. He'd died a monster.

"Where's Jenna?" Simon asked, peering around Sophie.

"With Oliver," Sophie said.

Simon exhaled deeply. "I'd better go and tell her."

Sophie nodded. "I'll take care of Buck."

Simon handed her the reins. Without another word, he headed inside the house and to Jenna's bedroom, knocking softly on the door.

"Come in," Jenna said, her voice low.

Simon pushed open the bedroom door and stepped inside. Jenna was sitting on the bed beside the crib, but she did not look up when Simon came in. He walked over to her and sat down next to her. Neither of them spoke for a moment.

"We found Jarrett," Simon said, and he felt Jenna's body stiffen. "He's dead. He fell."

Jenna turned to him, her face pale.

"He's dead?" she asked, mirroring Sophie's response.

Simon nodded. "He broke his neck."

Jenna did not speak for a long moment before she exhaled shakily.

"I thought I would be happy," she said, shaking her head. "But I don't think I am."

Simon understood. It was the cost of compassion, feeling this way. Despite everything Jarrett had taken from Jenna, he'd never been able to take her compassion. It was why she hadn't been able to take his life in the kitchen, and why she couldn't be happy that he was now dead.

"I can't believe he's actually gone," Jenna said as she looked into the crib.

Simon put his arm around her shoulders and she rested her head on his shoulder.

"What am I going to tell Oliver?" Jenna said, her voice small. "When he asks about his pa?"

Simon said nothing for a moment before he looked away from Oliver and down at Jenna.

"I don't know the answer," Simon confessed. "But what I do know is that we'll raise him to understand how loved he is, how valued, and we will create a home for him where he always belongs. We'll do all this so that if there comes a time to tell him the truth, he will know that he is worth so much more than that story. That he is, and will always be, so much more than where he came from."

Jenna looked up at Simon and her green eyes were full of tenderness.

"Thank you," she whispered.

She placed her head on his shoulder again and Simon rested his head on hers. They sat like that for a long while, staring down at Oliver as he slept peacefully in his crib.

Simon eventually got up and closed the bedroom door behind him as he stepped out into the hall. He turned and headed to the kitchen where Sophie was standing at the window, staring out into the night. Simon had no idea what time it was, but he guessed it was a few hours after midnight.

As Simon entered the room, Sophie turned and smiled, her brow slightly creased.

"How is Jenna?" she asked.

Simon sighed heavily. "She's going to try and get some sleep."

Sophie nodded. Simon walked over to her and put his arms around her waist; she melted into him, her head on his chest, and he closed his eyes, breathing in the scent of her.

"I am worried about her," Simon said softly.

"I know," Sophie agreed as she lifted her head and looked up at him. "It will take time, but Jarrett is gone, so maybe Jenna can finally stop looking over her shoulder and start living again."

Simon nodded. None of them knew how long it would take for Jenna to be able to close this chapter of her life, or if she'd ever be able to. Still, Sophie was right—Jarrett was gone and with him, the threat that had been hanging over all of them for months.

"We should probably try to get some sleep," Sophie said as she stifled a yawn.

"I don't want to let go of you just yet," Simon said, leaning down and kissing her.

"Then don't," Sophie said softly, a smile in her voice.

Simon kissed her again.

They stayed by the window for a long time as the world outside slept. Simon could not stop thinking how differently things could have gone for them that night. If Oliver hadn't woken at just that moment, if Jarrett had succeeded in enacting his revenge. They had been on the verge of losing everything, and yet by God's grace, they were all safe. Simon had never been so grateful for a new day with his family.

***

The house was quiet when Simon got up later that morning. He made some coffee, and drank it at the kitchen window. It was already midmorning and none of the chores had been done. They'd all slept in after the disruptive night.

Simon drained his cup and left the kitchen to get to work. As Simon entered the stables, both Buckaroo and Silver whinnied at him.

"I know I am late," Simon said apologetically.

He gave the horses their breakfast, which they ate hungrily. Simon then headed out of the stables and as he did, he turned to see Sheriff Duncan riding up the road. He stopped and waited.

"Mornin'," Sheriff Duncan said, tipping his hat as he brought his horse to a halt.

"Mornin'," Simon echoed.

Sheriff Duncan was still in the clothes he'd worn yesterday and his eyes were heavy. Simon guessed that with everything that had gone down, he'd not gotten much sleep, if any at all.

"Would you like to come in for some coffee?" Simon offered.

"Thanks, but I can't stay," he replied. "I just came to tell you that Jarrett Davidson's death has been ruled an accident. I sent a telegram to this family this morning."

Simon said nothing as he wondered how Jarrett's family would respond to the news.

"How's Jenna?" Sheriff Duncan asked.

"Haven't seen her this morning," Simon said. "But I think, all things considered, she's doing all right."

"She's a tough woman," he said gruffly.

"She is," Simon agreed.

The sheriff cleared his throat. "Well, I for one am glad this whole business is over."

Simon nodded. "Thank you, Sheriff," he said, with all sincerity. "For everything you did to help Jenna and those other women."

Sheriff Duncan nodded. "You look after yourself, and your family."

"I will," Simon promised.

The sheriff tipped his hat to Simon in farewell before he turned and headed back toward town. Simon headed to the barn to milk the cow and when he was done, he carried the silver pail into the kitchen. As he stepped inside, he found Sophie, Jenna, and Oliver.

"Good morning," Sophie said brightly as she took the pail of milk from him.

"Morning," he said as he looked at Jenna.

She had Oliver on her knee and as Simon caught her eye, she gave him a tight-lipped smile. She was wearing a white handkerchief around her neck, hiding the long crimson cut left by Jarrett's knife. Simon walked over to them and tickled Oliver under the chin, and he squirmed and cooed in delight.

"How are you feeling this morning?" Simon asked, looking down at Jenna. "Did you manage to get some sleep?"

"Some," Jenna said.

Simon nodded as he took a seat at the table.

"Was the sheriff here?" Sophie asked as she put a plate of eggs down in front of him.

"He was," Simon said, looking at Jenna, whose face remained expressionless. "He just wanted to let us know that Jarrett's death has been ruled an accident and his family has been notified."

Sophie nodded but Jenna did not react.

A knock at the door sounded, and a moment later, Rose appeared in the kitchen.

"Rose," Jenna said, getting up from her chair. "What are you doing here?"

"I came to see you," Rose said. "To make sure you were all right."

"Why don't you and Rose take a walk around the garden?" Sophie suggested. "It's a beautiful morning."

Jenna hesitated.

"I'll look after Oliver," Sophie said.

Jenna looked over at Rose and she was smiling. "All right," Jenna agreed.

She handed Oliver to Sophie and she and Rose headed out onto the ranch. Simon and Sophie watched them for a while.

"Do you think people can ever be the same after experiencing so much?" Simon asked, turning his head to her.

Sophie did not answer right away, her eyes thoughtful.

"Every experience changes us," Sophie said. "Both good and bad, but what I've come to realize is that we have a degree of control over how we change. I think at some point in life, after experiencing bad things, a person reaches a crossroads in their life. At this crossroads, they have two choices—to let these bad things become them or to try to let them go."

Simon turned his head back to the window, watching Jenna. He knew that she was at this crossroads, but he did not know what road she would choose.

***

After Jarrett's death, Jenna stood at the crossroads for weeks, existing but not living. Nothing Simon or Sophie tried seemed to work. She was present but not really there. Every day she went through the motions, dressing, eating, caring for Oliver, but she was empty, a shell.

Then, one day, after lunch, there was a knock at the front door.

"I'll get it," Simon said, getting up from the table. He walked down the hall to the front door. As he opened the door, he frowned at the stranger on his porch.

"Hello," the woman said. "Are you Simon Jones?"

Simon did not recognize the woman, or the carriage he spotted over her shoulder, parked near the barn

"Yes," Simon said after a moment. "I am he."

"You don't know me," the woman said. "My name is Margaret Pearson, I am Jarrett Davidson's sister."

Simon eyed her warily. "What can I do for you?"

"I was wondering if I could talk to you and your cousin about my brother?"

Simon hesitated. "I am not sure that is such a good idea."

"Please," she said, her blue eyes softening. "I've come very far and I only need a moment."

Simon was not sure that talking to Jarrett's sister would help Jenna, but there was something in her face, a gentleness that he'd never seen in her brother.

"Okay," he agreed.

He moved aside and Margaret stepped into the house; he led her down the hallway to the kitchen. As they came into the room, Sophie and Jenna turned and their eyes widened in shock.

"This is Margaret Pearson," Simon said. "She wanted a moment to talk to us about her brother, Jarrett."

Simon had not uttered his name in weeks and even now it left a bitter taste in his mouth.

"Why don't you sit?" Sophie asked as she reached over and pulled out the chair next to hers. "Would you like something to eat or drink?"

"No, thank you," Margaret said politely as she took a seat at the table. "My husband is waiting in the carriage outside and I said that I wouldn't be long."

No one spoke for a moment.

"My husband did not think it was a good idea, me coming here," Margaret continued. "But I needed to come and speak with you."

She looked across at Jenna, who had not spoken a word.

"When I read about what my younger brother did to you and those other women, I was sickened," Margaret said, her blue eyes full of sympathy. "But I was not surprised."

Simon raised his eyebrows.

"I did not come here to make excuses for my brother," Margaret said. "He was his own man and he made his own choices."

"Then why have you come?" Jenna said, frowning at her.

Margaret exhaled shakily. "Our father is a terrible man. Our mother left us to his mercy when we were just children, and for years we lived in subjection and fear. I managed to escape when I was sixteen; I got married and never looked back. I am not proud that I left my brother behind, but when it came down to leaving, he chose to stay."

Simon looked at Jenna, who was pale and had her hands clasped in her lap.

"I sometimes wonder what would have happened if I'd forced Jarrett to come with me," Margaret continued. "That maybe I could have saved him from becoming a monster just like our father, but I think a part of me knew that it was too late, the damage had already been done."

Margaret shook her head wistfully.

"I hadn't spoken to Jarrett for over ten years when I got the news of his death," she said. "But afterward, all I could think about were the stories in the paper, your story, and I knew I had to come and see you.

"But why me?" Jenna asked.

"Because of the baby," Margaret said.

Jenna's shoulders stiffened. "What does this have to do with my son?"

Margaret leaned forward in her seat, not breaking eye contact with Jenna.

"I thought that if you understood Jarrett better, what made him behave the way he did, that it might ease your mind," Margaret explained. "To know that Jarrett wasn't born the man he became. I needed to come and tell you this, in case you were ever worried that your child might be like him."

Simon glanced at Sophie, whose gaze was glued to Jenna, and when he looked back at his cousin, he saw something in her eyes—relief. Up until that moment, Simon had not considered that Jenna might be worried that Oliver would turn out to be like his father, but it was clear to him now that the thought had been weighing heavily on her mind.

"I am so sorry for what he did to you," Margaret said, her tone gentle. "And I will pray for you and for your son that you can find peace in this life, and happiness."

The room fell silent for a moment.

"Well, I'd better get going," Margaret said, getting up from her seat. "I appreciate you opening your home to me and letting me talk with you."

"I'll show you out," Simon said.

Margaret turned to follow him, but as she did, Jenna caught her by the hand.

"Thank you," she said softly.

Margaret pursed her lips and smiled as Jenna let go of her hand. She followed Simon back out of the kitchen and to the front door.

"I am sorry for the pain my family caused yours," Margaret said as she stepped out onto the porch.

"Thank you," Simon said sincerely. "And thank you for coming to speak with Jenna. I do think your words eased her mind."

"I am glad of that at least, and I am glad that Jenna's son will be raised here," Margaret said as she looked around the ranch, smiling faintly. "This is a good place, I can sense it in my bones."

Simon smiled.

"Well, goodbye, Mr. Jones," Margaret said. "I will pray for your family."

Simon nodded as she crossed the porch and disappeared around the side of the house. A few moments later, the carriage drove past and disappeared down the road.

Simon stayed on the porch for a moment, looking out at the blue mountains, and the pair of eagles circling in the cloudless sky. Margaret Pearson was right about this place; it was good.

He felt Sophie slide her arm around his waist.

"She gone?" Sophie asked.

Simon nodded. "How's Jenna?"

"As strange as it may sound, I actually think it helped, what Margaret said."

"Did you know that Jenna was worried about Oliver growing up to be like Jarrett?" Simon asked.

Sophie shook her head, sighing softly. "No, she never said anything to me. But I often used to wonder if Frank was the way he was because of his father."

"Things will get back to normal," Simon said, finally feeling in his heart that it was true.

Sophie looked up at him and smiled and Simon felt his heart skip a beat.

"I love you," she said.

Simon leaned down and kissed her. "I love you too."

They felt silent for a while, standing together on the porch together, Sophie holding him tightly. Simon did not know what their future would bring or what would happen with Jenna. Yet, at that moment, he wasn't afraid. He and Sophie were in love and they had chosen each other. They were a team, and together they could overcome anything.

Extended Epilogue

Shadow's Ridge, Southern Arizona, 1873

"Jeremiah Jones," Sophie scolded as she put her hands on her hips. "If you eat another blackberry, you are going to get a runny tummy."

Three-year-old Jeremiah Jones turned and Sophie saw his chin and mouth were stained purple with blackberry juice. Sophie could not help but smile; Jeremiah was the spitting image of his father, with big brown eyes and dark hair. He was tall for his age, and Sophie guessed that one day he'd been as tall, if not taller, than his father.

She sighed as she took his hand; on her other arm, she carried a large basket full of berries.

"Come on," she said. "Let's get these berries to your pa before you eat them all."

Sophie and Jeremiah walked back through the orchard toward the house. It was early fall and the trees were already laden with fruit.

Sophie and Jeremiah stepped in through the kitchen door and Simon turned from the stove. Sophie smiled at him and shook her head in amusement. It had been six years, six harvests, and she still could not get used to him in an apron.

"We picked some more blackberries," Sophie said, placing the basket on the table. "Although I think JJ might have given himself a tummy ache."

"I did not," Jeremiah said, his bottom lip sticking out.

"I never got a tummy ache from eating too many blackberries," Lily said.

Almost five-year-old Lily stood on a small stool by the stove. She was also dressed in an apron, which was much too big for her, but she had insisted.

Although Lily had Sophie's ash-blonde hair and blue eyes, Simon was her hero. She hardly ever left his side, and Sophie often teased that she was like his little shadow.

"Don't boast, Lily," Sophie warned.

"Well, it's true," Lily mumbled.

Sophie caught Simon's eye and the corners of his lips twitched.

"How's the jam going?" Sophie asked, peering into the pot.

"Good," Lily said, licking the end of the wooden spoon. She was the official taster.

"We should be finished with the blackberry jam today," Simon said.

Sophie nodded. "Then we can start on the peach tomorrow—"

A sudden wail from the bedroom interrupted Sophie's chain of thought and she left the kitchen and headed to the bedroom. As soon as Sophie leaned over the crib, eight-month-old Daisy stopped crying and smiled at her. She had blonde curls the same color as Sophie's, but in the past few weeks her blue eyes had turned brown.

"Hello, sweet girl," Sophie said as she reached down and picked her up, cradling her to her chest.

Sophie carried Daisy into the kitchen just as six-and-a-half-year-old Oliver came racing in the back door, nearly knocking Jeremiah off his feet.

"Slow down, Ollie," Sophie warned, placing Rosie on the floor near the table next to a pile of wooden blocks.

"Sorry," Oliver apologized, grinning sheepishly.

He was a handsome little boy, with his mother's auburn curls and striking blue eyes.

"Lily," Oliver said, turning to her. "Do you want to go down to the creek and catch tadpoles?"

"Can I?" Lily asked Sophie.

Sophie pursed her lips thoughtfully. "All right," she agreed. "But no wading deeper than your knees and no going into the long grass to look for snakes, either."

"We won't," Lily said as she jumped down from the stool.

"Can I go?" Jeremiah asked.

"No, you can't," Lily said. "You're too little and you don't know how to swim."

Jeremiah's bottom lip trembled.

"We'll teach you to swim in the spring, Jer," Simon promised as Lily and Oliver raced out of the kitchen.

Jeremiah continued to sulk but as Jenna stepped into the kitchen, his face brightened. Aunty Jenna was his favorite person in the whole world. Jeremiah ran to her and she picked him up and put him on her hip.

Jenna looked around the room. Her auburn hair was tied in a loose plait. "Has anyone seen Ollie?"

"He and Lily have gone to look for tadpoles in the creek," Sophie said.

Jenna sighed as she nodded. "I swear that boy is like a whirlwind, I never know where he has got to at any given moment."

"I can remember someone else being like that," Simon said, winking at her.

Jenna smiled and it was a real smile, one that made the corners of her eyes crinkle.

"Oh, Max says that when you are finished making jam, he could use your opinion on something."

Max Green was the most recent addition to their family. He and Jenna had met six months ago at church and had been married in the summer. For years, Sophie and Simon had hoped that Jenna might meet someone, but because of what happened with Jarrett, she did not believe a man would ever want to marry her.

Then she met Max, who was kind and gentle and made her laugh. What was more, he loved Oliver as if he were his own son, and Oliver loved him back. After everything that had happened, all the bad things she'd been through, things had finally started to align for Jenna, and Sophie could not have been happier for her.

"How is Max getting on?" Sophie asked as Daisy crawled over to her and tugged at her skirts.

"I think he's enjoying it," Jenna said.

Max had never worked on a ranch before, but a few months ago, Simon had offered him a job as a ranch hand.

"And he's finding enough time to work on the house?" Sophie asked as she reached down and picked Daisy up, putting her on her hip.

Max was a carpenter by trade, and was building them a house on the ranch. So far it was a lean-to with a kitchen and a bedroom, but when it was done, Sophie was certain it would be a handsome building.

"On the weekends, mainly," Jenna said. "Although he might have more free time if Simon were helping him."

Jenna shot a hard look at Simon, who turned from the stove.

"The best way to learn is on the job," Simon said knowingly. "Max won't learn anything if I am always there to do it for him."

Jenna rolled her eyes and Sophie smiled. She would never get tired of seeing Jenna like this—passionate, fiery, but most importantly, happy.

"So what are we doing for Lily's birthday?" Jenna asked.

"Simon has some big surprises," Sophie said. "He won't even tell me."

Jenna raised her eyebrows.

"All will be revealed tomorrow," Simon said mysteriously. "Actually, speaking of Lily's birthday, there is something I need to do in town."

"What is it?" Sophie asked as Daisy fiddled with the buttons on her blouse.

Simon smiled secretively as he walked over to her and kissed her on the cheek. "Will you finish the jam?"

Without waiting for an answer, Simon rushed out of the kitchen toward the stables.

"Don't forget to check in with Max," Jenna called after him. She turned back to Sophie and shook her head, smiling.

"Would you like some tea?" Sophie offered.

"Sure," Jenna said. She still had Jeremiah on her hip and carried him over to the table and sat down, shifting the little boy onto her lap.

"Lily and Ollie wouldn't let me play with them," Jeremiah said, pouting again as he crossed his arms.

"How about after tea we go down to the creek?" Jenna said. "You and me?"

Jeremiah nodded enthusiastically, his face cracking into a smile.

"JJ, why don't you go to your room and play for a bit?" Sophie suggested.

Jeremiah slid off Jenna's lap and hurried out of the kitchen.

"Pass me Daisy," Jenna said, putting out her arms.

Sophie gratefully passed the little girl to Jenna so that she could make the tea and finish Simon's jam.

A short while later, she and Jenna were sipping hot tea as warm sunshine poured in through the window. Daisy, who was cradled in Jenna's arms, yawned sleepily.

"How's she sleeping?" Jenna asked.

"She's good," Sophie said. "Better than Lily and JJ at that age."

"That's good," Jenna said, looking down at Daisy and smiling.

Sophie watched them for a moment and as she did, she saw something in Jenna's eyes, a look she did not quite understand.

"Jen?" Sophie said. "You all right?"

Jenna looked across at Sophie and exhaled shakily.

"I have some news," she said, lowering her voice.

"What is it?" Sophie asked, leaning in toward her.

"I am pregnant," Jenna confessed.

"What?" Sophie cried, her excitement causing Daisy's eyes to pop open. "How wonderful for you!"

"Do you really think so?" Jenna asked. "With Max's new job and the house being only half a house, it all just seems like bad timing."

"Oh, don't worry about all of that," Sophie said, unable to stop smiling. "We'll get it all sorted."

Jenna's shoulders relaxed a little but then she frowned. "I am worried about how Ollie will react."

"He will be delighted," Sophie said.

"Do you really think so?"

"Of course," Sophie said. "He's always telling Lily how lucky she is to have a brother and sister, although Lily tends to disagree."

Jenna giggled.

"Have you told Max?" Sophie asked.

"Not yet," Jenna said. "I wanted to wait a while longer."

Sophie nodded. She could still remember how nervous she was when she found out she was pregnant with Lily. She'd always wanted to be a mother, but the idea she might fail her children in some way was a terrifying thought.

"I am so happy for you, Jen," Sophie said as she reached over and squeezed her hand.

Jenna smiled, and it was hard to believe how far she'd come in the past six years. Sometimes Sophie thought about those early months and they seemed like another lifetime.

"You know, there was a time when I never thought I would be happy again," Jenna said softly. "And now happiness is everywhere I turn."

Sophie smiled. "You deserve it, after everything you've been through."

"And so do you," Jenna said, beaming at her.

The two women fell into comfortable silence and, not for the first time, Sophie thanked her lucky stars. Jenna had become a sister to Sophie, and she would always be grateful to her for placing that advertisement in the paper all those years ago.

***

Sophie lay in the bed next to Simon listening to the early morning sounds that she loved so much. With three young children, they did not get that much time on their own, and this had become one of Sophie's favorite times of the day.

"Hey," Simon said, rolling over to face her. "I meant to tell you there was a letter from your ma, I left it for you in the study."

"Thanks," Sophie said.

A year ago, Mr. Colton had died from a heart attack. Shortly after he died, Sophie's mother had reached out to her. Sophie had been hesitant at first to open that door after everything that had happened. But Simon had encouraged her to write back, and slowly they were starting to get to know one another again. Sophie had asked her mother to come for Christmas and she'd accepted. It would be the first time Sophie had seen her in over five years, and the first time her mother would be meeting her grandchildren.

Sophie's thoughts were interrupted by Lily, who pushed open the door and jumped onto the bed.

"It's my birthday!" she cried at the top of her lungs.

Baby Daisy stirred in her crib but did not wake.

"Happy birthday, special girl," Simon said, entrapping Lily in a big bear hug.

"Happy birthday, baby," Sophie said, joining in on the hug.

"When can I have my surprise?" Lily asked, her blue eyes bright with excitement.

"After breakfast," Simon said.

"Well then, we'd better get a move on," Sophie said as she climbed out of bed.

A little while later, they had finished eating and Lily was so excited that she was buzzing. Sophie washed the dishes while they waited for Jenna, Ollie, and Max to arrive.

"All right, let's go," Simon said once everyone was gathered together in the kitchen. He took them outside and led them all to the barn. "Wait here."

He opened the door and disappeared inside, emerging a few moments later with a white pony. Sophie did not know if

Simon had done it on purpose, or by accident, but that pony was exactly like the one her father had bought her as a girl.

"A pony!" Lily cried, her blue eyes shining.

"She's yours," Simon said, leading the pony to Lily. "I will teach you to ride, but she is your responsibility. You'll have to feed her, groom her, and make sure she gets plenty of exercise."

"I love her," Lily said, her round face bright with excitement as she hugged the side of the horse.

Everyone gathered around the pony to admire her. Sophie smiled as she watched them all chatting animatedly about what to name the pony and how much fun Lily was going to have learning how to ride. Oliver and JJ lamented about wanting their own horses soon, while Daisy cooed as she put her little fingers through the pony's soft mane. Sophie caught Simon's eye and he smiled, his brown eyes twinkling.

"I have something for you too," he said.

Sophie frowned. "But it's not my birthday."

Simon waggled his eyebrows playfully as he turned and disappeared into the barn, emerging with a brown cardboard box. Jenna took Daisy on her hip so Simon could hand the box to Sophie, and she peered inside. Looking up at her were two orange eyes, and she felt her heart skip a beat. The little kitten was gray with white feet, just like Mittens.

Mittens had died two years ago in her sleep, and Sophie had missed her so much since she'd gone. Sophie reached into the box and took the tiny kitten in her arms. She held it as she looked up at Simon, blinking back tears.

"She's perfect, Simon," Sophie whispered as she reached up and kissed Simon.

He put his arm around her shoulders and they watched Lily, Ollie, and Jeremiah arguing over names for the pony. In that moment, Sophie's heart felt so full, she was sure it would burst open.

Jenna caught her eye and they smiled at one another. Their family was growing, but no matter how full Sophie's heart felt, she knew there would always be room for more babies, more ponies, and more kittens. There was always room in their family and more than enough love to go around.

Simon nuzzled his head against hers and Sophie sighed contentedly to herself. After everything, all the hurt, the losses, and hardships, she had everything she had ever dreamed about. She finally had the family she'd always wanted, and she had Simon, the love of her life.

THE END

Also by Sally M. Ross

Thank you for reading "**An Unexpected Family for the Rugged Mountain Man**"!

I hope you enjoyed it! If you did, here are some of my other books!

Also, if you liked this book, you can also check out **my full Amazon Book Catalogue at:**
https://go.sallymross.com/bc-authorpage

Thank you for allowing me to keep doing what I love! ❤

Printed in Great Britain
by Amazon

26400636R00198